Eagle SHIELD

MILESTONE RISING

Carl Lakeland

First published in Australia by Aurora House 2018

Republished by the author 2019

Copyright © Carl Lakeland 2018 Web: carllakeland.com
Typesetting: Carl Lakeland
Cover design: Simon Critchell, Carl Lakeland, damonza.com

ISBN number: 9780648587026 (paperback)

Distributed by:
Ingram Content: https://www.ingramcontent.com/
Australia: Phone +613 9765 4800 |Email: lsiaustralia@ingramcotent.com

Milton Keynes UK: Phone +44 (0)845 121 4567
Email: enquiries@ingramcontent.com

La Vergne, TN USA: Phone 1-800-509-4156 |
Email: inquiry@lightningsource.com

Gardners UK: https://www.gardners.com/
Phone: +44 (0)1323 521555 Email: sales@gardners.com

Bertrams UK: https://www.bertrams.com/BertWeb/index.jsp
Phone: +44 (0)1603 648400 Email: sales@bertrams.com

A catalogue record for this book is available from the National Library of Australia

It may be he shall take my hand
And lead me into his dark land
And close my eyes and quench my breath—
It may be I shall pass him still.
I have a rendezvous with Death

And I to my pledged word am true,
I shall not fail that rendezvous.

~ *Alan Seeger. 1888-1916*

CONTENTS

CHAPTER ONE

Alice Springs 1996

She said nothing after I picked her up from the safe house and drove her away. Heading south out of Alice Springs on the Stuart Highway, all I had for company was the constant rattle and whine of the diesel engine. Not that I minded so much. I had no experience making chit chat with a ten-year-old girl. Most kids I considered a right royal pain in the arse.

When she *did* say something meaningful, we were kicking up long dust trails, several hours south on the Oodnadatta Track.

"Hey, mate, slow down!"

Mate?

Did she just call me that?

I glimpsed her from the side for a second while the Land Rover bounced hard over the ruts and potholes. "What's the problem?" I yelled over the noise of rushing gravel.

"You're going too fast, and my bum hurts!"

My Land Rover wasn't all that forgiving in the suspension. A road like the Oodnadatta Track tended to show its weaknesses. I slowed things down a pace, considering my arse was also about to fall off.

"Where we going, mate?"

"Don't call me mate," I said. "Away . . . We're going away."

I checked the rear-view mirror for the umpteenth time. Nothing but dust. No cars. We were on our own. My brain thumped hard thinking about all the things that must get done. When we get there. South, to the big smoke. About as far south as we could get.

"Then, what do I call you?" she asked in what I thought was an annoyed undertone.

"You mean, who. I'm Nathan. And you're Angelique."

"Maggie said not to call me that anymore."

"Yeah. I know. Angel is your name from now on."

"You still haven't said where we're going. And what's wrong with your leg?"

"You ask a lot of questions," I said. But then I realised kids must be like that. I reached down and tapped my prosthetic limb with my knuckles, loud enough for her to recoil in her seat.

"Oh my god! You've got a wooden leg!"

"Yeah, just like a pirate. My leg is somewhere on the side of the road in Iraq. And we're going to Melbourne." I expected a barrage of questions, but she took it on board and went back to being silent. She didn't even bother to ask where Iraq was.

Thank you, Jesus . . .

I shot another quick sideways glance her way. Angel, with big, orange, foam headphones on her head, positioned her camera lens through the window at the rushing landscape. She took a few shots. The motor drive whirred. Then, she placed her camera in her lap as though poised for another opportunity to take it up again. Pentax 35mm. And she appeared to use it like a pro. A ten-year-old photographer. An artist in the making, I thought.

"What's that you're listening to?" I asked. She didn't respond. I leaned over and lifted an earpiece away and repeated my question.

She gave me eyes that said, 'as if you would know', before saying it was Metallica. I hadn't previously partaken in music by Metallica. *Now was the time*, I decided.

"Hey," I said. "Go ahead and share your music." I tapped the dash a couple of times, then went back to eyes on the road. Angel smiled for the first time in hours, getting out the compact disc from a rather large-looking portable device with the word Walkman written all over it in big letters. I figured maybe I'd get one of those. But I was no big music lover. My collection stretched across a couple of LPs by Supertramp and that was about it.

"How do I play it?" she asked.

"Feed it into the slot. You'll get it."

"Oh. Yeah, I see."

No sooner did she do that; I was greeted with a most awful sound. Screaming guitars. Yelling voices. No way could I make out any lyrics. She liked it?

I moved to turn the volume down. She flicked my hand away. "Don't, Nathan. It's Metallica. It's supposed to be loud."

I rolled my eyes. *What have I gotten myself into?* But I had to ask.

"You like it?"

"It's cool!"

"Figured you'd say that. And no. You're not getting any tattoos. Forget it."

"Tattoos? Gross!"

"We'll check back in ten years. I'll still have the same answer."

Angel giggled and began to bounce her head around in time to the noise I knew would stuff my speakers in a minute. Oddly, after a while, I began to . . . like the sound. I found myself bouncing my brain in my skull, the same as Angel.

"What's the name of the song," I said. "I can't make out the words."

"*The God that Failed.* It's my favourite. Will you take me to see Metallica one day?"

"You never know. That depends on if Metallica decides Melbourne has a big enough crowd. Do you reckon they'll come?"

"I know they will. I just know it."

* * *

A few more hours driving the dusty track saw us pulling up at William Creek. A hotel and a roadhouse in the middle of nowhere was a welcome sight, and an opportunity to fill up with food and get a tank of diesel. The sun sat low on the horizon. The track to the blacktop at Marree would have to be driven through the night. Heading inside to pay for the diesel, I noticed a sign behind the counter. 'Rooms 30 bucks mate.' That decided everything for me. A dusty track through the night wasn't on the radar if I could help it. If someone was tailing us, maybe they'd drive on past.

"I'll take a room," I said to the woman with no front teeth and a dirty pinafore that looked as though it'd been worn while slaughtering pigs. "And a bottle of bourbon in a paper bag."

After giving her hands a good wipe with what appeared to be a dishcloth coated in filth, she said flat, "No likka after three. Them's the rules."

Jesus . . .

I forgot about the local laws.

Figuring what the heck, I tossed her a lie. "I've got a sore throat and a killer of a headache. Gonna use it for medicinal."

"No booze after three," she said again. "Those bloody government fellas will have me head on a stick. It ain't so much for me not sellin' it to ya. God knows the few bucks I make from it, just ain't worth me losin' me licence, mate. Them's the rules. Can't 'elp ya. Sorry 'bout that."

"What'll it take then?" I asked.

"Bribin' me won't do nothin' neither. Take a look 'round outside, what do ya see? Nothin' but desert out there, mate. You reckon I got any other chance for makin' a livin'? If those government fellas get to knowin' I've sold anythin' illegal, they'll shut this place down. Then what?"

She huffed and rolled her eyes. I laughed a little under my breath. Here it comes, I thought. She reached under the counter and got a plain glass jar with a clear liquid. "Locals round 'ere call it rocket fuel. Government fellas 'ave got no record of this stuff. And it's 'alf the price."

Angel was gone by the time I got back to my Land Rover. I placed the jar of clear liquid down on the hood and scanned a full three-sixty. No sign of her anywhere. Where had she gone? Should I panic? Why didn't she stay in the car like I asked her to?

I looked inside the window and saw her camera on her seat. She hadn't gone to take pictures. Damn it! I specifically instructed.

Angel rushed past me, grabbed the door handle, opened the door, and hopped inside. Just like that. No nuisance. No concern.

"Didn't I tell you . . ."

"I had to go to the toilet, Nathan."

I put my head down and carried on.

A couple of minutes later, I opened the door to our motel room with a brown paper bag containing the jar of so-called rocket fuel tucked under my arm. Angel went through into the dirty, but somehow as-clean-as-it-could-get accommodation. Musty smelling. Mildew, but that didn't make sense. Mould doesn't grow in the desert unless there's something in the ground.

Dead bodies . . .

I pushed the thought out of my head, but still the mildew. How?

Angel came back from inspecting the bathroom. "There's no hot water. And there's water all over the floor."

There it was. Leaking pipes. I wondered how long those pipes had been leaking. In the middle of the desert, where fresh water meant life or death. Surely someone would fix it quickly.

"Figures. That's okay, Angel. It's like we're camping tonight."

She looked at me with a set of sad eyes as I sat on the edge of the lumpy bed, rubbing the itch away from my left thigh. "What happened?" she asked. "*How* did you lose your leg?"

In my mind I wondered how to answer. All the things I've done. All the things I've seen. There was no short answer, I realised. Only the long. But she was too young to hear it. Her little mind would never process it. There'd be the day when I'd have to 'fess up. She'd have to be much older than she was today. So, I did the thing I thought was best. I avoided it. I deflected. I gave her something else. The guilt at just doing that - no way could I be a parent. Now, the question was rushing up in my head. Why me? I couldn't do it. But before I knew it, it was time to get ready for sleep.

* * *

I heard a muted yelp from the bathroom. The girl had decided a cold shower was better than none. Something I chose to avoid. Not only that, she'd sorted herself out with no prompting. No fuss. No bother. It was in that moment I realised her determination. I admired that. I admired it even more in a ten-year-old girl. When she was out of the shower with her hair wrapped high in a towel, she said words that forced me to the edge of tears.

"My mum and dad are dead." She stated it without any emotional attachment, as though reading words from a dictionary.

"Yeah," I said, not able to add anything further. Not knowing how to respond.

"Did you know my mum and dad?"

"Yeah." Again, my words came in the multitudes. As she stood there intensely eyeing me, I thought back to the time I'd met Franco and Alisha. Basic training. Kapooka, 1980. Franco was a young recruit, the same as me. Alisha, a civilian nurse, who on occasion would show up at the base RAP to administer inoculations. They instantly hit it off. After they'd married, their relationship went toxic and I asked myself why I didn't bother to come between them. To stop them from making the worst mistake of their lives.

Shit . . . Why didn't I do anything? I had the power. I didn't see it . . .

But, as a seventeen-year-old boy soldier, I couldn't have known the future. I couldn't have foreseen Franco's demise and the damage he'd leave in his wake.

Angel never left my gaze as I reminisced. For a moment it seemed as if she knew what I was thinking about. That fiery stuff in the jar stopped me from saying the right words.

I had a small sip but couldn't bear to drink any more. It burned from my throat right down to my stomach. It tasted like vodka with a tequila aftertaste that blasted the taste buds into numbness. The rush to my head was almost immediate. No wonder it was kept under the counter. Maybe I'd have reacted better without it. Maybe I'd have been a bit more comforting to her. But somehow, she was doing well on her own. She reached over and placed a tiny finger on my cheek. "You're crying?"

"This place is dirty. I must've got dust in my eyes."

I felt her tiny arms around me, and her head, smelling of motel soap, resting on my shoulder. She was there for a couple of minutes. I couldn't have helped it if I tried. All the demons I kept locked in my head erupted, and I wept for just a second or two. A moment of weakness. I knew all about them.

So many nights I'd spent in my solace with a bottle of Wild Turkey and a loaded Beretta. The barrel at my lips. Only a small amount of pressure on the trigger and those demons would be gone for good. All those memories whirled at the back of my mind like a silent movie. All the while, Angel held me close and tapped on my back with her little hands. Could it be in that precise moment her purpose was to extract all my woes?

"Nathan, please don't cry. It makes me sad too," she said, sobbing a little.

"Sorry, Angel. I'll be sorted in a bit. I have a lot of stuff in my head, y'know?"

"What should I do to make it better for you?" she asked.

How can a girl so young ask such a grown-up question? I was taken aback and immediately rose from that place I'd been. I'd no business being there. It was a moment of complete openness. A place I tried hard over the years never to venture. This wasn't about me. How could I have been so selfish? My mission was Angel. My mission was Eagle Shield. I pulled my head out and got on with it.

Standing before me, with her little eyes gleaming, Angel gave me the warmest smile. "You're all better now, aren't you?"

Bowl me over with a wet sponge. Immediately, I felt lighter.

She reached and lightly tapped my prosthetic limb with a tiny knuckle, in the same way I'd done only an hour and a half before. "You were going to tell me what happened to your leg."

"Yeah, I was, wasn't I? But that's for later. Plenty of time, Angel. Time for sleep. We need to get going early." Another deflection. I wasn't happy.

The deflections will only last so long. One day, I'll man up.

There was the typical ten-year-old's displeasure. But again, her disappointment seemed fleeting and she left to get ready for sleep with no argument. I wondered how my mission would turn out. Angel was no longer the pain in the arse I thought her back in Alice Springs. Franco and Alisha's legacy was far from that. As I realised it, there was something else. I felt my heart being ripped from my chest. How was I to know that kid would take my heart away? Something I never expected, nor imagined possible. I was so far away from being paternally capable. I knew it. I felt it. With Angel, I could already tell it was going to be a different relationship than I at first assumed.

* * *

Late in the evening, occasionally, a road train thundered past. Exhaust brakes rattled anything not screwed down and could be heard a kilometre or so up the track. With the sounds of the thumping road trains and Angel's snoring, which was similar to a two-stroke lawn mower, I tried to sleep but failed.

Under a single, dim light bulb, at the crooked and aged TV table, I lifted the paperwork from the yellow folder Maggie had thrust into my hand. Among the papers was a fresh birth certificate bearing Angel's new name; I had to wonder how it was made possible. A bank passbook account had been set up. A new passport due to run out in five years. A blue computer floppy disk. The decryption codes for the disk were printed on a single sheet of silk and placed in a plastic sleeve.

A document entitled Eagle Shield, and a mission brief that had an attached address in Melbourne, accompanied with a set of keys. Acceptance papers to St Michael's Grammar School in Melbourne. I poured over the paperwork and navigated through the objectives in my head.

My mind drew back to Maggie before we left Alice Springs. I'd met her out on the street, in front of the safe house. Who'd know if even safe houses were safe? "Nathan, above all, keep her from harm," she'd said. "Your charge is of the utmost importance. Eagle Shield can never be taken for granted. You must never fall behind in your objectives. The agency will continue to fund Eagle Shield up until it's concluded, or until further notice."

"Concluded? You've made no mention of a conclusion."

"The day Angel steps into the Ben Chifley Building is when Eagle Shield is completed."

"Ben Chifley? Maggie, what makes you think Angel will even *want* to be an ASIS player? Don't you think that's being a little presumptuous?"

"We don't have the luxury of choice, my boy. It is what it is. You must make it happen. You must guide and direct her into position. Your mission brief explains all of your objectives. After she comes of age and starts her ASIS training, only then is Eagle Shield regarded as mission accomplished. I know you well, Nathan. Better than you might think. If there's anybody up for the job, it's you. Your package has had a close call. Much too close. We cannot risk that again. Her parents are gone. We've lost assets. We almost lost Angel. A couple of millimetres to the right and that bloody sniper would've accomplished his mission. We don't get to decide if it was fate or just good luck."

"Hmm . . . That's why we're going to Melbourne. To hide among the masses."

"Not only for that reason," Maggie put in. "But also for what Alice Springs cannot provide."

"Investment in private schooling?" I asked as though I was surprised. I wasn't surprised.

"It's expensive, yes. The agency's budget will cover all of it."

"Lucky girl," I said. "If only for the education." What would've been the case if Franco and Alisha were alive? Maybe she'd get to grow up like any normal kid.

"Don't make me regret my decisions, Nathan," Maggie said, as though cutting through my thoughts. "The facts are Franco turned. He played us all. He murdered his wife," she trailed off, pausing a beat. "Look. There's a special something with that girl. I saw it from day one. Her mother was also astonished by her abilities."

"Abilities? What are we talking about here?"

"I could tell you . . . but discover it for yourself. Call it part of getting to know her. I'm quite sure she'll amaze."

Then Maggie handed over the disk. At that moment, I thought I caught a glimpse of someone through the window behind Maggie's rear. I took the disk, eyed it for a second, and placed it into the folder.

"The disk and codes were in Angel's backpack," Maggie went on. "How it got there, I'll never know. But I assume Alisha put it in there. I assume it was an attempt by her to get it to me. What I found almost caused me an early death, Nathan. At your opportunity, take a look and see for yourself."

I placed a hand on my chin and eyed Maggie. Why was I not surprised this would jump up and bite me all over again? Operation Matchbook in Southern Iraq was a success, but with the cost of two lives. Two mates. I'd made a silent oath – nobody would die on my watch – but stepping down range, two fell. I will always have their blood on me. So, here it comes. It starts once more. "Let me guess. The Milestone theory?"

"The centrifuges in Southern Iraq were destroyed," Maggie said. "It turns out that was a small piece of a much larger picture. Iran was the culprit, and the one that got away."

"Milestone is alive?"

"Oh, Nathan. My dear boy, Nathan. So much more. The theory of Milestone is alive as you stand before me. Unfortunately for all of us it is now an inevitability rather than a theory. Milestone will be fully initialised within twenty years. Added to that, a secret project called Amber. Some of the documents have been heavily redacted, but we've managed to get an understanding of what could...*will* happen. With you in play, we can begin to formulate our counter operations, to this . . . so-called Amber project."

"Jesus."

"Yes. Jesus, as you say. Now you can understand how important Eagle Shield has become. Angel is the linchpin. Our hopes revolve around her. Even though you may not see it as I do just yet, you will in time. We cannot afford to fail. We are essentially humanity's last hope. We were under the radar with the Guardianship. That has changed. We *were* the only agency that has managed to stay dark to those players. It'll never be that way again. That girl in your charge is . . ."

"I can see where this is going. It's okay, Maggie. I've got this."

Maggie paused long enough to take a deep breath. At the window behind her, the curtains moved again. I thought I saw the shape of Angel's face peering through, but then she disappeared. Maggie continued. I listened. "It is imperative the decryption codes are secured in a separate location to the disk. See to it they are both well protected. You'll be coordinating with CIA Special Agent Don Bosco in due course."

"Bosco? No shit."

"Surprised?"

"We go back a way. Operation Matchbook."

Maggie smiled briefly, then her gaze hardened. I needn't have said anything. She knew everything.

"How is it possible Bosco is now CIA?" I asked. "I never would've guessed. He's a good man, but it fails to register how Bosco and CIA can exist in the same sentence."

"I'm curious. Why would you say that?"

"He's eager on the trigger. Bosco fires from the hip. He doesn't think about things. He takes no prisoners."

"And *that* is the reason the CIA recruited him. *That* is the reason we have him on board," Maggie said. "Bosco is your exact opposite. Honestly, I don't know where you go in your head sometimes, Nathan. You're good at what you do. Bloody good. But you tend to overthink things. Bosco is the man for the job when only the dirty option exists. The thing is it won't be easy for you *or* Angel. Better to have friends close by, huh? Friends in the same circle."

Just then, it occurred to me. "You made that happen?"

"Amazing, the ASIS machine," Maggie said. "I even surprise myself at times. After reading Bosco's records, I realised Delta operators are trained in the same way as the CIA Special Activities Division. It was a matter of a phone call to Langley. Next thing, Bosco was willing to oblige. Oh, and Nathan. You must understand by accepting this mission . . . ."

"My private life is next to non-existent. It won't . . . *can't* get in the way."

Hmm . . . This is how my life plays out . . .

Again, cutting through my thoughts, "This is most probably for life. We can arrange for more time if you'd like to think further. But we'll have to kill you now, if you attempt to back out."

"Thanks for that. Let's get this started, shall we?"

I took all the documents in the yellow folder and thrust them into a leather zip-up briefcase Maggie handed me.

"A bit of cold war technology," she went on. "In the briefcase, you'll find a ballpoint pen. Do not take it out of the briefcase. It is a radio beacon and will activate if you and the briefcase are separated by more than fifty metres. Wear the ring I've given you. The ring closes the circuit to the radio beacon. It is not waterproof. When washing hands, take it off. I will *not* tolerate false alarms. Clear?"

I nodded.

"The bad news. If activated, the signal can be tracked by others. We've tuned a frequency that hopefully stays off radio scanners. Risky, I know. It's either that or a set of handcuffs. The best policy, I suggest you never leave the briefcase unattended. Keep it with you at *all* times. If the beacon never activates, that can only be a good thing."

"What'll happen if . . ."

"That's Bosco's job." Maggie cut in. "He's your actions-on. He'll be in the shadows, but always listening and never far away."

"Roger that."

That night was the last of my nights alone. At least up until Angel could manage her own life, I supposed. I slept in the Land Rover. For some reason I felt it better that way. Maybe I was savouring my own space for just a little while longer. Maybe being suddenly thrust into the position of being a parent was beginning to scare the shit out of me.

My mind dizzied with the taste of that awful rocket fuel at the back of my mouth. How I needed a good shot of bourbon. I sighed and put the paperwork away, thinking I could finally manage some shut eye.

CHAPTER TWO

William Creek

At first, I thought it was the rumble of another road train pushing past. At the edge of waking up nothing seemed real, and the motel room felt as though an earthquake was tossing everything about. It was no earthquake. And it was no road train. It was Angel, flailing in her bed as though struck by a seizure. She flew back and forth, hitting her head repeatedly with a god-awful crunch on the fake timber wall.

Alarm pumped through my veins. I didn't quite know what to do! I knew I had to do the dad thing. Step one: Don't panic. Step two: Panic. Wide-awake, I rushed over and cradled her head to prevent more damage. All I could do was wait until she awoke properly or went back to sleep. I held her as best I could. She whipped back and forth as though a demon had possessed her tiny body. Then she stopped abruptly. She sat upright, stiff as a nail. Her eyes red-rimmed and wide. "Nathan. Did I dream it?"

"You had a bad dream? You okay?"

She looked at me, ghostly pale with those big eyes. "They're here, Nathan."

"Who?"

"They're . . ."

She gulped back air. Her breathing laboured. Without a prosthetic limb on my stump, I flew awkwardly to her bag and got out her puffer. I gave the L-shaped device a shake and held it for her. "Breathe, Angel." She breathed back after a squirt. Then, she sat still and hung her head for a minute or two.

"Who's here?" I said, after I thought everything was over. I didn't know what I was dealing with. It could be epilepsy. Maybe it wasn't. I was no doctor. If it was, surely Maggie would've enlightened me about the condition.

She looked up. "The tall man with black skin. Did I dream it? Did I dream him?"

"You must've. Who's the man in your dream?"

"I don't know. Charlotte showed him to me. Charlotte, and Mum."

This can't be good . . .

Maybe it wasn't the right time, but I knew I had to get to the dream while it was still fresh in her mind. I sat at the edge of her bed, wiping the build-up of sweat from her distraught face.

I thought about Maggie telling me Angel was different. She didn't explain how. She said I'd find out. Was this it? I already knew my charge wasn't in any way ordinary. The dream. I must get to it. "What else can you tell me?" I asked.

"Mum and me. We were at the top of the hill where that big steel thing is."

I thought hard. Alice Springs. South. The MacDonnell Ranges. The telecommunications tower at the west peak of The Gap.

"What else?"

"Charlotte flew over me and I followed her."

"Who's Charlotte, Angel?"

"My eagle friend. Charlotte. Don't you know I called her that?"

She looked at me as though puzzled. I had no idea she'd given it a name. I had no idea she regarded it as a friend. How could that be? That eagle killed Franco. It mauled him. Franco's carotid artery was ripped out by a set of giant talons. A giant beak punctured his eyes and ears, and his tongue was torn from his neck as if the eagle had ripped a snake from a tree trunk. Franco's life was snuffed out before his body hit the ground. All this . . . and yet, a friend?

"I could feel the man standing behind me," Angel went on. "I thought it was dad. But then it wasn't dad. When I turned around, the man had black skin. He was really, really tall and he smiled at me with really, really big, white teeth. A smile like angry dogs get. He said something that scared me."

"What did he say? Can you remember?"

"Mmmm . . ."

She was thinking hard, I could tell. Her little eyes darted left and right. She hung her head. Her face became pink. The dream. It was getting away.

"What did he say, Angel?"

"He said . . . he said . . ."

"What?"

"Peace maker . . ."

It didn't make any sense. Dreams are like that. They never make sense.

"Then the tall black man reached out to gr . . ."

Angel sat still. Her little body froze into place. "What's that smell?" she said. "It's awful! What is it?"

"What smell?"

"Like that black stuff those men put on the road. I can taste it in my mouth. Make it stop, Nathan. Mak . . ."

Her body convulsed heavily. Her eyes rolled back and became white. She whipped back. Her back arched up and her head went into an awkward tuck. Her arms and legs wildly twitched and twisted. She foamed and grunted at the mouth. Holy shit! This *was* a grand mal seizure. All I could do was hold her and prevent any injury. She flailed on and on until finally her body relaxed and went limp.

* * *

I called Maggie at the first opportunity. Due to the isolation, the public phone from the street was the only line of communication available. The telephone number in the yellow folder came with a set of instructions. Someone answered immediately after two tones. "Hello." The voice of a man. American accent. Distant. "Do you have your laundry pick up number?"

"Docket number 774732," I said. "Make it quick."

"One moment please . . ." Click.

My mind numbed listening to the long ding-dongs at the other end of the line.

Click. "Your laundry will be available after two p.m. sir."

"That's not good enough. I need it now."

"One moment please . . ." Click.

Oh, my lord, I thought. More bloody ding-dongs. Fury rose in my veins.

Click.

"Canter?" Maggie said. "One moment please, patching a secured line."

Click.

Christ!

Click. "Go ahead, Canter."

"It's Angel. Not good!"

A long pause at the end of the line. "You know, Canter, I thought I wouldn't be getting a call so early into the mission. What's the matter?"

"You weren't forthcoming with her medical, Mag . . . err, Shilo."

"Canter. Protocols!"

"I apologise, Shilo. I'm a little flustered."

"Tell me what happened?"

"Epilepsy. She had a grand mal seizure. Twice actually. In the space of thirty minutes."

"You're kidding."

"I shit you not. Tell me you have the condition on record."

"I . . . we don't. She's never had one. You must get her medical assistance. ASAP."

"I don't have any of her medical records. Not even a Medicare card. You should've supplied it with the documents."

"I told those idiots in Canberra to include everything. Are you sure?"

"Would I be making this call if it were all there?"

I heard her huff at the end of the line. "Where are you?"

"On the Oodnadatta," I said. "William Creek."

"Bloody hell, Canter. What in god's name are you doing there? Why didn't you take the Stuart Highway!"

"I thought I had a tail and diverted."

The line went silent.

"Shilo. Are you there?"

"Let's get our heads back, shall we? Where is Angel now?"

"Sleeping," I said. "In a motel room."

"And what started this? Any ideas?"

"A bad dream. She said some black man tried to hurt her."

"She said that? A black man? Did she describe him?"

"Yeah. Tall. You sound as though you might have a clue."

"I do. Those black people she refers to are documented in the intelligence you have with you. However, I have no idea how she could have known. Have you managed to access the disk?"

"I have no computer."

"Canter. If you went on the Stuart . . . anyway . . . do you have access to facsimile where you are?"

"Not until Marree. A good day's drive."

"Get there. Immediately. And call me when you arrive. I'll facsimile her medical and Medicare details. Let's hope Canberra is forthcoming with what you need. Other than that, journal everything. Every small detail. We need to know what kicked this off. A bad dream is unlikely to cause epilepsy. Can you think of anything she did or said that is out of the ordinary?"

I thought about it. Then I remembered. "Peace maker. She said the person in her dream said it."

Another moment of silence.

"Shilo?"

"I'm here. I must admit, I'm very surprised. And shocked, I must say."

"You know about that? What she *means* by that?"

"It depends. Peace maker? Or Peacemaker, all one word?"

"That's unclear. What difference would it make?"

"It makes every bit of difference, Canter. Just get to Marree and call me. Out!"

Click.

I shuddered, standing there after hanging up the phone, and the recollection came. Black man. Tall. I'd seen one. Exactly as Angel described in her dream. It seemed so long ago.

On that first day of enlistment into the army, Franco was es-corted into the recruitment office by someone matching Angel's description. He entered the hall where we were all to take our oaths to flag, Queen, and country. The lanky black man was wear-ing what I thought at the time was an American military uniform. He was so tall he bobbed down slightly, entering through those Tasmanian oak double doors.

And there was a connection somewhere else, but where? Franco wasn't alone. There were two from Alice Springs joining up on that day. And they were the only two that made their way down from the Northern Territory. The other guy had introduced himself as Scotty-Blue, as he sat down in the chair next to mine. It was from that moment I knew there was something sinister go-ing on.

Franco and Scotty-Blue were never on any record. Their names were never called off on a roll. They were never issued dog tags, or the service numbers to go with them. It was as though Franco and Scotty-Blue were training as completely anonymous individuals.

CHAPTER THREE

Breakfast

My head still reeling from the phone call to Shilo, I went back into the motel room to find Angel fast asleep. Thank god for that. I wouldn't have known what to do if she had gone wandering on her own. I went straight for the kettle and switched it on. At the same time, I poured the rest of that wretched so-called rocket fuel down the toilet and flushed it away.

I reached for the overhead cupboard and opened it, looking for some coffee. No sooner had I opened it; the door came away. I was left standing there like an idiot, holding it in my hand with the hinges and screws hanging. But there was coffee in little sachets and others containing sugar. The kettle began to boil. I was only a moment away from getting a hot brew. I wasn't counting on the whistle. I held my hand over it in an attempt to stop the noise and burned my hand. Angel awoke from her sleep and sat up in bed. "Nathan?"

"Making a brew. Sorry for the noise."

"Coffee? Can I have some?"

"What? Not bloody likely. A cup of tea is better for you. Green tea, maybe. But there's none. Maybe just drink water. How are you feeling?"

"My head hurts. I'm getting a headache."

I thought about quizzing her further about the dream, but realised she'd need more rest. "We'll go out to the front for breakfast if you like. I'm sure they'll have something there. Don't expect miracles. Maybe they've got some pies."

"Eweee, gross," she said. "I don't think I'd like a meat pie for breakfast. What about chocolate?"

"Don't even think about it. That's not something to have first thing in the morning."

I checked my watch. It wasn't early. It was getting close to 1100. We'd have to get a move on if we were going to reach Marree before sundown.

"But Nathan. Chocolate makes my headaches go away. Same as coffee."

"Nice try. Not happening. Gonna make you a cup of tea. No sugar. No chocolate. Nothing. Got it? You need to get ready, Angel. We're out of here soon."

After getting up from her bed, Angel walked slowly toward the bathroom with her little shoulders hunched forward. "I don't feel good, Nathan," she said as she turned her head across her shoulder, walking past me as I poured hot water into two cups.

From the bathroom she called out, "How long does it take to get to Melbourne?"

"Two days from here."

"I don't want to go today. Can we stay here for another night?"

"No. We need to be in Marree before sundown."

"Oh, pleeeease."

"Nope."

"Oh, Nathaaaannn."

Here we go. I had no idea how to recover from an inbound tantrum. It left me wondering how I'd cope when her teen years finally hit. That was only three years away. I attempted to end the inbound sulk-fest by changing the subject altogether. "What if we make it a slow trip and do some sightseeing? We can stop at Lake Eyre and you can take some pictures with that snazzy Pentax of yours. You'd like that. I'd like it as well." It blew me away how Angel seemed to be so accomplished in using such a camera at her age. On the drive down from Alice Springs, I'd caught her muttering to herself as she made her selections with aperture and shutter speeds. So amazing. But then, there were eight-year-olds playing Mozart's symphony No. 14 on Steinways.

I remembered Maggie's instructions to get to Marree. Maybe it wasn't such a great idea to hang about. Angel didn't answer. I called out. "Angel, are you hearing me?" No answer. The words 'oh no' suddenly whipped through my head. I couldn't remember hearing a toilet flush. I certainly didn't remember any water flowing.

I went to the door and knocked. "Angel," I said. "Open the door."

I pushed the door, noticing a weight behind it. I pushed harder and caught a glimpse of her hair on the floor. "Angel!" I pushed the door further so I could get in and bent down at her side. Yellowish sputum was around her mouth. Another seizure. Good Christ!

This is not good!

I picked her up and carried her to the bed, grabbing a towel on the way. "Angel!"

Her eyes opened. "What happened?"

"You've been sick." I checked her over and wiped her clean. "You good?"

"Nathan, my head hurts."

I sat by her side and gazed down at her, cleaning her up a bit more. I pulled the covers up to her chin and tucked her in. "Rest a bit," I said. "Maybe we'll stay here for another day. Try and get some sleep, huh?" I was not looking forward to explaining this to Shilo.

She closed her eyes, at the same time smiling a little kid smile that said she was content and happy. I tucked her in and stayed by her side up until I heard the first sounds of her snoring. I lingered a bit more and for some reason, my mind drifted back to a much younger me. And to the time Angel's parents first met.

CHAPTER FOUR

Kapooka, 1980

By week three of basic training, we were snapping together like a bunch of magnets. We'd been up to the barbers and had the humiliation of a crew cut. We'd been down at the Q-store to collect our uniforms.

Finding a uniform to fit me was an exercise and a half. It seemed either the length was right, but the width made it appear as if I was wearing parachute, or if I got something to fit my frame, the length was down around my knees. Eventually, something was found that would have to do. The rest of my uniform was destined to be tailor-made and would arrive by courier, so the Q master had said.

We'd been down to the armoury, issued our SLRs, and were trained with them. We'd set up and zeroed in sights. We'd even drilled with them.

I didn't know it then, but the rifle range was all the way up and over the top of a steep hill they called Heartbreak. Getting there in greens, boots, and kit was going to be a major pain in the arse.

On the roster for the day, however, was a trip to the Regimental Aid Post. Inoculations. Something to *really* look forward to.

We'd go in squads of four, then report back to continue with our training.

I was at the RAP with Scotty-Blue, Franco, and a stocky guy we called Beef. A civilian nurse was to do the honours. As she walked into the room, the whole place lit up with her presence. Something happened to Franco. It seemed he went away somewhere in his head. It was as though he was struck dumb. His mouth hung open. His eyes went wide. We all knew it was love at first sight. Bloody Franco. I've never seen anyone fall so hard.

The nurse introduced herself as Alisha Falkner. She gave us a good bit of background on her story as a kid growing up in the town of Wagga Wagga. After our shots had been administered, Franco was reluctant to leave without the prospect of seeing her again. He put the hard word on her and managed to get a telephone number. Smooth as a crooner. All the way back to our barracks, you couldn't take that smile off Franco, even if you wanted to.

* * *

It was just after midnight. The silence in our room was suddenly broken by a rustling sound, as though some idiot had decided to get out of his cot and get dressed. It was Franco.

I saw his shadow and heard a set of footfalls pad out of the room, down the hall, and then he was gone. His disappearance could be nothing but bad and meant the entire platoon now had to suffer the prospect of one of its members going AWOL. If Franco didn't get back before reveille, the dire consequences would be felt by all, and the lucrative Vasey Trophy our platoon was chasing would go to another. Worse, if he got caught, he'd be on the next call to back-squad. I wasn't about to let that happen.

Scotty-Blue was snoring like the bugle call that would get us up in a few hours.

"Blue. Get up," I whispered, at the same time giving him a hefty shake.

"Cripes, Franco. I was just 'avin . . ."

"It's not Franco. It's me. Canter," I said in a low whisper. "Franco's gone."

"What?"

"Blue. You know where he went. We gotta get him back before it's too late."

Scotty-Blue sat up in his bed, looking as though he wasn't yet fully awake. Moments were getting away. I asked again, "Where do you reckon he's gone, mate?"

"That bird 'e met at the RAP," Scotty-Blue whispered. "I reckon he's gone to meet up. He rang 'er before, when we were up at the boozer. So, he's probly arranged to catch up somewhere, knowin' that bloody wanker."

"Where?"

Scotty-Blue appeared to think for a while, then answered, "The road 'ouse out on the 'ighway. 'E said somethin' about it. I didn't think 'e was serious though. Bloody 'ell. What a flamin' galah."

"Jesus. We need to get there and drag his arse back, Blue."

"Yeah . . ."

"I'll go wake up Beef. We'll need him," I said. "Get your kit, and let's get out of here." Then it struck me. We had no access to our civilian clothes, which were locked away in the security room at the end of the hall. We only had our greens. That meant Franco was in greens as well. He'd be lit up like a beacon out on civvie street. MPs were all over the place during the night, and they'd patrol places like the roadhouse out on the highway.

"We'll also need Lemon," I said. "I'll go get him up."

Getting Lemon out of his cot was an experience. The oldest in the platoon, Lemon had re-enlisted just for the money. He'd obviously learned the art of sleeping with his ears open during his time in Vietnam. I slunk into his room and crept up beside him. No sooner did I do that than his hand was squeezing around my throat. "It's Canter." I gagged. "Need your help."

"Canter? What in the . . ."

"You can let go if you wanna."

Releasing his death grip, he sat up and wiped the sleep from his eyes. I told him everything that transpired and saw his facial expression harden. "No. That can't happen," he whispered.

* * *

The four of us padded out of the barrack in greens, with camo cream that Lemon had painted in diagonal lines across our faces. It wasn't until we were a fair distance away from the Alfa Company barrack that we placed boots on our feet. Lemon suggested we take a bit of cash. Not to buy something, but to bribe the night picket if we got sprung. A few bills would easily persuade them, Lemon said. Who'd know if those so-called night picket duty recruits used the opportunity to get away for a while themselves?

By the time we got to the fence line, the lights of the roadhouse across the highway shone through the early morning fog with an eerie glow. A slight breeze was pushing in from the north, enough to prickle the skin on my forearms. The fence was no problem getting over. I expected to see a six-footer that was at least electrified. To my surprise, the fence was four-foot rural consisting of the usual four strands of wire. Not even barbs.

We climbed over and moved through the native shrubs and noxious gorse on the side of the road. We waited in the shadows, choosing a moment when no headlights could be seen in either direction to move again. No cars in sight, we slunk diagonally like black cats crossing a suburban street. Reaching the other side, we found shadows among the shrubbery and waited there for a bit.

From our position in the shadows, I could at last see through the window of the roadhouse. There was Franco, as suspected, in a cubicle with Alisha chatting her up. He wasn't wearing his green shirt – instead a white t-shirt, like the one we all wore at PT. Franco had thought this out. The real beacon was his haircut though, and he'd easily stick out to any patrolling MP.

We were about to make our move from the shadows when a set of headlights came over the rise. Lemon got us down as it approached. We'd have to wait a bit more. But as it drew nearer, it slowed down. The light from the half-moon hit it, and from the shape and sound of the vehicle I could tell it was a coach. Tourist coach probably. And heading straight for the roadhouse. It was going to make Franco's extraction even more difficult. Who knew if there were military staff on board inbound for Kapooka? If there were military on the coach, Franco was knee-deep in a hefty fine and back-squad. Perhaps even a dishonourable discharge.

From roughly a half kilometre away, I could see the coach had stopped. The odd thing was the absence of any sound of exhaust brakes, plus the fact the bus wasn't pulled over to the side. It was just stopped in the middle of the road. Stopped for no good reason. Just stopped.

"That's weird," I said to Lemon.

"Yeah," he agreed. "With those lights on, we've got no hope of getting to Franco."

"It's like it saw us," Scotty-Blue said.

"Bloody hope not," Beef said. "We're all fucked if it has."

"Roger that," Lemon said. "We don't have a choice. Until it leaves the area, we stay put. Got it?"

We all double-tapped Lemon's arm, and the waiting began. A few moments passed and I just happened to notice the headlights of a motorist in the distance heading our way. Another car sped past us going the opposite direction but it was too late. What I thought was certainly a head-on collision was only narrowly avoided.

"Holy crap! That was close," I said. "That can't be right. There's something wrong down there."

"Majorly," Scotty-Blue agreed. "I reckon we go take a bo-peep."

"Our prime mission is Franco," Lemon said. "We'll make the coach our secondary."

Something in my brain told me it had to be the other way around. "No," I said to Lemon. "I dunno what it is. Those lights down there need to be dowsed. Blue, you're on me. You two, when the lights go out, go get Franco."

Beef double-tapped my arm.

Lemon huffed. "Get down there fast and see what's going on. Then back here. We'll wait."

"Oscar Mike," I said, and moved through the shadows with Scotty-Blue behind me, toward the strangely stopped coach.

The pilot light in the cabin was on. From roughly forty metres, we could tell the engine was idling, but even more horrifying was the sight of the driver slumped over the wheel. My heart pounded hard at my breastbone. I instructed Scotty-Blue to run as fast as he could go back to the roadhouse and raise the alarm. The coach headlights drew long shadows on the road as he sprinted away.

Running toward the coach, I could see it was full of sleeping passengers. The air-conditioning unit on top was silent. That was one thing that should never be shut down. Then, it hit me between the eyes like a live 7.62mm full metal jacket. Carbon monoxide. Those people in there needed fresh air and fast.

I tried to pry the door open, but it wouldn't budge. I considered my options. I could break a window or two, so I could get in. But if I did that, maybe I'd cop a whiff of the deadly gas, and that wouldn't do. It hit me with the speed of light that the breeze was coming from the north. I'd need to smash the front windscreen and then the rear. The carbon monoxide would flush out.

But how could I smash it? There were rocks around the place, but none big enough to do the job. Nonetheless, I tried it. The biggest rock I found was about the size of my fist. I threw it a couple of times. No good. The rock bounced off. My mind was on the edge of panic; I worked hard at keeping my logical brain in check.

Reaching into my pocket, I pulled out a dummy 7.62mm round I kept as a lucky charm. The tip wasn't as hard as diamond, so scratching at the glass was no good. Instead, I positioned myself at the front of the windscreen and placed the tip of the round up to the glass. Using the rock I'd found, I hit the back of the round with a good solid whack. SMASH!

Glass everywhere. All over the place and all over me in small fragments. I immediately raced around to the rear and did the same there. SMASH!

Being so tall and agile meant getting inside was just a short climb from the rear bumper. I cut my hands getting in. The oozy sensation I put to the back of my mind. Adrenalin pumped inside me and made me lightheaded. Either that or it was the carbon monoxide making me feel as though I was about to tip over.

From the rear, I moved down the aisle, checking for vitals on seated individuals as I went. Unfortunately, a few sitting toward the rear had none. A few more were faint. I needed to think fast.

A slight breeze was pushing through, but not enough to flush the gases from inside. I tucked my mouth and nose under my shirt collar and raced to the driver's seat.

Had the bus been manual, I wouldn't have known what to do. As luck would have it, it was auto, which meant I could get it going. Hauling the driver from his seat took a little effort. Then it was a matter of climbing in and driving. The wind coming through would flush out any trace.

Pulling up at the roadhouse on a section of concrete big enough to handle an evacuation, I flipped the switch for the door and screamed out. "Need help in here!" Then I immediately went to the first person I saw to my rear.

By the time I hauled out half a dozen or so, Scotty-Blue, Beef, Franco, and Lemon had a few more down on the driveway. Alicia was pounding on someone's chest, trying to bring him back. We were all giving CPR when several ambulances and police cars turned up. Two MP Land Rovers screeched to a stop and the occupants scattered and went to work on those lying on the ground.

The guy I was working on had a familiar face. That he was dressed up in civvies was probably the reason I couldn't place him. I changed from giving him breaths of life to jumping on his chest with the heels of my hands, giving it heavy thrusts.

Soon, I heard the thumping blades of choppers, and after a few moments of tricky manoeuvring, it landed nearby. Paramedics jumped out from the choppers and scurried like mad hens around the place. At that instant, civilian police cars arrived and their V8 engines screamed past the location. I watched them skidding broadside, red and blue lights flashing through the fog, blocking off both directions of traffic. And there I was, with striped diagonal lines of camo cream over my face, getting down to the task of bringing life back to the familiar guy at my knees. As I thumped and pushed at his chest, his body shook like jelly. Then back to the breath of life, over and over again.

More thumping. More pushing. Pinch the nose. Tilt the head. Breathe and check. Do it again. I didn't stop. Then the horror of who he was suddenly struck me. The guy started to breathe and colour came back to his lips.

Lying before me, he slowly came back from wherever he'd gone. He looked up at me. He recognised me. I was sure of it. Camo cream and all. He closed his eyes again. A slight curl at his lips. He squeezed my hand and gave it a bit of a shake. I was now deep in the shit with our platoon sergeant, Sergeant Sheen.

Out of the forty-odd people on the coach, we rescued eighteen. Out of those eighteen, six were critical and airlifted away. Six more were transported by ambulance to Wagga Wagga Base Hospital. And the last six came around as though they'd just been asleep.

There was more military on the coach than I realised. I later learned they'd spent the day in Albury for business, along with military personnel up from Puckapunyal. The army had lost two officers and two NCOs that night. But among the survivors was the Battalion Commanding Officer, the eccentric Lieutenant Colonel Willie White, who two weeks later pinned the Distinguished Service Medal to my chest.

CHAPTER FIVE

Lies and Secrets

It was a lot colder after the adrenalin wore off. A cell in a 'place of brief incarceration for petty crimes', they'd called it. Not jail. Not even military jail. But that's what it was so far as I was concerned.

A washbasin and a toilet. A roll of toilet paper hung from a bit of wire. Two bunks. A couple of blankets and the same green-grey painted walls that were everywhere else. A single light bulb in the centre, hanging, swinging slightly on a long cord. Sitting opposite on his bunk was Scotty-Blue, eyeing me intensely.

The others were elsewhere. Most probably in another cell, I thought.

Out at the roadhouse, before we were chucked into the back of the MP Land Rovers, the media arrived. A journo thrust a microphone into my face. Someone standing beside the journo snapped off a couple of pictures that dazed my eyeballs for more than a few seconds.

I was about to answer the journo who'd asked me to describe what happened when an MP came between us, then manhandled me away, my mouth still hanging half open. Manhandled all of us away. Franco, Beef, Lemon, and for all I knew, maybe even Alicia. I don't know what happened after that.

I assumed there'd be a shit fight to deal with. I assumed the coroner would've been flown down from Sydney. The place would've been shut up tight until the scene was cleared by the coroner's office. After that, I could only speculate.

Families had lost someone. A mother, father, brother, or sister. Perhaps I could've done more, but I failed. I rewound the whole scenario in my mind and played it back, looking for the critical moments I could've used to do more.

As I sat there, Scotty-Blue sat up and got himself to my side. I felt Scotty-Blue's arm about my shoulder. "Ya did good, mate," he said. "No point beating yourself up."

"Can I ask you a question?"

"Yeah, of course, mate. Go for it."

"What if Franco didn't go AWOL? All those people, all the military . . ."

"Yeah mate, dead as a doorknob."

"Nail," I said, correcting him.

"Canter. Sometimes things just 'appen," he said. "Sometimes things get served up for us and we deal with it. It's just 'ow it is. Shit 'appens, eh? Just like what we're in right now."

"What do you think will happen from here?"

Scotty-Blue sat back and appeared to think it over. "I reckon we might get a bit of a fine."

"Then back-squad?"

"Yeah. Probly, mate. Confined to barracks. Who'd know? We just 'ave to sit it out and see what eventuates, eh? In the meantime, try an' cheer up a bit. That was intense, but fun. Don't ya reckon?"

"Fun?"

"Yeah well, probly not the best choice o' words. But now we're 'ere, let's just see, eh?"

It must've been close to reveille. The darkness outside of the miniscule window was starting to get lighter. I'd expected the call to rally, but it didn't come. Instead, a set of keys jingled outside and the lock was unlatched. An NCO appeared wearing a red beret. "You blokes need something to eat. I've been instructed to get something for yas. Anything you want, apparently. We'll make it happen."

"Shit, eh?" Scotty-Blue said. "In that case, I'll 'ave some lobster. Never 'ad that before. Maybe some oysters too."

"Within reason, recruit," the MP smiled wryly. "But go for it. What else do you blokes want?"

"I'll pass," I said.

The MP nodded, then looked at Scotty-Blue. "You?"

"Bangers and scramble will do just fine, eh?"

* * *

Footsteps stopped at the door and it was again unlocked.

The big steel door squealed open. I thought it was food. It wasn't. In marched our platoon CO, 2nd Lieutenant Gustafson, dressed in full parade uniform including a sword at his hip.

"Stand fast," I yelled, snapping to attention. Scotty-Blue also stood fast.

"Thank you, men. As you were," Gustafson said after a snappy salute and removing his hat. An MP turned up, balancing a steel tray containing a decent serving of sausages and scrambled eggs.

"It appears you men have gotten yourselves knee-deep," Gustafson said. "Sorry for having you locked up in here. Rules are rules, and you were, after all, AWOL. That said, some of the circumstances are in your favour. After you mess, get yourselves a hot brew and back to lines. Clear?"

"Yes sir," we both barked.

"Both you lads will report to the RAP for counselling at 1800. Understood?"

"Yes sir."

"Good! Carry on then." And then he was gone as quick as he came in, while leaving the cell door open.

* * *

Gustafson was dressed up in his shiny boots and brass for a reason. It all made sense after we'd made our way up Heartbreak Hill after leaving our cells. Me, Scotty-Blue, Franco, Lemon and Beef approached our platoon who were lined up in full parade uniform and standing at attention. Gustafson bellowed out the order to present arms. They all responded, slamming boots into bitumen. Gustafson quick marched to the head of the platoon, about-faced, then presented his sword. I held my head up. The very first day pride burst up and through my body. Pride. I never knew it could feel so good. But Scotty-Blue milked the moment, shouting 'eyes-right' as we marched past them and beyond.

* * *

After 1700 up at the boozer, it was tradition to break your belt and remove your hat before stepping in. I didn't know where the tradition came from and how many times I'd screwed up before I got the message. Pubs weren't my thing, and as a seventeen-year-old I only spent a handful of hours in such places. If it wasn't for Lemon and Beef, Scotty-Blue and Franco, I don't think I'd have ever considered going there.

I was sitting at the table in the corner, glass of beer in my grip, when a green clad recruit I never knew put a newspaper over my shoulder. The coach tragedy had made the front page. However, there was no mention of any military involvement with the rescue. I was relieved, and at the same time baffled at how our involvement managed to stay out.

Scotty-Blue, sitting opposite, took the newspaper and scanned it. He huffed and laughed before passing it to Lemon, who made a crack comment, then placed it back on the table upside down, placing his beer on it as a coaster.

"Welcome to the world of lies an' secrets," Scotty-Blue said.

There was always something about Scotty-Blue. From day one, he and Franco were whispering to each other like they were hiding something. Me being me, I took the moment and seized it. "Now's a good time to tell us about the lies and secrets *you're* keeping, Blue."

To be honest, I didn't expect a response. I thought Scotty-Blue would shove my question aside and deflect like he always did.

"You 'aven't worked it out yet, have ya, Canter?" Scotty-Blue said.

Lemon looked up from his beer with a set of birdlike eyes. Maybe I should've waited to get Scotty-Blue by himself. However, I knew with a few beers under his belt, Scotty-Blue would be more likely to go with the moment. What he said next took me *completely* by surprise.

"Haven't ya noticed me an' Franco aren't on any rolls," Scotty-Blue went on. "We're not on any records. We don't exist 'ere. We don't even get to march out with you blokes. When we're done doing what needs doin', we'll just be gone. Without any warnin'. You'll wake up with two empty cots beside ya. An' there won't be no talk about it, neither."

Scotty-Blue lifted his glass of beer and took a big swig, not taking his eyes off me. After giving his mouth a wipe with his shirtsleeve, his gaze hardened. "Look, if I 'fess up to it, one: You probly think I'm a nutcase. Two: Once you know, there's no coming back. Believe me when I tell ya, it's a big weight to bear. But before I begin, I have ta ask yas to make me a promise that can't ever be broken. Can I trust yas?"

I nodded, the same as Lemon who was looking as though he'd already decided Scotty-Blue was a nutcase. "What promise?" I asked.

"You need to swear that you'll never claim to 'ave known me."

"What do you mean?" I said, sitting back, thinking how stupid this conversation was turning.

"What I'm sayin' is, no matter what, I'll always be a stranger. You've never known me, ever. Even from after we leave this place. Should we ever meet up again, you don't know me and I don't know you. Get it?"

I nodded, but half-heartedly.

"Well, I'm glad we've reached that understandin'. You don't realise the stuff I 'ave in me 'ead. It ain't nice. An' I live with it every day. Me an' Franco both do. This is serious, Canter. Bloody serious. This shit will make your skin feel like leather when I'm finished. You blokes ready for this?"

I was beginning to feel the same as Lemon. Maybe I was wasting my time. But one thing Scotty-Blue said couldn't be ignored. Scotty-Blue and Franco were never on any records. From the moment we arrived at Kapooka, their names were never read off anything. They had no pay book. They didn't even have dog tags or the service numbers embossed on them. They'd been training alongside us as anonymous individuals that were never there.

Lemon and I leaned in as Scotty-Blue started with his story.

"It's about the Guardianship. The Guardianship of Milestone. An' some kind of a secret project they've got going, which is the reason why me an' Franco are 'ere in the first place."

Lemon chose the wrong moment to take a swig of beer. He sprayed it all over the table and tried not to choke. But there it was. Lies and secrets. I wondered where this was going. I didn't know whether to laugh out loud or not.

Scotty-Blue leaned in. "You know about Jimmy Carter's nukes. An' you know about them Ruskies an' what they're up to, don't yas?"

I nodded, as did Lemon. But at the same time, I wasn't completely up to date with American politics.

"The thing is this," Scotty-Blue went on. "There's been big loads of enriched uranium goin' someplace. Someone's been buyin' it up from the Russians. There's keyhole intelligence showin' the uranium is leaving Russia, but from there no one knows where it's been endin' up."

"Keyhole intelligence?" I asked.

"Bloody hell, Canter. That's a term used to describe intelligence that ain't all there. What we've got is just a small snippet of something much larger."

"Okay . . ." I felt a yawn coming on. I even snuck a peek at my wristwatch.

"Anyway. Our government fellas 'ave been trainin' up blokes like me an' Franco, so we can lead the way to gettin' the bigger picture of what's been goin' on, from up there in Pine Gap."

"So, what's the Milestone thing about?"

"The Guardianship of Milestone we reckon are the blokes who's been getting hold of the uranium. Again, it's keyhole stuff. We think it's been endin' up in underground gismos called centrifuges and gettin' turned into weapons-grade plutonium."

"So, what?" I said. "Carter's got nukes. So has Brezhnev . . ."

"Mate, where's ya head at?" Scotty-Blue said. "Haven't you ever 'eard of M.A.D. theory?"

"No. But something tells me you're about to tell us."

Lemon laughed. He didn't say much. It appeared he was happy just to listen as things went on.

"M.A.D. Mutually Assured Destruction," Scotty-Blue said. "Nations that bear nukes are to 'ave no advantage over any other, so no nukes can ever be used. The theory is this: Say someone gets to launch nukes on another country, with early warnin' stations dotted around the world, the aggressor ends up gettin' pummelled as well, so the need to be an aggressor goes away. No advantage."

"Makes sense."

"Yeah but say someone has more fire power than others. The advantage swings in their favour. M.A.D. is out of the question. Now that arsehole gets to be a world dictator. Imagine it, if that ever 'appens."

"So, whoever is stockpiling the uranium is making a move to world domination?"

"Exactamundo," Scotty-Blue said. "We need the bigger picture, mate. So we can stop it from 'appening. That's where Pine Gap comes in. We intercept what's goin' around on the airwaves. Get the bigger picture. Find out where this uranium is goin'. Oversee and coordinate operations to shut that shit down."

"Pine Gap is American territory," I said. "Prime Minister Gough Whitlam tried to close it down."

Scotty-Blue stopped and glazed over. I saw his facial expression harden.

"Canter," he said. "Where in the fuck did ya 'ear that?"

I was about to answer. I remembered back to the time I was a kid, watching the World Heavyweight Wrestling. Killer Carl Cox was about to wallop Mario Milano for the last time when the doorbell rang. Father was at the table, tucking into his black bread with caraway seeds, stinky cheese, cabanossi, and pickles. Mother ran to the door, and Uncle Lennie rushed in urgently, his hands visibly shaking.

"It's on the ABC. They've gone and sacked the bastard," Uncle Lennie said, loud enough to get father up from the table. I saw father swallow his food with force and, at the same time, reach and twist the selector to channel two.

On the TV, Prime Minister Gough Whitlam stood on the front porch of Parliament House in Canberra. "Well, may we say God save the Queen . . . because nothing will save the Governor-General . . ."

I saw the look on father's face. He drew white as paper and his jaw swung open. Mother went still, shocked the same as father.

"Told ya, didn't I?" said Uncle Lennie, breaking the moment. "Those CIA blokes would get their way in the end. And now Whitlam's got the arse."

"The Gap?" Father said.

"Yeah. That bloody Pine Gap stuff . . ."

"Shoosh. The both of ya!" Mother shouted. "You won't say those things in my house!"

Lemon's ears pricked up the moment I got my headspace back. He looked incredibly surprised. Lemon was no fool. I already knew his bullshit tap didn't even have a handle. He placed his beer down and leaned in with a slight smile on his lips.

"My father and his brother talked about Pine Gap all the time when I was a kid," I put in.

"You gotta be kiddin'," Scotty-Blue responded, then sat back in his chair with a hand up to his chin, glaring at me with eyes squeezed into slits. He seemed gone for more than a few moments. I sipped at my beer, waiting for Scotty-Blue's next words.

Scotty-Blue smiled before finally coming back with his response. "Don't tell me. Don't fucken tell me your old man was Eric Masters. An' his brother. That crazy nutcase, Lennie."

A voice in my head kept telling me, 'get him to repeat that, in case you didn't hear it.' I went over Scotty-Blue's last words almost in slow motion. I rewound it in my head. Played it back. Rewound it again. Then, it was like someone lit a firecracker under my arse. It hit home.

Holy crap! If there was an earthquake, I felt it. I shook in my seat. I said nothing. My mouth went dry. I needed to go for a run. Anywhere. Just to get away. Away from what I was hearing. I commanded my legs to work and lift me from my chair. But they weren't there - a couple of jelly sticks attached to my torso. I said the only words I could think of. "How . . . did you know them?"

I shot a glare at Lemon. He looked just as shocked as I felt. His mouth open and swinging. Blowflies could've settled on his tongue and I doubt he would've noticed. His glass, empty. If Lemon sat there with an empty glass in front of him, there was a reason for it. The reason for him to stay seated now must've belted him in the head.

Scotty-Blue leaned forward and eyed me harder than ever. "Your old man oversaw a repeater station in the Blue Mountains. A place called Linden. The repeater station bounced signals from Pine Gap across the Tasman. But that repeater station is due to be scrapped. There's a new networkin' technology comin' up that's gonna replace all repeater stations. Internet, they're gonna call it. Everything goes down telephone lines. No need for them bloody humongous radio towers anymore."

"My father died not long ago," I said.

"Yeah, I know, mate. That was unfortunate. We 'ad 'im pegged to go off and do other stuff."

"You *are* a fucken nutcase, Blue!" I shouted. Heads turned.

"Hey, quieten down, Canter. All I'm doin' is giving you what you need to know."

"So, you're saying my father was a player?"

"That's the long and short of it," Scotty-Blue said. "Not just a player. But your old man made it possible for us to get some of the keyhole intelligence I was speakin' about. He was a soldier. In the true sense of the term."

"No. He had his own business. He was never a soldier."

"Cover story. Ever figure out how he could afford all that kit he owned?"

Can't be true . . . it's impossible . . .

"Cripes!" Lemon finally said something.

"Then what about my Uncle Lennie?" I said.

"Mad as a hatchet, your uncle. He got 'imself chucked from intelligence. The bloody idiot. Couldn't keep 'is mouth shut. Gobbin' off classified crap to everyone 'e knew. So, 'e was put into a home for the mentally ill."

"Yeah. I remember it," I said. "I thought he had a nervous breakdown."

"He did in a sense. He was pushed into it."

Before I could add anything further, Franco made his way over to the table, through crowds of recruits, with a big grin on his face. When he reached us, he didn't bother to sit. He stood there with a hand on Scotty-Blue's shoulder, smiling that big cheesy grin.

"Gawd, strike me, Charlie," Scotty-Blue said. "You look like you're ready to go for a root."

"It's gotta be love, mate. Gonna marry that woman."

Franco was about to step away when Scotty-Blue grabbed his arm. "Hey. You're not gonna believe this, mate. Canter's old man was Eric Masters."

Franco paused and stood there, biting his bottom lip. He put his hand down hard on Scotty-Blue's shoulder. I saw the tips of his fingers squeeze and disappear around Scotty-Blue's collar-bone. "Blue. Pow-wow, mate."

"Cripes. I'm in the shit now, eh?" Scotty-Blue said, wincing with obvious pain before getting up and stepping away.

I sat there watching Franco and Scotty-Blue as they exchanged words. I knew it was serious when Franco ground a finger into Scotty-Blue's chest. Scotty-Blue's face went as red as his hair. Lemon, in the chair opposite, took the opportunity to get another schooner. "You look like you need one too," he said.

"Make it a bourbon. No ice. Straight up."

"Like that, huh?"

"This is doing my head in, Lemon. What the fuck is going on?"

He slapped a hand on my shoulder. "Can't believe it myself. And I've been around for a long time. Anyway, we'll sort it. Take a breath, mate. Something tells me this is far from over."

I should've left it alone. I should've left things with Scotty-Blue where they were and not gone there. Regrets. I hated them. But now it was out, there was no turning back. Scotty-Blue was right. It was a weight I had to bear on my shoulders. Lies and secrets. I was left wondering how things would be different if I just *never* went to the boozer in the first damn place.

I continued to scan Franco and Scotty-Blue from where I sat. Their talking broke into shouts, then Scotty-Blue swung one at Franco, connecting with his chin. He fell backward into a few recruits having a drink. Then, the whole place lit up. Things went crazy.

A brawl broke out and stuff went flying. Chairs flew. Tables turned over. Glass smashed everywhere. Just as I thought it was time to get the hell out, someone aimed one at me. I managed to block it and send one back. That's when the MPs ran in, shouting and yelling to break it up.

CHAPTER SIX

Codan

Angel's vitals were all okay. I checked them over and over and over again – I had to be sure. I had to be certain. I felt her forehead and cheeks, which were cold to the touch. Too cold. Stuck in the middle of the desert with no hope for medical assistance, I wasn't sure what to do next. Raising the alarm was out of the question, and I couldn't stomach the idea of another call to Shilo. That would play out just as bad as having a sabre-toothed cat latch itself around my throat.

Angel's eyes opened slightly. "Nathan?"

"I'm here. Try to relax."

"That water you put in the jar wasn't nice. It burned my throat."

Every cell in my body went still. I tossed that stuff down the toilet. I didn't notice how much had been drunk. I thought it was me who'd taken at least half of it. Maybe a bit more than half, not sure.

"Angel, couldn't you smell it?"

"My nose is blocked."

Figures. The dust in the place also blocked mine.

"Why didn't you spit it out?"

"I was thirsty. I took a big drink. I don't like the water from the tap. It tastes funny and it's brown."

Crap!

"Angel, open your eyes. Can you see me?"

"I can see you. Why are you so scared?"

"Stay here and don't move a muscle. I'll get some clean water from the front."

I ran from the motel room, half limping around the corner. After punching the door open and leaping inside, I saw the lady with no front teeth busy with another customer. I didn't care. "Need the flying doctor," I yelled.

Heads spun and eyed me. "What for?" the toothless lady said.

"That stuff you sold me. My kid drunk some of it."

Instantly, she echoed my terror. She pointed with a finger. "The airstrip across the road," she said. "The tin shack with the red cross on it. That's the clinic."

My mind was in overdrive. Who'd know if the flying doctor was moments or hours away? Hours, I didn't have. That stuff in Angel's system needed flushing out and I had a job on my hands.

Springing through the motel room door, I saw Angel was mid-flight with another seizure. I raced over in time to save her head from colliding with the bedpost. At the end of the fit, she projectile-vomited onto the wall. Traces of blood. Angel was teetering on the edge of something catastrophic. I held her in my arms. Blood vomit dripped from the corner of her mouth. I opened her airway and checked her vitals. The tips of her fingers, lips, and tongue were tinged blue.

I raced with Angel's body being nothing more than dead weight in my arms across the stony street to the clinic with the paint-peeled red cross. Busting through the door, I yelled "Help!"

Two Aboriginal male nurses erupted from a cards game. I put Angel down gently on the nearest gurney. One nurse spoke in native tongue to the other while checking her over. He pointed to something and the other nurse went blurring away, sidestepping equipment with the prowess of a rugby player.

"The flying doctor," I said.

The nurse said some words in broken English that I thought contained the word 'Codan'.

"Where is it!" I yelled.

"Know how to use it?" one of the nurses asked, at the same time checking equipment.

I nodded and ran to the corner, where on a table sat a Codan HF Radio. "What's the call sign?" I yelled over my left shoulder, then I noticed it written on a Dymo label attached to the radio's hard case. I reached down to the Codan and activated the emergency request button for at least ninety seconds as per protocol.

A voice crackled over the speaker. "Victor zulu eight victor juliet bravo. Please state the nature of the emergency."

I picked up the mic and pressed a button. "Ethanol poisoning!"

"Roger. Inbound to your location, ten mikes. You guys are the luckiest arseholes alive. Patient delivery heading your way."

I couldn't help but roll my eyes. "Is the MO on board?"

A moment of silence, filled with radio background static. "Who is this? Identify yourself," the voice crackled.

"It doesn't matter. Get here. Out."

Back through the plastic curtain, Angel lay on the gurney with an IV already attached and an oxygen mask over her face. The two nurses regarded me, then went about their business with Angel.

It was at that moment a muffled bang rang from somewhere outside. The nurses looked up, regarding each other with a smile.

"When is 'e gonna get that truck fixed, eh?" one said. A backfire I thought and put it out of my mind.

Angel's IV drip was changed the moment the aircraft touched down. Stepping into the clinic, the doctor was followed by three others, including a woman in a wheelchair. The doctor ignored me and went to Angel to begin emergency care. An Aboriginal nurse instructed me to take a seat out in the foyer, and the awful waiting began.

Roughly twenty minutes—that felt more like hours—passed before the doctor came out of the room and into the foyer, almost nonchalant to the emergency. Finally locking eyes, he asked, "You're military?"

"That obvious, huh?"

"Takes one to know one," he said, then stuck out his hand. "Captain Will Bryant, 6RAR. That was then. Now, this. Not that I mind so much. The isolation suits me better. And I'm away from the bullshit grunt mentality."

"Shit," I said and shook his hand. "Nathan Masters."

"Where from? Or don't say. It's totally fine by me."

"152 Signals Squadron SAS," I said after a split second of weighing it up.

"152 Sigs? Impressive. That explains your knowledge around the Codan HF," he said, before stepping away slightly. Over his left shoulder, he asked, "Which group?"

"Special Sigs Intel." Maybe I shouldn't have said it. But I did. I was flustered with all that was going on.

"Intelligence man!" he said as though genuinely surprised. "You blokes are still out chasing down mobile scuds. But you're here."

"Slightly injured down range," I said, then lifted my jeans leg to show him.

He eyed me intensely over the top of his spectacles. "I see. That's unfortunate. But it also means you must be home soil deployed. Intelligence doesn't get to retire if you can still eat and defecate."

I said nothing. His probing was getting too personal. I shut up shop from that point on, telling him any further words would mean his death, to which he lightly laughed. I was absolutely serious.

"Your girl is lucky," he said. "She'll not need a medivac and will be fine after twenty-four hours on a saline drip. However, the question remains about her eyesight. We'll know more as she begins to rehydrate."

"What about the seizures?"

"A reaction to ethanol poisoning. They won't reoccur."

"Thank god for that."

"We're not out of the bush yet, Nathan Masters," he said, while checking his clipboard. "Two things. One: How did she get ethanol in her system? Two: Who is she to you? If you're home soil deployed, I find it hard to comprehend how a child her age is in your company." He lifted his gaze from the charts, scrutinizing me with a set of eyes that told me I needed a good answer, or he'd shut me down.

What could I say? "I'm her legal guardian."

"If that's the case, you'd have her Medicare and official papers showing you are who you say you are."

I paused. He looked back at his clipboard as though waiting for a response. I had the papers. Everything was in the briefcase.

Shit! The fucking briefcase! Was I more than fifty metres away from it?

The bloody radio beacon . . .!

The doctor went on. "Unless you can come up with the documentation to explain how she's in your care, I can't release her to you. Do you have anything? Birth certificate, passport, whatever?"

"Yeah, I do. But . . ."

"But? You're either her legal guardian or not. What aren't you telling me, Nathan Masters?"

"I'll be back shortly," I said, then made for the exit; at the same time someone busted through the door in a mad flap. "Doc Bryant! Where is 'e?"

Doc Bryant eyed the panicked local from across his medical charts. "What is it?"

"It's Lilly. She's got 'erself shot!"

* * *

Stepping across the stony road toward the hotel, Doc Bryant and the local guy strode quickly over. On entering the hotel, I realised the backfire I'd heard moments before was no backfire at all. Lying in a pool of blood, with two hotel patrons standing over her, the woman with no front teeth stared up with eyes fogged over. A shotgun blast to the chest had opened her dirty pinafore with red. A neat hole in the forehead said nine-millimetre projectile. An execution, gangland style.

Leaving them there to handle the situation, I retraced my steps to the motel room. The sight of everything turned over was something that I had only lived out in the worst of nightmares. The horror of the situation struck me. The radio beacon had activated. Someone had tracked it. Someone had zeroed in on it. Even worse, Shilo would know.

I searched for the briefcase and yellow folder. It didn't matter how hard I looked, nor for how long. Whoever had ransacked the place got what they came for. The briefcase and yellow folder, with all its contents – the documents, the disk, everything had been stolen.

Getting my head together, I began the process of looking for clues. Outside the motel room door were tyre tracks in the dirt. By the tread pattern, I knew it could only be BF Goodrich off-road tyres, and that said four-wheel drive. It didn't say *what* kind of four-wheel drive. It could've been any number of makes and models, and there were more than a few around these parts.

I also noticed more tyre tracks. The dirt between the tread pattern lifted and was sharper than the BFGs, indicating more recent activity. I guesstimated it had to be an SUV. I followed the tracks to the road and found both sets were headed south.

To the front of the hotel, Doc Bryant and the locals stood in a circle, discussing how to proceed. The woman with no front teeth called Lilly was still on the floor with a blanket tossed over her body. I had moments to react. Precious time was playing against me.

I needed to get into the air and head in the direction of the tyre tracks. Immediately. But Angel. Could I leave her? I'd have to forget about being her dad for a short time. I struggled trying to decide which way to go. I needed the briefcase. And I needed Angel to be safe. I needed to be there for her as she recovered. But without the briefcase, there was no Eagle Shield. The dire consequences and the repercussions of the disk falling into the wrong hands were too horrifying to imagine.

"Doc," I said urgently. "I need to get into the air. And I need a weapon. The guy who did this is heading south on the track."

"You can't use the RFDS aircraft, Nathan Masters. And I can't help with a weapon. But I can get you into the air with our helo."

"It needs to happen right now." I looked away as thoughts of how this would play out went whipping around in my head. "Angel. I need to know she'll be safe!"

"Of course, she'll be safe," the doctor said. His words reassured me. Somehow, I knew I could trust him. I'd only be away for a short while. An hour at the most. I'd be back. We'd be making our way south by the end of the day. Shilo wouldn't need to know the finer details. I'd have something worked out. I'd have something ready to report and everything would proceed as planned.

The local guy spun towards me, then said, "I 'ave a single shot bolt action 303 if that's any good. You can take it and kill that mongrel who's done this to poor Lilly."

"Get it for me!"

* * *

Stepping into the hangar, I was expecting a Black Hawk. It wasn't a Black Hawk. It wasn't even a Huey. It was a tiny Robinsons that would struggle in the effort of chasing down a four-wheel drive doing top speed on the track.

Up in the air, I pointed the barrel of an ancient 303 from the helo's open window. No scope. A single round chambered and ready to fire. As the helo reached its top speed, I was surprised how quickly we picked up the tail end of a long dust trail. I felt a rush of adrenalin to my head, as we got closer to a black SUV racing south. "Take us down," I said to the pilot over coms.

The black SUV raced on the track, I assumed as fast as it could go, as the pilot positioned the helo within range. I aimed my weapon at a tyre, then I noticed the driver's hand signals from out of his open window. Military hand signals. "Do we have Citizens Band UHF?" I said to the pilot, to which he gave thumbs up, then switched to channel eleven.

"The driver in the black SUV. Identify yourself," I shouted into the mic.

"Canter? Could that be *you* up there, big hoss?"

"Bosco!"

"Hey, Canter. Got yourself into a bit of a pickle?"

"Bosco? What the . . .?"

"Yeah. Thought you might say that. It seems I picked up the radio beacon, but a little too late, isn't it? Didn't you even know you *had* a tail? I've been tracking the bastard. Slimy sucker, this one. Slippery as cod in soap water. Time to get him shit-canned. What do you think?"

"Roger that," I responded. "What's the vehicle?"

"He's in an F100 Bronco. V8 probably. You've got your work cut out. Reckon he's making a run for the airstrip at Marree."

I thought about it. It was unlikely he'd use a civilian airstrip to get away. My mind ran through all the options he'd have.

Bosco came back. "You still got ears on, Canter?"

"A civilian airstrip is out of the question," I said over the CB. "I know these guys. He'll have an aircraft waiting somewhere. Somewhere an aircraft can land."

"What're you thinking, Canter?"

I thought hard. Where could an aircraft, most likely a Lear jet, land in the desert? Then it came to me.

"Bosco. Hang a left and make for Lake Eyre."

"Good thinking. I'll catch up with you there. Stay on the coms, Canter."

"Copy that."

Without any prompting, the pilot tilted the control stick, rolling the helo left. I instructed him to stay low and hug the terrain toward Lake Eyre. As the helo snuck up from behind the huge herds of cattle that were lazily grazing, they scattered in all directions as though their lives depended on it. In the distance, the white open space of Lake Eyre came into view—and there was the dust trail we'd been chasing down. As if reading my mind, the pilot flew down lower and positioned the helo behind the racing Bronco. We'd spring from the dust and take him down with the one and only round I had. Or I had another tactic to work with. "Take us up and straight on," I yelled. The pilot gave thumbs up.

The moment we blasted over the top of the Bronco; I could see the aircraft standing stationary on the white salt pan. Lear Jet, just as I thought. My one shot, I decided, would have to be at an engine to disable it. From there, I could only imagine what we'd do next. At least with the aircraft out of action, the documents and disk had no hope of getting away.

Moving in closer to the Lear Jet, I aimed the 303 at an engine. On the ground, two guys in black suits scurried and launched themselves up a set of stairs and lept inside. Waiting for a shot, the pilot slowed the helo. "No!" I yelled over the noise of the rotors. "Keep the forward momentum. We don't know if they have us painted. Assume it to be the case."

The pilot gave a thumbs up and increased speed.

"On my mark, roll left and I'll take the shot," I shouted. I trained my eye down the weapon, holding it steady as much as I could. "Ready . . . Mark!"

The helo rolled left. I breathed in and held. I pulled the trigger and immediately the recoil shoved the stock hard into my shoulder. Looking on, the one shot I had chambered missed the engine, but it must've pierced the fuel tank; the Lear Jet promptly erupted into a fireball and exploded, spitting a visible shockwave across the salt pan.

"I was *not* expecting that," yelled the pilot.

"It wasn't the plan," I yelled back, realising I had no chance to gather any usable intelligence. Maybe it was a good thing. Who'd know what would've occurred had those guys in black suits put up a fight. Without any firepower to give the bastards something to think about, the situation could've turned out worse than anything I could imagine. Briefcase or no briefcase.

After the pilot swung the helo back around toward the west, the incoming Bronco broadsided on the salt pan, stopped briefly, then sped off with wheels spinning back in the direction it came.

"Bosco. Got your ears on?" I yelled into the mic.

"I'm here. What's your status?"

"The aircraft has been destroyed. Tango heading your way."

"Roger that. Oscar Mike."

CHAPTER SEVEN

Lake Eyre

Up in the air, the pilot again leaned on the control stick. The helo changed direction and followed the Bronco's dust trail toward Bosco's SUV. Bosco had already broadsided his vehicle in the dirt and had jumped out, using it as cover. I saw the repeated flashes of the muzzle as Bosco began peppering shots at the Bronco, the moment it came into his range. The Bronco steered out of control, veered off the road, and turned over.

"Get us down there!" I yelled to the pilot.

As soon as the helo hit the dirt, I sprang from the door. I sprinted, limping toward Bosco as fast as I could go.

Bosco pulled the G-man to his feet, then raised his handgun, pointing the muzzle at the G-man's head.

I screamed out, "No! Bosco. No!"

When the shot rang out across the silent desert, the hope I had for gleaning intel was dashed for good. I moved over to Bosco, feeling my shoulders hunch forward with the disappointment. I stood there, looking down at the dead guy with the words 'yet another stuff-up' racing through my brain.

After a pause, Bosco casually turned and walked past me to the pilot somewhere at my rear. Bosco moved without any bother, as though it was of no consequence, raised his weapon, and K-POP! – put a bullet into the pilot's head.

"Bosco! Are you fucking serious!" I yelled.

"Can't risk it, big hoss. What option do we have?" Bosco said, as he took a red bandana from his jacket pocket. Using the bandana, he began wiping his prints clean from the handgun. Stepping back to the deceased G-man, Bosco placed his handgun into the hand of the dead guy on the ground. "Dumbass just took the easy exit," he said, while at the same time reaching and retrieving what I thought was a Glock pistol from the dead G-man's holster.

"Here, you take this one," Bosco said, passing me the Glock. "Something tells me this ain't over, and you're gonna need it."

I stood there stunned, not knowing how I'd report this one to Shilo. I took the Glock from Bosco without a second thought. I checked for rounds, then tucked it at the small of my back. Bosco rifled around in the Bronco wreckage. "Oh. Here it is." Bosco grabbed the briefcase from within the wreck.

He took it, walked to me, then slapped the briefcase hard on my chest. "Don't lose it this time. I ain't doing this shit again. I'll organise the clean-up crew with Shilo. Reckon that sits a little unsavoury with you."

"Let's just glean as much as we can, Bosco."

"There won't be much. These G-men don't carry anything of use. Exactly for that reason."

I sat in the passenger seat of Bosco's SUV while he drove at an easy pace, north toward William Creek. The briefcase containing the yellow folder, disk, and documents was safe in my possession. I placed the briefcase on my lap and ran my hands over the textured leather, thinking how I'd report back to Shilo.

I thought about Angel and somehow knew she'd be okay. However, the guilt over abandoning her played heavily on my mind. I needed to be there for her. But I also needed the briefcase. How I wanted to be two people at the same time.

I glimpsed sideways at Bosco. His dawdling was really starting to piss me off. Something told me that until I got back there, Angel was in danger. Maybe I should've stayed with her and let Bosco handle everything on his own. But then, there was the Lear Jet. I'd hate to think what would've occurred had I *not* been there. It made me shudder thinking about it. How frustrating it all was with Bosco, driving with an elbow hitched out of his window, cruising along like he was on some kind of Sunday drive.

C'mon, Bosco. Step on it. Fa Christ's sake . . .

But then there was another thought. A question to which I needed an answer.

"The woman at the hotel," I said. "Was that you?"

"What! No! Of course not! I don't do innocents. That was the G-man looking for you. That woman probably didn't give him anything."

"Oh, and the pilot wasn't an innocent?"

"Heck, Nathan. Told ya before there's no choice. It had to play that way."

Hmm . . .

I went back to being silent, weighing things in my head. Bosco was right, I conceded. There could be no leak. No loose ends. Had the pilot spoken of anything, even a slight hint, it would blow everything and there'd be a price to pay.

I caught Bosco eyeing me as he drove. He had that look on his face. I knew what he was thinking. I had thought this time he might let it rest, but Bosco being Bosco, there was no chance of that. How did I know he was going to bring it up all over again?

"What!" I finally said.

"How's that leg of yours going?"

That's how the conversation normally started. He'd bring the goat thing up and rub my nose in it all over again. "Operation Matchbook was a shit fight. How many times do I need to say it? Don't you think we need to move beyond what happened down range?"

Operation Matchbook. How could I forget it? How could I put it behind me? Once the smell of death gets up the nose, it never leaves. Burned and charred bodies only sometimes were aired in the media – and even then, briefly.

Looking at those articles, I wondered what kind of life they'd left behind. Their lives didn't make the papers. The details didn't reach civvie street or get viewed by the average Joe on CNN.

The movies tried to reproduce incidents like theirs. But how could Hollywood replicate something they'd not witnessed? How could they know about boiled-up, expanding brain matter that punched its way out of eyes, ears, and noses? Some of those guy's heads literally exploded from the immense pressure of a rapidly expanding organ. The average Joe will never see it. Never know of it. It was better that way.

Bosco sighed openly and then said, "You're right, Canter. Let's forget all that stuff and put it away for good. But tell me something. Where in the heck is your package?"

"That's a story for another day. But I'll give you the short. Angel is at the medical clinic. What a stuff-up I've made of it so far."

How could I explain all the things that led to Angel being taken into medical care? It *was* a stuff-up. The dad thing again. Why didn't I have it in me to be a father? It should've never happened.

I should've never left that awful so-called rocket fuel within the reach of a minor. It made me think about those labels printed on things that were bad for kids. 'Keep out of reach of children.' But there was no label on that jar. There wasn't even a childproof cap, for god's sake.

"Just tell me she's safe and I'll leave it," Bosco said, drilling into my thoughts.

"She's safe . . . I stuffed up. That's all I'm saying."

The way he eyed me and gave me *the look* told me he wasn't impressed. But to his credit, he didn't say another word.

Bosco stopped the SUV south of William Creek. I grabbed a jean leg, tossed my prosthetic limb to the side, and got out. In my hands was the briefcase and the local guy's 303. Walking back to William Creek, there would be at least three kilometres of thinking to do.

"You know they're gonna ask about the pilot," I said, peering back through an open window.

"You'll think of something. I've already given you the clues. I'll make it easy for you, Canter. Whatever you report back to Shilo, I'll back it up."

Then he was gone.

I was left there in the silence. I forced my steps forward and broke into a light jog, all the while thinking about Angel. I hoped the trust I'd put in Doc Bryant wasn't betrayed.

CHAPTER EIGHT

Matchbook

At last, we found ourselves where we should've ended up
in the first damn place. No more dead ends. No more wrong turns.
No more getting into a trajectory away from the target. I stood
agape at the colossal concrete structure housing the centrifuges
we were about to destroy.

I wondered how we'd manage it. A few slabs of plastic explosive. A handful of detonators. That's it. How in the heck could a
half-dozen blocks of C4 even scratch it? Even make a dent in it?
There were thousands of the cylindrical uranium-enriching devices, as far as my eyes could reach. Trailing off into the distance,
they didn't seem to end.

"Well, Canter," Bosco said. "We'll go looking for a weak spot.
Everything's got one."

"Yeah. And where do you suppose we start?"

"Easy, mate," Scotty-Blue said. "At the beginning."

"You fucking idiot, Blue," Franco put in. "This isn't the time
for clichés."

"Fan out," I said. "Look for anything that will make for a chain reaction."

Scotty-Blue said words that stopped everyone. "You don't wanna say those words chain reaction 'round 'ere, mate. Bloody unlucky in a place where they make nukes, don't ya reckon?"

I nodded. Bad choice by me. "Move out," I ordered. "Stay on coms."

Moving forward with my M-4 trained down range, I kept walking in a straight line. Franco and Scotty-Blue ducked left. Bosco and Granger ducked right. Smic went off in another direction altogether. As I traced the edges of the centrifuges, I was already getting a picture of the weak spot Bosco suggested.

"Bosco. You seeing what I'm seeing?"

"That depends, Canter. I'm not psychic. I don't have a crystal ball either."

"Smart-arse. Take a look. The centrifuges are arranged into banks."

"Yeah, I noticed. The banks are channelled into what looks like a main supply conduit?"

"Correct," I said. "I'll follow an MSC to see where it leads. Oscar Mike."

"Roger that."

I counted them just for good measure. Sixty centrifuges connected to a bank. Each bank on an MSC. I followed the nearest MSC to what appeared to be a tiny control room. A shack, small enough to house as least one individual. No one in sight, which was odd. Moving silently to the door I peeked inside. A column of switches in there.

It was no good. Planting explosives on a single control room would only dispatch roughly five hundred banks. I did the math. Our available C4 would never cover it. There had to be another option.

"Canter. Smic."

"What have you got?" I responded.

"Green gooey shit all over the floor. Rad counter off the bell."

"Step away for Christ's sake!"

"It's too late, mate. I'm afraid I've taken a big punch."

"Fa shit sake, Smic!"

"Sorry, Canter. But I think I've found that weak spot. The trouble is, you'll all get lit up and glowing by the time you get down here. I recommend yous all stay back and let me handle it. I have an idea that just might work. Copy?"

"Make it quick," I said. "And Smic. Maximum dial, okay? Rendezvous at checkpoint kilo."

"Roger that."

"Everyone but Smic. Fall back to checkpoint kilo."

Maximum dial was only two hours. Two hours to get far enough away. I hoped it was enough. Maybe it wasn't. We'd be dead either way. Each way I looked at it, the same result. A quick death, or a slow one. We weren't coming out of it alive and that's all there was to it. But then, from somewhere outside, the crackle of AKs opened up.

* * *

"Hardball! Come in, Hardball! This is Matchbook! Over!"

Surrounded. Boxed in. They were all over us, at every hour of the clock. It didn't matter which way we faced. We somehow found a wadi and tracked the edges, finding cover. Granger pushed on in front. A step too far. The earth opened up as an IED was triggered. Granger's body was left shattered into a horror I was not able to describe.

We hunkered down in the IED crater with AK fire zipping past. I screamed into the mic again. "Hardball! Come in, Hardball! This is Matchbook! We are a ground call sign, and in the shit! How copy! Over!"

Silence from the radio. I tore it off my back and noticed a hole big enough for my fist. The radio was as useless as a rubber beak on a magpie. I threw it down hard.

"Bosco!" I screamed. "TACTBE!"

Bosco immediately grabbed the tactical beacon from his chest pack and tossed it, at the same time firing from his hip.

The TACTBE in my grip, I brought the mic up to my face. "Turbo! Turbo! Turbo! This is Matchbook! We are a ground call sign! Over!"

A ping-zip over my right shoulder. I shot a stare back at Bosco and shook my head. A sharp shot ricocheted across the top of his kevlar helmet. I caught his smile, and he was back to what had to be done. I yelled again into the TACTBE. "Turbo! Turbo! Turbo! This is Matchbook! We are a ground call sign...In shit-state-fubar! Over!"

Within seconds, a voice crackled over the speaker, "Matchbook. AWACS . . . Reading you two by three . . . Send . . . Over."

"AWACS. This is Matchbook . . . Request immediate air support. Grid to follow. Flash . . . Lima. Golf. Oscar. Danger close. Wait! Out!"

"Roger Matchbook. Flash . . . Lima. Golf. Oscar. Danger close. Grid to follow. Wait. Out."

Bosco scooted over to my side, slapping a hand on my back then pointing his gloved hand. "Get the incendiary LGO on that ridge. Eleven o'clock, Canter. Clear it. Then let's get the hell out." He was gone. Back to six.

I immediately read off the grid under night scope. "AWACS. Matchbook. Grid. Over."

"Matchbook. AWACS. Send. Over."

"AWACS. Ten-digit grid . . . November. Echo. Six. Seven. Three. One. Two. Zero. Niner. Four. One. Five. Tangos in the open. Flash. Lima. Golf. Oscar. Danger close. How copy. Over!"

"Solid, Matchbook. Flash . . . Lima. Golf. Oscar. Five mikes. Out."

My heart dropped. Five minutes. We were dead in three. The crackle of AKs from the top of the ridge. A zip cracked past the side of my face. Another shrill of a projectile past my shoulder. That was close. Too close. Death was a moment away. Pinned down, running out of ammo. I was at eleven. Bosco at six. Franco at three. Scotty-Blue at nine.

We closed ranks on the two KIAs at our feet. Smic and Granger. Granger bled out. Nothing we could do. Smic was there, minus the top of his head. Bosco peppered shots to his front and flank. The same as Franco. The same as Scotty-Blue. Franco called out for another mag, to which there were none.

"Canter!" Bosco screamed over his shoulder. "Where is that Flash LGO!"

"Two mikes," I screamed back.

Over the noise of battle, the tinkling sound of a bell. A goat bolted down into the wadi. Down into the IED crater. It pushed up to my side, looking for cover. Its slitted pupils were wide. Its mouth hung open. It was silent and shivering. The look of shock in its eyes.

"I'm out!" Franco screamed.

On my last mag. Bosco at six, I knew he'd run out in a few. We could no longer afford rapid fire in bursts. Every shot fired would have to mean a kill. Then the sound. Angels on our shoulders.

"Incoming!" I screamed.

"Incoming!" screamed Franco and Scotty-Blue.

The ear-splitting scream of F-16 Fighting Falcons punched overhead. Fire support had arrived not a split second too soon, dropping their laser-guided incendiary ordnance exactly on the grid. The ridge at eleven. The night sky lit up with incredible explosions, raging with fire and flames. A hole had been punched through the line of fire. But down in the open wadi, down in the IED crater, we were still pinned at six, three, and nine.

"Bosco! Smoke flanks and let's get the fuck out!" I screamed at the same time as I saw Scotty-Blue picking up Granger's remains and doing his level best getting him across his shoulder. A full mag was under Granger's body. My eyes focussed. There were two. I kicked one across to Bosco. He picked it up and slapped it into his M-4 in a precision movement. I kicked the other to Franco.

"Smoke out!" Bosco screamed. His voice was drowned out by the noise of peppering automatic weapons in the distance, and the shrill of projectiles passing, cracking by.

"Leave the KIAs!" Bosco screamed. "We have to move now!"

Franco picked up Smic's body. "We don't leave 'em, mate. They don't get to be haji propaganda bullshit!"

"Fuck!" Bosco screamed, at the same time hurling a few more smokers.

I slung my M-4, picked up the horrified goat, and pulled it into my chest.

"Are you serious!" Franco called out.

"Hearts and minds, brother," I yelled. "Hearts and minds."

We moved out of the IED crater and tracked the edge of the wadi. Up over the ridge, we began to leapfrog in an echelon formation. The goat under my arm, I fired from the hip when it was my turn. Then, dead trigger. I thought it was a failure to eject, but no. There were no rounds left in my magazine.

Dropping my weapon, I grabbed my sidearm and opened up until Bosco, Franco, and Scotty-Blue made their way past. They settled and began firing shots. That's when I knew it was my turn to leapfrog. That's how it went for the next kilometre or so. Drop down. Turn and fire. Wait for them to pass. Then leapfrog again. All the while, the goat I had tucked under my arm had no argument. The shocked creature was still and silent, not so much as a bleat.

By the time we reached the same rammed earth huts we passed on the way in, the imminent danger was over. Every round we had at our disposal was spent. There was nothing left to answer a fight apart from the blade I kept in my chest pack. The handle was within easy reach and I was ready to do the job if it ever came down to it. We tabbed on, hoping to Christ haji wasn't around the next corner. The thought of getting into shit all over again wasn't far from my mind.

With the goat slung over my shoulder, we passed the familiar rammed earth huts and headed toward our designated extraction point, where I'd use the tactical beacon and call in. We'd get out pretty much quick smart.

A voice called from somewhere behind, and the goat all of a sudden wanted to get away. It was the herder, and his happiness at the sight of his goat coming home was everything I'd been working toward. The goat kicked and bleated. I let the thing go.

The herder beckoned us closer. I thought he just wanted to show his appreciation. Then there was a massive thump at my side. That's all there was.

* * *

I opened my eyes. A woman in desert fatigues was standing at my side. As my eyes focussed, I saw she was with someone else; they were talking in Arabic. The woman checked off things on equipment that clicked and beeped.

I felt stuff over my face. Tape. A mask. And something down my throat. I tried to speak but gagged. The woman appeared startled and looked down at me. She bent over and pulled something out. I saw it. A long plastic tube. I felt it rip up from my guts as she pulled it away.

I tried again with more words. "Water." All I could manage. It came out raspy and garbled. It probably didn't make sense, but somehow, I knew the woman understood what the word was. Even though I felt incredibly thirsty, she moved away without giving me any and my eyes closed again.

* * *

Someone shook me.

"I'm Teresa," the voice said. "Hello, Nathan. Wake up. Good boy. Wake up."

My eyes opened. The woman I'd seen before.

"Nathan. I'm Teresa. Your doctor."

The pain in my left foot was intense. I moved my toes and the pain went away for a second or two. Then the pain came back more intensely than ever. I moved my toes again and relaxed as I flexed them forward and back. Forward and back. The fiery pain left again, but then erupted in my left knee. Penetrating. Forceful. Fierce. A fire under my body. I placed my hand down on my knee to give it a rub.

A horrible realisation struck me: There was no knee there. Not even the toes I flexed a moment ago. Everything gone. A stump… A stump wrapped up in bandages. And a firestorm of pain racing up my back and through my head.

I felt a cooling sensation rip up my arm. Then into my shoulder. The pain left. I closed my eyes.

CHAPTER NINE

Marree

The goat thing was always the subject of banter. Catching up with Bosco again, I thought he might let it be. As I walked the dusty road back to William Creek with the local guy's 303 tucked under my arm and the briefcase pulled to my chest in the same way I'd taken that goat away from danger, I caught myself smiling briefly with the memory. Smiling, but with a certain amount of embarrassment, I supposed.

Getting my head together, I thought about what was next: To continue the journey south to Melbourne. I thought about what had recently transpired and it suddenly occurred to me. The weapon I had tucked at the small of my back was the one used on Lilly, the lady with no front teeth. The G-man's murder weapon. I reached around and pulled it out. I scanned it and thought about tossing it. The moment I thought it, a Police Landcruiser belted over the rise toward me with blue lights flashing and siren blaring. My next urge was to toss the handgun as far away as I could get it. Too late. I couldn't do it without being noticed. I thrust it back behind my back, hoping they'd drive on past.

The Police Landcruiser belted past me. Rising dust got up my nose, causing an inbound sneeze attack. But my sense of relief was short-lived. I spun on my heel to see the taillights of the Land-cruiser light up. I heard the rush of its tyres locking up in the gravel. I saw the silhouette of the vehicle in the late afternoon sun as it slowed and did a long U-turn. I heard the engine accelerate toward me, siren still blaring. Lights still flashing. Panic swept up my body and I stood rock still. The Landcruiser rushed to a halt, ten feet away from where I stood. I dropped the rifle. I dropped the briefcase and automatically put my hands in the air.

The door of the Landcruiser opened. "Get on the ground!" one cop yelled; gun drawn. The other bowled me over and pushed the side of my face into the dirt. I felt my hands being forced up my back. I heard the click and zip of handcuffs. I felt hands pat me down. Then one of the cops retrieved the handgun.

Fuck!

"Stop. Stop. Stop!" I said as loud as I could, under the immense pressure of someone with a knee between my shoulder blades. The words I said appeared not to be heard. No words were ex-changed between the cops, even though I shouted STOP once more. "I can explain everything." The moment I said it, I realised any explanation needed to be far from the truth.

"Plenty of time for that, sunshine," one cop said while drop-ping the handgun in a plastic evidence bag, his pinkie finger delicately stuck up in the air. The situation was *bad*. If they dropped their eyes to the contents of the briefcase, Eagle Shield would become compromised. There could be no explanation. None at all.

In the back of the Police Landcruiser paddy wagon, being tossed about as it thundered south down the Oodnadatta Track, I thought about getting the ring off my finger. I needed to do some-thing – anything – to activate the beacon. Water. I needed water. Water would do the trick. But what choices did I have? My hands were cuffed. At my back. I felt the smoothness of the ring on my finger and played with it a little. My mind twisted with the options. I could get the ring off. Easy. Then what?

I reached with my fingers and the ring came off in my hand. I sat sideways and tossed it onto the steel bed of the Landcruiser paddy wagon. It bounced with the bumps and the forward momentum. From there, I just had to get it wet. But how? Piss on it, my mind thought, then tossed out the idea. How could I manage it with cuffed hands? I manoeuvred over to the bouncing ring. I knelt down and the side of my face hit the cold steel floor. The ring bounced up and landed between my teeth. Immediately, the ring started to burn in my mouth. The beacon had activated.

I put up with the burning pain in my mouth for more than a couple of hours. The sun had long slunk under the horizon, and stars like jewels danced in the sky. My mind went back to Angel. I wondered where she was and hoped she was being cared for. Maybe Bosco was with her right now. I hoped that to be the case, seeing as he wasn't responding to the activated radio beacon. All I could do was wait and hope for any signs of change. Looking through the window of the Landcruiser paddy wagon, I saw the streetlights in the distance and I knew it had to be Marree.

* * *

The two cops reached in and grabbed me by the upper arms. I was desperately waiting for an opportunity to spit out the ring from the back of my mouth. That opportunity came. A few moments later, I was manhandled away. They chucked me into a small cubicle behind paint-peeled metal bars with more than enough graffiti etched into cold, grey walls. I kept thinking that maybe

Bosco would be around somewhere. Maggie's words sprang to mind.

He'll be in the shadows, always listening, but never far away.

Maybe Bosco was dragging this out intentionally. His sense of humour was something I struggled with most of the time. It wouldn't have surprised me if his stalling was meant to be funny. It wasn't funny, not even if it was supposed to be sarcastic. But as the hours dragged on, no sign of Bosco. No sign of anything. I called out down a lonely and empty corridor a couple of times. My words went ignored.

With the first signs of the sun's rays peeking through the miniscule window just above my head, at last a cop, who I'd not previously met, appeared at the cubicle with a set of jingling keys. He smiled down at me, at the same time twisting the key in the lock. "Toilet break, sunshine," he said dryly. As he reached through the bars and locked my hands around my back, I wondered how in the heck I'd manage it.

"You're gonna have to either take the cuffs off, or hold it for me," I said. As soon as I said it, he reached into his pocket and got out a set of blue latex gloves. I knew it was the latter. I rolled my eyes.

"The joys, huh? This job really sucks sometimes. Just make sure you aim it straight and we won't have any issues."

"Don't look at me. You're the one who gets to aim it."

After I emptied my bladder, the cop ushered me into an interview room and locked my cuffs around a metal loop on a plain old table that was etched with the same graffiti I'd seen everywhere else. The cop, without so much as an acknowledgment, closed the door and left. I sat there and ran my eyes over the place. No cameras I could see, but I knew they'd be there. No two-way mirror. Just a plain old table. A bin thrust in the corner, overflowing with empty paper cups. A couple of chairs.

I sat and wondered why nobody bothered to put fresh paint on the walls. Grey as a storm cloud. Plain as ever. A clock on the wall sat askew. It wasn't a happy place. Maybe it was that way for a reason.

Within a minute, the door opened. A fat guy came in, wearing a grey suit two sizes too small and a necktie that should've been kept solely for the Melbourne Cup races. Dragging out a chair that squealed across the dirty lino floor, he plopped himself down. The button on his blazer struggled to break free. I wanted to cover my face in case it did. He eyed me with a turned down brow and said, "I'm Detective Senior Sergeant Falconbridge. At a minimum, you'll be charged with being in possession of an unregistered firearm. It goes up from there. Talk, and let's get this thing sorted out."

"What about my phone call?"

He laughed. "This isn't the movies, sunshine. Start talking and we can see about where this will go. One: Make me happy, and I'll let you have that phone call. Two: Don't make me happy, and it means going back to one."

"Where's my stuff," I said.

"I assume you're talking about the briefcase?"

"Yeah. Where is it? Give it back," I said. My gut clenched at the thought that they'd already seen what was in it. That being what it was, it spelled out nothing but bad.

"That's where things get a bit twisty," he said. "Imagine my surprise at what we found in there. Lots of things. Weird things. But if it were all above board, all those documents should've been accompanied with a 'law enforcement on hold' order issued by the Federal Police and the High Court of Australia, which there wasn't. Your explanation?"

I said nothing.

"So, you're some kind of flashy government fella. You'd expect a guy like you would be issued with the order. But make no mistake. It's not a licence to kill. You're either kosher or a nutter. I've seen many things in my time. I've heard and seen everything. Maybe start by telling me what I should believe. I reckon that's a pretty good place to start. Don't you think?"

"Easy. I'm kosher. And the order is pending through the High Court. Now, get me out of these cuffs so I can go about my business."

The detective looked down and laughed as though his mind was already made up and that I was the nutter. Why was I not surprised? The man had on a red necktie with dancing, hip-thrusting Elvis's. If I was the nutter he claimed, it forced me to believe I was in the company of an idiot.

"The grazier at William Creek gave us his statement," he went on. "From that, we have reason to believe you weren't involved in the murder of one, Lilly McPherson. From the information we received from a second witness, one Doctor William Bryant, it appears your alibi is rock solid. However, it still doesn't explain how the alleged murder weapon was found in your possession. My gut tells me ballistics will match the handgun to the bullet found at the crime scene. Should that happen, and by all assumptions it will, you'll have a whole lot of explaining to do. I suggest you cut the crap and get your head in it. As I keep saying, start talking. I'm all ears."

It occurred to me that the police had not travelled the road out to Lake Eyre. Had they been out there, the conversation would've turned out differently. Or perhaps they had. I knew any further words would dig me in deeper.

Bosco . . .

Where in the fuck are you? You son of a bitch. This isn't funny any longer . . .

"I need a phone call to my lawyer," I said.

The detective laughed the same as before. He laughed so hard his big round belly shook. I looked down and saw the stressed button on his blazer. That thing was going to shoot off, I was sure of it. I wanted to cover my face.

"Holy crap, sunshine. Did you think that one will work?"

"I know my rights. One is a phone call. Are you going to deny it after you've already given me my rights?"

"Actually, no. We haven't done that step. Where did you get that idea?"

"Well, you'd better let me have them. Because anything I've said to this point can't be used."

"What exactly did you say? I've heard nothing."

Hmm . . . playing for time . . .

"Am I not under arrest?"

"Detained for questioning."

"Then take the damn handcuffs off!" I shouted.

"Okay . . . okay . . . Easy, sunshine." The detective reached into his pocket and got something out that looked like a steel pin; with it he began unlocking my handcuffs. When my hands were free, I sat back and folded my arms, hoping my body language would tell him I was in no mood for bullshit. "Where's my brief-case? You have no right taking it!"

His eyes went to slits. Poker face, maybe. Now was the time for formalities if he was going to do it. Either return the briefcase, or I'd have a phone call. After a heavy sigh, he left his chair, closing the door quietly behind him. My mind went to Bosco. Now's the time.

I shit you not, Bosco . . .

The detective returned. No briefcase in his hand. I looked away, knowing how this was going to play out. A second fat, uniformed cop with three stripes on the shoulder waddled in behind him, an A4-sized laminated yellow card in his grip. We were now going formal, I realised. But by the end, I'd get to make at least one phone call. The thing was, how in the heck could I explain all this to Shilo?

The detective sat down. The constable behind him read off a couple of words from the laminated card. A knock at the door. It opened with the face of yet another cop staring in. "Pardon Boss. Feds are here."

I knew in my heart the exit was near. The two immediately disappeared from the interview room and I was again by myself. I kept my eyes on the clock as the minutes ticked by slowly. It wasn't long before three uniformed Federal Police officers entered, appearing dazed from an emergency flight I assumed was out of Canberra. They were followed by another extremely young-looking guy wearing a black suit. Eyeing him from where I sat, I was hard-pressed to believe he was older than eighteen. Maybe he just looked that way. A baby face. He stuck his hand out for a shake.

"Nathan Masters?"

"Yeah. I'm him."

"I'm Andrew Mack. I'll be escorting you back to William Creek."

CHAPTER TEN

The Young Gun

A sigh of relief left me the moment the RAAF Challenger 604 lifted gracefully off a lone Marree runway. I gazed out the window, thinking about how things got so bad and if there was a way I could ever get back on track. I wondered if Angel had fully recovered from the predicament I caused, and I imagined her smiling face after we reunited.

After getting it all together, there'd be the simple matter of the continued trip south. But would it be simple? As I gazed at the diagonal landscape and horizon out the window, I wondered if it would go smoothly from this point. I needed it to be so. Something in my gut told me it wouldn't. I readied myself for any possibility.

Sitting opposite me in his luxury leather seat – with the three federal police officers just out of earshot – the young ASIO officer sat staring out of the aircraft window. It was as though he was away in his own internal world. Studying his expression told me he'd much rather be elsewhere, as though to him, the escort back to William Creek was a pain in the arse. Maybe it was. I cast a critical eye across him. His face looked familiar. A younger version of someone else I knew in the dark recesses of my mind. I remembered his name. Andrew Mack. It can't be true, I thought. It didn't stop me from enquiring.

"You're a little young to be in the game," I said, getting him back from his contemplations. He smiled and nodded, locking eye contact. "I get that a lot. I *am* qualified. Just in case you were wondering."

"I make no judgments," I said. "So long as the man can do his job. The rest is bullshit."

Saying those words appeared to brighten him up. He smiled with genuine warmth. "I know what you're thinking," he said. "I'm nineteen. ASIO pulled me in at eighteen."

"ASIO player at nineteen, huh? Most your age are still at university…"

"I graduated from university at fourteen," he cut in, his expression suddenly hard. Why was he was getting all defensive? Maybe he'd had this conversation a thousand times. Okay. A bit touchy. Maybe I'd try something a little different.

"A prodigy?" I'd never met one. For some reason, Doogie Howser from the seventies television show came to mind.

"I don't do the pigeonhole thing," the young Andrew said. "I never wanted to be in the game. I always thought quantum physics and microbiology was my calling. Step-mother changed all that."

"Your step-mother?"

He smiled wryly. "Gimme a break, Nathan Masters. As if you don't know."

In truth, I didn't know at first. I made the connection only a minute later. Maggie's husband, Theo. Theo, the Alice Springs police officer who'd been taken down . . .

And then it went thundering through my mind as I made the link.

Theo was killed in the same way as Lilly McPherson. Gangland style. A shotgun blast to the chest. A small calibre projectile to the head. His murder was never resolved. Was his assailant the same man who'd killed the lady with no front teeth? Could there be a connection? The more I thought it over, the more the two incidents resembled each other.

No way could Lilly's murder be a copycat. Theo's demise was never put out publicly. And now, in both instances, Angel was the target. In Theo's case, his murder was the result of something he had in his possession. A bullet fragment. The bullet fired at Angel that almost took her life. It was Theo who found the fragment. It would've led to an investigation into finding Angel's attacker. It didn't get that far. Theo was killed, and the bullet fragment stolen from him. It was only after that event; Eagle Shield came into being.

Even more than before, I realised Angel *was* in danger. Until such a time as she got to the safe house in Melbourne, she would always have watchers on her tail. Her life would always be threatened. I should've never left her alone.

Sitting there, I ran my hand over the textured leather of the briefcase in my lap. Andrew was still eyeing me as though on the defensive. It was as though he knew my next words. It was as though he was almost daring me to speak them. So I spoke what was on my mind. "I'm assuming you know all about Eagle Shield?"

"I know everything, Nathan. I knew before you."

There it was. His prodigy nature beginning to show. How could he know about everything before me? Matchbook was in play while he was most likely in primary school. But going by his earlier statement, he'd have already left primary school and gone on at a much younger age. Did he even *go* through primary education?

"How is it you know everything?" I asked, knowing his answer would somehow surprise. But his next words went far beyond surprise; they revealed something completely unexpected.

"Matchbook, and now Eagle Shield, were first considered out of the collaboration between Shilo and me."

"You started this?" I felt my eyes bulge almost agog. I tried hard to keep my astonishment in check. I thought everything we started, even from years ago, was out of the thinking minds of the closed community of intelligence officials locked up somewhere in Canberra. I couldn't – no matter how hard I tried – imagine such a young soul as the top brain behind what we went through.

"Eagle Shield was . . . *is* always about Angel's safety. We need her to be safe. We need her with us," Andrew went on.

"You need her with you? What do you mean?" This was something Maggie never explained. Or perhaps she did. Maybe I missed it. Did I read about this in the mission brief? That bloody stuff in the jar. How I regretted it. Regrets. I hated them.

"When she's older," Andrew said matter-of-factly.

Then it dawned. Maggie *did* explain it. The wish for Angel to join ASIS as an adult. Now Andrew was making this point as urgently as Maggie. It made me think about the disk and what it contained. All over again. "You know about the disk?" I asked Andrew.

He nodded vigorously. "Yes, I know what's on it."

By now, I was no longer surprised. I checked my attitude at the door. Something I should've done in the first place. The young Andrew was gaining my respect. I found myself leaning in and believing the words coming from someone so young. "Do we have a laptop computer?"

"There's no need," he said. "I can explain it all. Only God himself knows the shit fight we're in. Thanks to the Guardianship."

"Guardianship of Milestone?" Here we go again. It appeared I'd never escape.

"Yeah." He sighed loudly. "That . . . and the Amber project."

"Maggie has given me some info on Amber. The intel is on the disk, which I haven't yet had a chance to scan. I know about the Milestone theory. I know about the enriched plutonium and assumed Matchbook shut it down. That was the plan. It's come to light that not all the centrifuges were destroyed. And now Milestone is a clear and present danger?"

"Not so much as an immediate threat. Intel suggest things will ramp up around 2016. Your Eagle Shield mission with Angel will become part of Milestone's undoing."

"Part?" Part. I thought I had the whole. I must've missed something. Maybe I was out of the loop for some reason. Another hate. Intelligence can be such a dog.

"There are other objectives that go on behind the scenes. Away from Eagle Shield. None you need to concern yourself with. Not yet, anyway. After Eagle Shield has been accomplished, all the pieces will be put together and we'll stop Milestone."

"Let me guess. By destroying the Amber project? Without Amber, there can be no Milestone. And Angel will lead the way to Amber?" That was the assumption I had in my head. Now, let's see how close I was.

Andrew nodded in agreement. "That's why Angel needs to get in the program. You don't realise the job you have, Nathan. But I think you're starting to get a picture."

Hmm . . . so everyone tells me . . .

"My guess? Angel won't go willingly," Andrew said. "She has a strong personality and a mind of her own. I think she'll be wanting to end up somewhere else. You'll need to change that. I suggest starting early. Give her some inspiration and desire. I don't know what you'll do. Maybe spark her interest by watching spy movies and reading books."

I thought about it. Bugger thinking about it. I bloody well came out and asked it.

"Just *what* makes Angel so special? She's a ten-year-old kid. She doesn't know anything. Why her? Why is she such a target? Why does she need to get with ASIS?"

Andrew paused before answering. When he *did* answer, it was without expression and was a statement that didn't seem to have any sign of a struggle. "Angel is part human. And part Oudarretian. That's the reason she's in danger. And that's the reason she needs all this protection."

Andrew reached into his pocket for a biro. He got a notepad from the side pocket of his seat. He scribbled something down. He held up the notepad with the word 'Oudarretian' written and double underlined.

I'd not heard the word Oudarretian before. After Andrew said it, I imagined it was some undiscovered race on Earth. A lost civilisation, I supposed. But Andrew had said the word human. As I put it together, I realised he was making a comparison. If it was a lost civilisation, would they not be referred to as human as well? Now, there was a division. An us and them. My mind twisted. He was speaking of these Oudarretians as otherworldly beings.

Andrew went on and confirmed it. "Not from this world," he said. "But they're human in appearance. It's hard to tell the difference. You must know what to look for to tell them apart. They all have one thing in common. They're black."

He passed the notepad over. I held it briefly in my hand before he leaned forward and snatched it away. Then, he scribbled something else down. "This is the interesting bit," he said before giving the notepad back. I looked down at the scribble. The word Oudarretian was written backward with the first few letters omitted. 'Terraduo.'

My eyes focussed. I couldn't believe what I was seeing. Out of what was written down, I saw 'Terra-Duo.' Then I realised the Latin translation. 'Earth-Two.'

"Are you bloody kidding me?"

"Not a bit," Andrew said, smiling. "Oudarret is their home planet. Earth Two. Black people from a world similar to ours. Ten light years away, to be exact. Their host star, or sun, is much closer to the surface of Oudarret in comparison to our sun to our Earth. They've evolved with a protective enzyme that they host in their skin. The Oudarretian black colour results from this. The enzyme absorbs white light. White light isn't reflected. This enzyme also protects them from cosmic radiation and therefore melanoma."

It erupted in my mind like a strobe light. The black person in Angel's dream. And the black person I'd seen on that first day I'd enlisted into the army. The black guy with the American uniform.

Tall as tall. I took a moment and pondered what Andrew had told me. Pieces were finally coming together.

"These Oudarretians are part of the Milestone theory?" I asked.

"One: It's no longer a theory. Two: Yes, they are. They instigated everything. They've been among the human race for decades. Perhaps centuries, who'd know? You have to wonder about the technologies humans have to this day, Nathan. On the disk, you'll find out what those technologies are. One is nuclear. There'd be no nuclear weapons if it wasn't for the Oudarretians."

"They gave us the technology to quite possibly destroy ourselves?" How shocked was I to hear this? I always thought it started with Einstein. Then Otto Hahn. Then Oppenheimer. Then Edward Teller. The list goes on. They weren't black. They weren't tall. I found it hard to believe these men were otherworldly beings. I must've missed something – but what?

Andrew punched through my thoughts with his answer. "They gave us that technology. Absolutely. The Oudarretians aided our best-known scientists in the race for weapons of mass destruction."

There it was. The bit I missed. It still didn't seem real. Andrew went on. "That's what Milestone is about. They'll destroy us all. Part of their plan."

". . . Why?" I had more words. They wouldn't come. It was as though they were lodged under the lump at the base of my throat.

Andrew held his breath briefly as though somewhere in his mind he was at odds with admitting the reasons why. As I sat back in my plush leather seat, I began to understand humanity's rise in technology and a marked acceleration in knowledge. Things were beginning to make sense in a way I never previously imagined.

Andrew finally answered why. "We've got our hands on a document that points the Oudarretian's motivation toward world oil reserves and the balance of power it brings. You have that intelligence with you. But there's also a glimpse of intelligence to suggest their need for helium-3. They want it. They need it to survive."

"Helium-3? I know about helium-3, Andrew. I also know helium-3 is dangerous in the wrong hands. What on earth would they be wanting the stuff for?" Helium-3 said nothing but huge explosion. I quickly thought back to the Oudarretian motive Andrew addressed. Where was the connection? What was I not seeing?

"What would they be wanting it for? That's easy to answer," Andrew went on. "Earth humans metabolise sugar and complex carbohydrate for energy. The Oudarretians metabolise helium-3 in the same way. Without it, they can't survive."

The explanation was simple and straightforward. But also, helium-3 on Earth was rare. On Earth, it could only be harvested out of radioactive decay. Knowing there was little if any radioactive decay on Earth, I wondered how the Oudarretians were getting it? And from where?

I asked Andrew what I was thinking.

"That's unknown," he said. "But it's obvious the Oudarretians are getting what they need to survive. We've been able to ascertain the enzyme in their skin is also dependant on helium-3. Otherwise the enzyme will degrade over years. They'll lose the protection it gives them. They'll also become vulnerable and lose their connection to time and space. Then, it'll be a slow death for every one of them."

"But what of the quantities?" I asked. "Surely, there'd not be enough found on Earth for their purposes. I mean, look at the amount of complex carbohydrates humans consume on average. That's a vast quantity, Andrew."

"It's all relative. In the plain old language, the amount of energy released in five tons of processed sugar is equal to a quarter of a teaspoon of helium-3. Not only that, relatively small amounts of helium-3 can be used to power cities for centuries and also be used for weapons far greater than anything imaginable. Then, and only then, bigger quantities are needed. They already know where those quantities exist. Make no mistake, Nathan. The Oudarretians have their sights set on getting it. Even as we sit here and talk about it."

"Where?"

"On the moon," Andrew said. "The Oudarretians see the human race as an infestation. An infestation to eradicate. They're evil fucks, every last one of them. The plan is to wipe humanity away using the technology they gave us during the mid-twentieth century."

"Nuclear war?" Holy shit. I remembered back to the conversation I once had with Scotty-Blue. The theory of M.A.D. This could be the one thing that threatened the balance of power, tipping it into the favour of a sole player. Scotty-Blue was right, even from all those years ago. How did I not see this? How did I not realise this even from the days of Matchbook?

. . . Iran is the culprit, and the one that got away . . .

Maggie's words. It all went spinning around. A cyclone. Spinning, making me feel lightheaded. The eye of the cyclone hit me. Something didn't add up. Surely if a nuclear war loomed and became reality, no life would survive. It just made things appear contradictory to what Andrew explained. "That doesn't make sense," I said. "If they are going down the road of nuclear annihilation, they'd be also wiping themselves out in the process."

"As I've already explained, the Oudarretians are not affected by radiation fallout. Unbelievable, isn't it?"

Now it made sense. It made *perfect* sense. The post apocalypse would never hinder them. Never distract them. They'd get on with doing what they came for. Without Earth humans, it would be easy. The moment I realised it, I came out and said it. "They're gonna kill us all so they can mine the moon?"

"It's a done deal if we can't stop it. We need Angel with us if there's ever gonna be a chance, Nathan. That's the short and long of it. And guess what? It's your job to make it so. You have the entire globe and humanity itself in the palm of your hand."

Was this supposed to make me feel important? This was making me feel extraordinarily small. The entire length and breadth of humanity sat with me. I wished I'd never heard it. My mind kept telling me, I'm no good for this. This was too big for me. I couldn't do this on my own. Whichever way I looked at it, it *was* going to be on my own.

Andrew busted through my horrible thoughts with one word. 'Guardianship.' I focussed on what he was telling me. "The Guardianship needs nullifying," he put in. "Without the Guardianship there's no Milestone. And the way to do that is through the destruction of the Amber Project."

Angel again. She'll lead the way to this so-called Amber Project. To destroy it. How, was the question. I tried to imagine the day she'd lead us there, but not knowing exactly what Amber physically was or what it would entail to nullify the threat. I failed trying to get my head around it. My mind went somewhere else.

I wanted to know about the Guardianship. Who were these guys? I knew Andrew was privy. I asked him.

Andrew sat back and smiled as though the subject was his own pet. "At the top, the Guardianship have retired political officials and former secret intelligence officers from a gathering of countries," he went on. "Down the bottom, a collection of thugs, as well as underworld and organised crime figures, who are rich enough to bankroll the Guardianship's activities."

Crime figures . . .

"Mafioso?"

"Bet your arse they're there," Andrew replied still with the grin. "Bonanno, Gambino, Genovese, to name a few. Lucchese, Colombo . . ."

"Jesus, Andrew! Are you shitting me!"

"Now you know what we're up against. The Guardianship gets around cloaked under the infrastructure of world intelligence organisations. They're so deep under, the legitimate world agencies don't know they're there. But with the help of the crime families who are financially involved with their activities, they have power far beyond our better understanding."

"But the Guardianship is dead with the rest of us, Andrew. They're human. They don't have the Oudarretian's enzyme thing."

"Glad you said it. That brings us back to the Amber project. We think it's the Guardianship exit strategy. The exit strategy for the so-called 'ticket holders'. If we don't destroy the Amber project, everything is lost."

"Tell me what we know about Amber?"

"Little is known. The intelligence we've intercepted hasn't given up much other than to tell us Amber is solely conducted within Australian shores. Amber is out there, somewhere in the desert. Where, we don't know. We've got a handful of years to find out everything. Why? Because of the time needed for the Guardianship to perfect their exit strategy. That says genome engineering to me. And that brings me to Angel and why she's so important. Angel is the result of an early experiment. Perhaps an early attempt at procuring an exit strategy. Perhaps Angel didn't turn out as expected. And that's why the Guardianship has a clear directive to capture or to kill her outright."

Stunned, I sat back. I placed a hand to my face, not believing. This was pure and unconceivable madness. Andrew went on, looking down as though he, himself, was at the edge of his better understanding. "The Guardianship had Franco's help in this." Then Andrew looked away. Probably out of disappointment and disgust, I assumed. But his next words confirmed it was disgust. "Franco was behind Alisha's abduction. Alisha was artificially inseminated against her will. Everything moral about this scenario goes out the door backward."

I put my hand up to my forehead and tried to hide from Andrew's words. I said nothing. I couldn't. I almost felt sick. Now I was fully aware why Franco needed the disk so desperately. Franco turned and crossed the line. However, I didn't know the circumstances of what led to his temptation. My guess, Franco knew what was in the future. He wanted a guarantee to be included in the Guardianship exit strategy. The same as the crime families. The same as those caught up in the temptation to get away, who were willing to sell their soul.

How dark was the man, Franco? How cold and calculating? Certainly, he was not the Franco I once knew. Now, all the intelligence Andrew brought to light lay digitally etched onto a magnetic plate no bigger than the palm of my hand. Someone had mysteriously called end game and downloaded everything. Who? I wondered. Who wanted to blow the whistle? Who wanted to leak the data? In the end, lives had been lost trying to recover the disk in an attempt to stop the leak.

The hard nature hit home, clear and direct. I now had a job on my hands. To Angel, I was both guardian and protector. Now and forever. Being away from her, I realised she was now vulnerable to any attack. If I could've increased the speed to get back to William Creek any faster, I would've made it possible. The urgency to get there couldn't have been more crucial. More vital. I found myself urging the momentum forward. Willing it onward. I leaned forward in my seat, trying to speed up the fabric of time.

"She's in danger right now!" I said loud enough to grab Andrew's immediate attention.

He shot me a hard look. "We can't get there any quicker. Let's hope all is okay when we arrive. Your road trip is done, Nathan. We'll be flying you and Angel down to the safe house in Melbourne."

CHAPTER ELEVEN

The Seven

I pushed my face up to the aircraft window the moment the RAAF Challenger 604 came to rest. The tarmac was empty of souls. I could see the tin shack with the paint-peeled red cross. Beyond that, the main dusty track. The hotel was sitting lonely in the distance with no patrons out on the veranda. My Land Rover was parked where I'd last left it, still standing alone on the dusty car park.

A flock of birds were perched on the roof, seemingly basking in the sun. Then horror hit me at the sight of Bosco's SUV parked next to mine. That couldn't be good. Everything I'd dreaded had become real. Looking further out from the window, Bosco was running toward the aircraft, running at top effort, waving his hands wildly in the air.

I shot a glare at Andrew. He locked eye contact and echoed my concern. I couldn't have said any words to take the truth away. Angel was gone, my mind said. Andrew got up from his seat and went for the exit; at that exact moment, I pushed up with my one good leg. I made urgently for the aircraft door, which swung down and became a set of stairs. At the foot of the stairs, Bosco was already there. Red faced. Ranting in his panic. "She's not here!" he shrieked.

Stunned, I managed some shouted words while stumbling down the stairs. "Have you got word back to Shilo?"

"I have," Bosco shouted at the edge of his breath.

"What did she say, Bosco!"

"She didn't. She hung up on me!"

Panic. I didn't know it could feel so bad. Out of all the times panic came to visit, I shunned it away. I pushed through it. I used the energy, turning it into something positive. But this time…This time it was as though panic was an ugly black dog biting at my calf muscle. It had sunk its teeth right in. I could not shake it away.

I turned to Andrew who was at the top of the aircraft stairs and appeared to be frozen in his own shock. "Get me the fucking satellite phone!" I screamed at him. He spun and disappeared into the aircraft, not a word said.

Bosco and I walked straight lines on the tarmac, back and forth, heads down, waiting for Andrew. When Andrew arrived after bouncing down the steps, I took the phone from Andrew's shaky, trembling hands. I tried to dial. My hands shook probably worse than Andrew's. My fingers quivered back and forth, not able to dial anything. Bosco snatched the phone from my grip. His fingers went to work, then passed the phone back to me. Placing the cumbersome phone to my ears, it toned twice and then answered.

"Hello. Do you have your laundry pickup number?"

"Just connect me to Shilo!" I screamed into the handset.

"One moment please, sir . . ."

Swear words and profanities that I couldn't verbalise swept around my brain. I thought I'd heard my inner voice speak vulgarly before. Now, I winced at the words I was thinking. Four letter words. Multiple four-letter words.

"Canter!" Maggie yelled from the other end of the line. "Sloppy, Canter! Sloppy, sloppy . . . Bloody sloppy!"

"Shilo . . . I'm . . ." Holy crap! I was lost for words. I thought I had them. They were gone!

"Are the federal police still with you!" Maggie shouted.

"Yes . . . I . . ."

"Pass the damn phone to them, will you please?"

I passed the phone to the higher-ranking federal cop. He took it and didn't speak. He appeared only to listen to Maggie's words, which I could just make out. She was screaming! Her penetrating voice erupted from the tiny speaker and I was at least five feet away. I saw the federal cop's expression harden. After a moment, he handed the phone back to me. I placed the phone to my ear, at the same time watching him sprint away with two others at his heel.

"Maggie . . ."

"Canter! Its bloody *Shilo* for god's sake!"

Good Christ! I was digging in deeper. How cold was this ground that swallowed me?

"I . . . I'm . . ."

"I suggest you get your backsides back here! All of you! FORTHWITH! Do you hear me!"

Click.

She was gone.

"Jesus," Bosco said in a low tone. "I reckon she's pissed."

"No shit, Bosco!" I gritted my teeth and said nothing further beyond a low growl. I stomped past Bosco; my hands curled into fists. I wanted to belt something. Anything!

"Give me something to hit!" I yelled.

Bosco grabbed Andrew by the shoulders. "Here! This one! Hit him!"

It would've been funny if it hadn't had been so serious. I even wound one up and aimed it squarely at Andrew. Andrew shrunk back. He didn't know what to do. Nor did I. I got myself together. Only just.

I moved past Andrew, who was still standing as though stunned, his complexion almost matching his auburn hair. I turned to get in the aircraft. At the top of the stairs, I looked toward the hotel. My attention turned to the birds sitting on the roof of my Land Rover. "Birds," I said out loud. "Out of everything, I now have a job cleaning my canvas roof!"

"The weirdest thing," Bosco said, staring up from the foot of the stairs. "They're eagles. They've been sitting there for hours. You'd think they'd be off doing things eagles do. But not them. I ain't never seen seven in a pack before. I thought eagles only got around in twos."

"You sure they're eagles? From where I stand, one is white. There's no eagle that's all white."

"I already told ya it's weird. You think maybe they're trying to tell us something?"

I thought going over and pushing them into flight was an option. At least I wouldn't have to spend an entire day scraping bird business off the canvas roof. But then, something else occurred to me. "Maybe you're not that far from the truth, Bosco."

I walked back down the few stairs, past Bosco, at the same time the aircraft engines began to spool. Bosco shouted something. I tried not to notice as I walked away. Bosco shouted again at my rear, "You're not serious, Canter? Hey…Big hoss? Remember Shilo? Oh, shoot! Canter! Get back here!"

I ignored him. I ignored the sounds of the engines. As I got closer to my parked Land Rover, I began to realise how big those eagles were. The pure white eagle had something in its beak.

Albino?

I pushed the silly thought away.

Walking a bit closer, I realised what that thing was. A bullet. The bullet caught the light of the sun and glinted. Another eagle had something else. My curiosity wanted to know.

A metre away, the seven eagles towered above where I stood. Huge and ominous. Staring with heads cocked sideways. Not flinching. Not moving. Rock steady and watching me, as though beckoning. The albino eagle with the bullet clasped in its beak hopped forward on a set of giant talons. They were huge, much larger than I'd expected from the distance. I'd never seen birds so big.

Reaching up, its massive head tipped forward and it dropped the bullet into the palm of my hand. I studied it. Clean. Undamaged, but with the usual markings suggesting the make of rifle it came from. Another eagle hopped forward, dropping something else. A lock of hair. Not Angel's hair. Hair the colour of ginger.

Its talons were encrusted in dried blood. Lots of blood. Lots of ribbons of flesh still clung to its spurs as though the eagle had made a clean kill. As soon as the lock of hair was delivered, the seven eagles took flight. I felt massive bursts of air pressure as they pushed away with their enormous wingspans.

It was a moment that couldn't be ignored. With the clues the eagles had given, I knew there'd be more. I turned and hop-sprinted back to the aircraft with the fresh evidence thrust deep in my pocket.

Reaching the foot of the aircraft stairs, I waved a hand to Bosco who was in his seat. He eyed me from the window with an expression of disbelief, and then got up. A moment later, the engines spooled down and Bosco came prancing down the stairs.

"C'mon, Canter. We're wasting time," he said, as though out of patience.

"There's something around here, Bosco. We can't leave without investigating."

"I saw you push those eagles away. Good! Now, let's go."

"I can't leave just yet. Don't ask me how I know. I just know." I took the bullet from my pocket and showed him. He took it from my hand and studied it. "Nine-millimetre. The markings look like Glock. You're thinking Glock?"

"Yeah."

"You know, nobody has them around here."

"No one but G-men."

Bosco ogled me with a set of enquiring eyes. "Where'd ya get it?"

"Don't ask. You wouldn't believe me anyhow."

"Oh, Christ . . . alright! Let's get to work."

I walked to the front of the aircraft and signalled a cut-throat to the pilot. Then I hand-signalled twenty minutes. I saw the pilot reach to his console, then lift the seatbelts from his shoulders. Twenty minutes. Any longer would not go down convincingly with Shilo. Passing the row of windows, I signalled to Andrew. I needed all hands. The more the better. Within a moment, he was stepping down the stairs and the three of us left the area. I noticed the federal police, who were busy pinning up crime scene tape around the tin shack. I kept thinking I should go there and look further for clues. But I relented and pushed on with my hunch.

"Where're we headed?" Bosco asked, as I kept the pace going forward, finally pushing past my Land Rover, which radiated the incoming desert heat.

"The eagles went in that direction," I pointed. "Let's keep going that way."

Bosco reached and grabbed my arm, spinning me around. "Now, wait just a goddamn second. We're chasing eagles now?"

"You said it yourself, Bosco. Maybe the eagles *were* trying to tell us something."

"I was kidding. You realise how ridiculous that is?"

"Ridiculous. Maybe. My gut tells me we keep walking this direction."

"Yeah. How did I know you were gonna say that?"

Then, another thought. "Bosco, you said you'd been here for how long?"

"A few hours. I can't remember exactly. Why?"

"Did you check out the clinic?"

"Yeah. Of course. A couple of dead Aboriginals. Killed the same way as that Lilly."

"Find anything unusual?"

"Lots of things. There was one heck of a firefight in there. Oh, that reminds me. I found this. I figured it would mean something." Bosco retrieved a compact disk player from the inside of his jacket. He passed it over, and I took it and scrutinized it. Walkman. Orange foam headphones hung from a wire. But Angel had left her compact disk player in her bag. I'd left everything in the motel room. How did she get it?

"Sorry, big hoss. I meant to give it to you straight away. But things got a little out of hand with Shilo going off her face."

"That's okay. But I wonder how Angel got hold of the thing when it was left in the motel room."

"Hey, that's not all, big hoss. Take a look inside."

I flipped the lid open. A compact disk. Metallica. The music Angel enjoyed the most. "Yeah, it's a compact disk," I said. "Something I missed?"

"Flip it over," Bosco said.

I took the disk out and flipped it over. I sucked back a gulp of air as I saw what was written in black marker pen. Angel had written those words. *'blue man not a nice man.'*

"Get over here, Bosco. I wanna kiss ya."

"Shit. No thanks. Now we'd better get out of here, like we were instructed by Shilo . . ."

"Not yet. I still have my hunch."

Andrew butted in. "Nathan. Bosco's right. We have to get going."

I ignored him and Bosco. I turned and walked away. Their footfalls behind me told me they were coming after all.

We headed in the general direction of where the eagles had gone and it wasn't long before Andrew crouched down with a knee in the dirt. "Tracks," he said looking down, poking around in the earth with a stick.

I moved closer to Andrew. A set of fresh footprints led off into the distance. I crouched down and inspected the tracks more closely. I could see at least four sets. One set of footprints were small. My instincts told me they belonged to Angel. I shuddered all over again. I felt bile rise in my throat.

We walked on, eyes dropped, and followed the tracks up a small rise. At the top of the rise, a body lay spreadeagled in the dirt. Getting closer, I realised it was the body of someone I knew. Dried blood and a portion of skull were missing from the back of the head. I knelt beside the already-bloated form and turned the body over, revealing a clean shot to the forehead. Through and through. "Oh, fa shit sake," I said as I swished the multitude of desert blow flies away.

Bosco knelt down beside me. For some reason, he put his hand to the dead guy's throat. Maybe he did it out of habit. But the guy was gone and gone for a long time. "You knew this guy?" Bosco asked.

"Yeah. He was the doctor treating Angel. He must've given chase. He was one of us, Bosco. A brother. 6RAR."

"6RAR, huh? Vietnam 6RAR?"

"He was a good man, Bosco. He didn't deserve this. Who knows what he saw during his time? Checking out like this just isn't right. Not for this guy"

"Especially if he was a Long Tan vet."

"Long Tan? Who knows. He was certainly in the age range. I didn't get the chance to be all chatty. Maybe he *was* at Long Tan. We'll never know now."

"That's a crying shame."

"He was the real deal in my opinion. And you're right. It's a shame regardless of the fact. Let's move. We're in the right area."

We didn't have to walk more than a hundred metres. The tracks led to a large pool of now-dried blood in the dirt with more than enough flies making a meal. Blood and remains were everywhere. Flesh remains. Skeletal remains. One of the eagles, I thought, looking down. The eagle with the blood and flesh stuck on its talons. I could only imagine what took place. My logical brain took over. "Fan out," I said. "We're close."

It wasn't long before Andrew called out. "Over here!"

CHAPTER TWELVE

The Grazier

I ran over to Andrew, Bosco's footfalls and heavy breathing behind me. I looked down to a set of depressions in the dirt. I knew straight away what they were. Bosco confirmed it.

"Goddam-it! A helo!"

"Yeah. A helo," I agreed. "By the looks of the markings, probably a Black Hawk. That says money. And that says…"

"Guardianship," Andrew put in as he stood up and scanned the area, cuffing a hand above his eyes. I wasn't sure what he was looking for. The thing was, we were too late. They'd taken Angel. Judging by the foot impressions, several more individuals were involved in this now. Who knew how many. Somewhere in the back of my mind, I'd already decided how this was likely to play out. The horror of it all. I reached down and inspected the depressions further, thinking there wasn't much more to glean.

"Look guys. I think we've got as much as we're ever gonna get around here." I began to walk back to the large amount of blood spatter we'd found earlier. "Anyone got a plastic bag or something?" The blood samples would go a long way with forensics. Maybe they'd lead somewhere. Just as I thought it, Andrew offered his help. "Good idea. I'll get to work on the samples as soon as we get back."

Let's see how that young prodigy mind of his can sort this out, I thought. Bosco dug into his pocket and got out his prized red bandana. "Here, scoop some up and put it in this."

I took Bosco's red bandana and after tying the corners together, I filled it with samples of bloody dirt. Walking back, I thought about what must've happened in William Creek. The town was empty of the few people I'd seen wandering around earlier. Those people had all but disappeared, and William Creek itself resembled a ghost town, something similar to the town of Kingoonya after the British government nuked the shit out of Maralinga during the fifties and sixties.

As we approached the motel, the air drew silent with nothing but the whizzing sound of the outback breeze pushing past fly-screened doors and windows. The dust eddies kicked up on the track. The little whirl-winds brought back images of the Wild West movies I'd seen as a kid.

Getting closer to the aircraft, I stopped for a second and cast my eyes toward the blue and white-checked crime scene tape the federal police had pinned up. Bosco must've sensed my hesitation. He reached and grabbed me by my shoulder and steered me onward. But I had unfinished business. I needed to see for myself what had taken place in the tin shack with the paint-peeled red cross. "Not now, Bosco. There's more." I knew there had to be something else. I wasn't going anyplace without the complete picture, or other things I could use.

"Bullshit! Shilo will have you nailed on a plank." Bosco started going off. I ignored him and ran toward the clinic. I heard him at my rear. "Canter! Jesus H Christ!" Before I knew it, I had Andrew stepping up beside me, pacing out in front of Bosco, who continued to sound off. Then Bosco's steps caught up with us. We were lined abreast, bearing down on that checked blue and white crime scene tape.

Entering the place, the scent of hospital ammonia was thick in the air. The three federal cops were bent forward, going about their business, bagging and tagging anything useful they could find. Those cops eyed me momentarily, then without a word got back to what they were doing.

I only half-expected to see the two Aboriginal male nurses on the floor. Dead the same as Lilly, just as Bosco described. Dead the same as Theo, I realised. Both with a shotgun blast to the chest and a neat hole in the forehead. Blood pooled under their bodies as they lay there staring up, eyes fogged over, at some unknown point of interest in space. I was beginning to feel nobody had any hope in this town when it came to the Guardianship arseholes who'd caused all the bloodshed.

The first thing that came to mind was to go to the gurney Angel had been on. I placed a hand down on the empty bed sheets and tried to imagine what had taken place. From there, I scanned the area in a full three-sixty. I said to Andrew, who was standing at my side, "What is it about this place that doesn't make sense?"

He put a finger up to his lips in thought. But as he stood there thinking things over, something came to mind. The Aboriginal nurses on the floor. Both killed gangland style. As the thought came, it set off tiny shockwaves that went rippling through my head. Bosco turned up at my side. I turned to face him. "It's odd, Bosco. When I think about all this, it doesn't add up."

"What doesn't add up? Guardianship assholes came in. They executed the Aboriginals, then made off with Angel. What's odd? How about getting back to the aircraft like we're supposed to."

"Bosco. The nurses were executed gangland style."

"Yeah."

"Why wasn't the doctor?"

"I'm afraid *you're* not making sense. The doctor wasn't killed here. He was killed out there," Bosco pointed.

"That's right, Bosco. Why wasn't he killed the same as the Aboriginal nurses? If you can imagine what must've happened, how did the doctor get away? He'd have had no chance ordinarily, if the bad guys came through the door guns blazing. But he was way out there, where we found him. What does that tell you?"

"It means he was away from this place when shit went down."

"That's my point. Why wasn't he caring for Angel?"

"Maybe he went to the bathroom."

"Even if that was the case, there's a toilet here."

My mind went back to the compact disk player. Could it be that Angel was bored and asked the doctor to go and fetch the player from the motel room? It would explain the absence of the doctor when everything went bad. Coincidence? Or was there something more sinister to it than I imagined?

And why did Angel suggest a 'blue man' when we were all looking for black guys? I closed my eyes and thought hard. But as hard as I thought, nothing else came. Finally, I conceded. There was nothing more to be found and the feds would have gleaned anything else. "We're done here, guys. Let's go," I said, then left the federal cops to it.

Outside, I pulled out the compact disk player and discussed my thoughts with Bosco and Andrew. Both agreed there could be more, or less even, depending on what really happened. But one thing was for certain. From the moment Bosco found the compact disk player, the clock had started and would keep ticking until such a time that Angel was back in safe hands.

I shoved the compact disk player in my shirt, ignorant to Andrew's requests to let him have it as part of the evidence we'd recovered. I didn't know why I refused to give it up. Maybe it was as simple as wanting to be close to Angel, knowing it was one of the last things she touched.

Heading back to the waiting aircraft, I heard a voice call out from somewhere behind me.

"Oi . . . you there!"

I spun, the same as Andrew and Bosco. The local grazier I'd met a day before raced toward me. I knew straight away what he wanted. My mind snapped backward, remembering his 303 rifle the cops had taken and confiscated back at Marree. His words confirmed it when he got close enough.

"Bring me rifle back, did ya?"

The moment the grazier said it, I caught Bosco eyeing me sideways; he was ignorant to the grazier, who smiled, with his hand stuck out for his rifle, like a kid waiting for a treat.

"Sorry. The cops confiscated it," I said. "It wasn't registered to me."

"Shit. Now how am I ever gonna get rid of the rabbits? I got nothin' to control the pesky shits."

"Maybe the cops will ship it back if you contact them. Now, if you can excuse me, I have things on." I apologised again and turned to step away. But then stopped. Maybe he witnessed what had happened. But something else hit me and made me start slightly backward. I got myself up to Bosco's side and whispered, "See what I'm seeing?"

"Yeah . . . I see it."

. . .blue man not a nice man. . .

I turned to the grazier. "I never figured out why outback guys like you always wear a blue singlet and blue King Gee shorts," I said. "Must be some sort of code thing going on?"

"Mate, it's always been that way. Where've *you* been?"

I turned to Bosco and gave him a quick wink. I turned to Andrew. Andrew mouthed back silent words in the shape of 'code orange'. I winked a quick response.

I turned back to the grazier, keeping code orange protocols in my head. "Tell us what you saw? Did you see anything?"

I tried desperately to keep my composure. I tried desperately not to take him down right there and then. Code orange meant caution. Code orange meant be aware. Code orange meant interrogation, but he must be willing to submit. At first, at least. How I wanted the situation to be code red. I'd take the fucker down, no argument. No hesitation. But that had the side effect of shutting the door on Angel's whereabouts. We'd need to nab him. Code orange. I'd play this one with care.

"Seen it? I lived it!" the grazier said. "They took everyone, whoever the hell they were. They loaded them all on the helicopter and shot through. I hid in that wheelie-bin over there," he said and pointed with a fat, calloused finger.

Here we go. Bullshit . . .

I shot a glance to Bosco, then back to the grazier. "I apologise. I never got your name."

"Me? I'm Doug Walken. I run stock not all that far from 'ere. I came into town to collect supplies for me dogs, y'know?"

More bullshit. . .

"I'm Canter. This is Bosco and Andrew," I said with my hand out. Yeah. I was going to shake the man's hand. He took it and shook. I'd never met anyone with such heavily calloused hands. But I squeezed it. Hard. I wanted to break the fucker's fingers. He eyed me curiously without so much as a wince. "Canter, eh? That's not your real name, I take it? Not unless you were in a 'urry to get out into the world."

I ignored his comment. "Did you see if the helo had any markings?"

"Markings? Nah, mate. All black."

"No numbers or anything?"

He appeared to think for a while. Both hands on hips, head down. Yeah. What an actor. This guy was playing it up big time. He went on. "There were the usual alfa-numeric numbers you'd normally see but buggered if I can remember any now."

I faced Bosco. He looked down. I knew he was the same as me, trying to keep a level head. Trying to keep things in check.

I turned back to Doug, looking past Andrew's poker face as I went. "What else can you tell us?"

"I heard a couple of those blokes talking as they walked past me hidin' in that wheelie bin. One of 'em said somethin' about somethin'. Buggered if I can remember it though. I stuck me head up for a bit. They'd already got hold of a few locals and chucked them in that helicopter. Martha Birch from the general store. Garry Penrose from the bottle-o. Mick Kettle from the barber shop. They must've done somethin' to 'em cuz they were goin' in no struggle. That's the reason why I went and hid. But there they were. Those black blokes."

"Black?"

"Yeah, mate. I don't reckon they were Aboriginal. Too bloody tall. Never seen any Aboriginal as tall as that."

"What else?"

"That's when it happened. They were walkin' away with that little girl you brought in yesterday. The doc came beltin' across the street and the chase was on. Then there was the shot. I stuck me head up in time to see them eagles come out of the sky. Shoulda seen it. Like angels of death, those eagles. Anyways, dunno what happened after that. I heard some commotion and that. A bit after, the helicopter took off. That's all I know."

"Did you get a good look at those guys?"

"Too bloody right I did, mate. Put me in a line-up. I'll peg 'em."

This guy wanted a line-up. The only way to do that was to take him with us. Maybe there was an ulterior motive. My guess, this guy was set up as an infiltrator. That gave me an idea.

"You need to come with us. We'll make sure you can have that line-up. Of course, we'll get you sorted with accommodation." I felt Bosco's protests. I ignored him.

"I dunno about that, mate. Got me herds to attend. And me dogs need their tucka."

"I'm sure your herds will be there when we get you back. Let's go," I said. As soon as he was in the aircraft, we'd have him and code orange would play out. Maybe it would get me back on board with Shilo. Or maybe not. I had to try.

"But me dogs . . ."

Now I was at odds. Maybe it was a better option to just grab him and bail him up. I shot a quick glance at Andrew. He shook his head slightly. It wasn't going to go my way. The grazier had to be willing. That's all there was to it. Law shit. Civil rights shit. How I wished those feds were close by. But then he'd belong to the feds. And that would shut the door on everything. I put my head down and walked a few paces closer to Doug. I locked eyes with him, hoping to give him something to think about. I was no longer in the mood for his bullshit. "Doug. We've got cops all over this place," I pointed to the tin shack.

"Yeah. What's with the clobber they're wearin'? Cops wear khaki. Are they interstate?"

"They're federal cops," I said. As if he didn't know. He was playing. "You have the choice of coming with us or going with them. Either way, you won't get back to your herds in a hurry."

"Who *are* you blokes?"

"We're with the government." Again. As if he didn't know. "I strongly urge you to come with us. The feds won't go easy on you. As soon as they see you're around, you'll be hauled in for questioning. Is that what you want? Now, you can come with us and we'll help you get back to your herds. Or go with them to Canberra. Who knows what after that."

It was no good. The grazier wasn't about to get in the aircraft. My options were none. I turned to Bosco and Andrew. "You two get on the aircraft and go. I'll drive up after we get sorted with the man's dogs," I lied.

Bosco and Andrew nodded in unison. Bosco got out his car keys and tossed them. I reached out and caught them. "Don't take your Land Rover, big hoss. Look after my Chev, won't ya?" Bosco hand-signalled. 'Firearm in the compartment.'

I pulled the items of evidence out of my pocket. The bullet and the lock of hair. I passed them to Bosco, hoping it was enough to get me back on board with Maggie. Holy shit! Where *was* I with her? The evidence we gathered might just save my arse. It might not. Maybe my new package would change things. I hoped it to be the case.

"You'd better give me that thing on your finger, big hoss," Bosco said, at the same time holding out his hand.

I almost forgot about the ring. I took the ring off my finger and passed it over. "Take care of the documents and everything else."

"Canter, you know how this is gonna play out?" Bosco whispered so lightly I struggled to hear him.

"Don't even go there. She's just a ten-year-old kid," I whispered back.

"Yeah, but there are three other civilians in this now. My guess, one will be executed before they even *come* to the table."

"Not if we liberate them first."

"Yeah," Bosco said, heaving a loud sigh. "How did I know you were gonna say that. See you back on the grid."

CHAPTER THIRTEEN

Ingress

I drove Bosco's black Chevy Suburban north on the Oodnadatta Track, having a hell of a time getting used to the left-hand drive. Every now and again, the grazier gave me a shove if I got too close to the centre of the road. I hated him shoving me. I hated him touching me. Added to that, Angel's compact disk player tucked inside my shirt was quite uncomfortable. I ignored it as I drove. Regardless of everything, we were already two hours into the trip heading north.

"I thought you said your property wasn't far away."

"It's not. We got about an hour to go before we turn off at Oodnadatta. Then to Coober Pedy."

"Coober-bloody-Pedy! We won't get there until after sunset. Are you bonkers?"

"Not all the way to Coober Pedy. Just after the turn off, about half an hour south east of Oodnadatta."

I knew somewhere in my mind he was taking me to some bull-shit location. That being what it was, I began to prepare for any eventuality. I sighed, thinking about whether to keep going or not. The RAAF Challenger would've long since touched down in Alice Springs. Maybe this wasn't such a good idea after all. I could only imagine Maggie's reaction when I didn't turn up. But the prospect of a live code orange would change it. I pushed the thought from my mind.

The grazier gave me a good bit of his story as we travelled. The last of the knuckle men, he boasted. He supposedly grew up on the knuckle, bare fisting at shearing sheds from Paratoo to Roxby Downs. Nose jobs were many, so he said. His teeth had been broken and some were missing, much the same as Lilly McPherson back at William Creek. A sideways glance revealed a nose bridge shaped like that of a seasoned Wallabies player. He'd told me everything, but already I'd heard enough.

I switched on the radio, hoping to drown out any further gas-bagging. The only station to pick up a signal was the local country ABC. It had to do. But he went on with the gasbagging and I tried not to listen. My mind was elsewhere. He droned on. I smiled occasionally, not fully knowing what about. I figured I needed to give him some input to keep him happy, even though my attention was in a different place.

He stopped talking at the exact moment a tone erupted from the centre console at my right elbow. I lifted the arm rest. Bosco's satellite phone. It toned on as I pulled it out and answered.

"Canter? It's Shilo."

I gulped back. "Shilo?" I said, pausing a beat. I was stuck for words just like before. Maggie must've sensed it.

"Let's put it away for another time. We'll discuss it later, Canter. More important things on. Well done getting the blood and hair samples. I don't know how you managed it, but it doesn't surprise me in the least. The bullet fragment, I'll send to Interpol. Somehow, I get a feeling the rifling won't match anything on a national databank. I've got T working on the blood and hair."

"T?"

"The prodigy, you referred to him as."

"Oh. Roger that."

Maggie went on after a short pause. "Moments ago, our friends from Detachment 421 in Swartz Crescent picked up a seismological event. A small one. But enough to spark their interest. Having tracked where it was, they forwarded the GPS coordinates to me and requested an urgent investigation. I have a strange feeling about this, Canter. After everything that has recently transpired, this can't be ignored. In my opinion, it's got Guardianship all over it."

"You want me to get to the coordinates?"

"Have you got anything else on?"

An awkward pause. Not sure how to answer. "I'm transporting a witness . . ." I said out loud just for the sake of Doug hearing me.

"Yes, I know. Bosco has brought me up to date on your code orange. I hope I don't have to remind you he needs to be a willing party all the way to our front door?"

"Understood."

"Take extra precautions with him, Canter. Play it by the book and we won't have anything further to discuss later."

Jesus. I hoped the grazier didn't hear that. I glanced sideways. He was none the wiser.

"I suggest getting to the coordinates and waiting for Detachment 421 to arrive," Maggie went on. "Bosco will deploy with them."

"Roger that. What do we know about the location?"

"It could be anything. It may even be the location of a Guardianship base of operations, for all we know. Oh, and one more thing. Stay back from the area until Detachment 421 arrives. Am I making myself clear?"

"Copy that, Shilo."

"Good. I've sent the coordinates to Bosco's GPS receiver, which he has told me is in the floor compartment. Check it now, will you please?"

"One moment, Shilo."

After pulling up on the side of the track, I lifted the carpet away from under my feet and reached into the compartment. I grabbed the receiver. The monochrome monitor blinked with the announcement of a set of new coordinates. I noticed the weapon Bosco had left there. A suppressed nine-millimetre Beretta. I left the Beretta where it was and closed the compartment, knowing this one was going to be by the book as Maggie had stressed. No more stuff-ups.

"I can confirm I have the coordinates."

"Where are you now?"

"Ten clicks south of Oodnadatta."

"Use the receiver to work out your ETA, will you please?"

"Already on it," I said while requesting a search. The ETA came back. "Jesus. Eleven hours at an average speed of a hundred kilometres per hour. ETA 0217."

"Better get a move on then. I suggest a brief stop at Oodnadatta. Get a full tank and supplies. Lay up until daylight a kilometre back from your ingress. I'll instruct Detachment 421 to rendezvous at your location. You'll need to transmit your standing position when you stop. And Canter, after the Chinook arrives, it is technically correct to assume the helo *is* our front door. Get your code orange willingly on board. Then he's ours. Clear?"

"Roger that. Understood."

"Good. Who knows what's out there. Be careful, Canter. Out."

I positioned the GPS receiver on the dashboard above the steering wheel. Already, I felt my passenger's eyes scanning me. I needed a moment. Just a moment to get my head together. Everything that needed doing was swirling around in my head. What was at the coordinates? What caused the seismological disturbance that got the attention of those dark souls in Detachment 421?

"Anyhow," Doug said. "That look on your face says we're not goin' to my joint."

"No. You're a witness and now in protective custody."

Right there and then, I wanted to grab the gun and blow his bloody head away.

"And you're my bloody bodyguard, eh? Sheesus!"

"Don't make me regret it," I said. "Whatever happens, stay close and keep your head down. Do as I tell you and we'll do fine.

If you don't, you might just get yourself a neat little hole some-where on your person for your trouble. Got it?" *That* might happen anyway. I kept that thought well to myself.

He said nothing. Doug sighed at the same time as he reached into the pocket of his faded blue King Gee shorts, pulling out a bag of tobacco. With a cigarette paper hanging from his lip, he began to mould a wad of tobacco in his hand. "Wanna rollie?"

"Yeah. May as well." I didn't smoke. But what the heck. I needed something. Anything. I didn't have any bourbon. Maybe a rollie would help settle my mind.

"What's the thing you stuck on the dash?" he asked while lick-ing the edge of the paper and completing a work of art. I thought about not telling him anything. But what the heck. In my mind he was dead anyway. One way or another. I'd get my chance after we'd finished pulling intel out of him. I'd make sure I'd be the one to dispose of him. However, when answering his question, I played it up for my own amusement.

"It's a global positioning system receiver." I grabbed the de-vice from the dashboard and brought it closer. Time to nerd out. "You input your longitude and latitude and it will guide you to the location. The four lights on the handset get you there. The green means you're heading in the right direction. The red means you're heading away. The ambers on the left and right mean the location is either side. The idea is to keep the light green. Maybe one day, there'll be a set of maps to make it easier and more user-friendly. It's for military use only for now."

"Holy shit! Never seen one o' them gismos before."

"Yeah. And expensive. It also has GSM and CDMA recep-tion."

"What in the heck is that?"

"Mobile network coverage. It's new tech. One day, everyone will have a mobile phone. Maybe one day everyone will have a GPS."

He passed me a lit rollie and I sat back, took a drag, and coughed up a lung. Now I knew why I didn't smoke in the first bloody place. The stuff was vile. I immediately tossed the cigarette out of the window.

"Better get out and put ya foot on it," he said. "You don't wanna start fires, mate. It'll end up being a firestorm and we don't need that 'round here."

After putting out the cigarette, my mind returned to the objectives my mind ran briefly away from. Now it was time to get back into the game. My code orange eyed me as I climbed back into the vehicle and dragged the seat belt over my shoulder. "Better git," he said as though not caring where we were going.

"I'm Nathan. That's my real name," I said, at the same time twisting the key in the ignition.

"Nathan, huh? That's better than Canter. Since when does a verb get to be someone's name?"

I killed the ignition and eyed him, wondering if I should go there. That was so long ago. The memory came back and I momentarily decided I'd give him a throwaway line for the hell of it. But I sat back in my seat and folded my arms with the memory. "When I was a kid before I enlisted, the name Canter was given to me by a guy who lived next door. Billy Butcher. Fat Fuck Billy I used to call him. I'd go out for a morning run knowing enlistment wasn't far away. I wanted to get into shape, I guess."

"So you were . . . cantering?" Doug smiled, then started to laugh. But his laughter didn't last. I shot a stare at him that shut him up. I went on. He listened.

"That's what Billy Butcher yelled out to me as I ran past his house. Canter! Yeah. Exactly that. But the name stuck and I have it as a handle or call sign. It reminds me how close I got to killing the prick. That bastard wore a knife in a scabbard on his belt. A big letter B was embossed into the leather; he was such a show-off. He dared me once. A game of stabscotch. Damn he was good at it. But when he gave the knife to me, I showed him I was in no mood for his bullshit."

"What'd ya do?"

"Another time, Doug. But I'll just say Fat Fuck Billy came off second best." Again, I reached forward and turned on the engine. "Will your dogs be okay?" I asked, hamming it up for his benefit.

"Nah, dun worry about it, mate. They're off the chain. I wouldn't pass up an adventure if ya paid me. So, what in the heck are ya waiting for? Let's git!"

CHAPTER FOURTEEN

Sometimes They Come Back

The moment after I switched off the engine and dowsed the headlights, I leaned forward and peered out of the windscreen to the wonderful night sky. Jewels of stars and galaxies sat there on a deep black canvas, twinkling and dancing. It'd been a long drive through the vast empty outback, avoiding roos and emus that bounced out in front without any warning. Even the odd camel crossed the track, which made for a speedy correction and a skilled touch of the brake pedal.

I slowed to avoid the many rutted patches and sped up with four-wheel drive engaged to escape the claws of muddy bogs. Doug was fast asleep and slept for most of the way. Thank god for that. I was in no mood for the chatter. Had I been a passenger, I don't think I could've slept for a second. My mind was live wired with the imaginings of what we were up against, not including the added responsibility of being Doug's so-called bodyguard.

Reaching down and lifting the carpet away from the compartment at my feet, I retrieved the Beretta. After checking for rounds, I sat back and rested the suppressed handgun in my lap. I fought the urge. I fought it hard. A bullet through the brain, he'd be shit-canned. Then my thoughts went to Angel. A bit of finesse was required here. Every step was crucial.

Grabbing the GPS handset, I requested my standing position and transmitted the data, knowing it would arrive within a second back at Alice Springs. Then the waiting began.

I checked the time on my wristwatch again and settled into place. Four hours until first light. It was cold out there. I put my finger up to the glass just to check. I rubbed my hands together then tightly folded my arms, knowing the cold from outside would enter in a few moments. I glanced sideways at Doug; the cold didn't seem to make any difference to him. King Gee shorts and faded blue singlet. Why was it outback guys seemed to wear nothing else?

0322.

I got out to stretch a leg. I had a piss by a tree while studying the edge of the Milky Way. Awesome. Back in the car.

0341.

It seemed like hours since I last checked.

0357.

0412.

I got out. Vapour shot away from my breath. Back to the tree. Maybe I shouldn't have drunk so much water. Back in the car. I looked at Doug while thumping the door closed. He didn't move. Out cold, so it seemed.

0432.

This time I took my wristwatch off and threw it on the floor. Within what seemed like thirty minutes I checked the time again. 0441.

I pulled Angel's compact disk player from my shirt. Metallica. Not my thing, but better than nothing. I placed the headphones over my head and pressed play.

I pressed play . . .

I checked the battery. All good. Pressed play . . .

Shit . . .

No disk would ever work with black marker pen scrawled over the data surface. I took the headphones off and placed the player in the glove box.

Doug, next to me, was fast asleep. I'll kill the bastard right here and now. I grabbed the handgun and brought it up point blank to his temple. That's when I heard it. And at the exact same time, Doug woke up. I lowered the handgun as Doug eyed me curiously. But the noise. A low thumping. The noise of turbofans. The sound of rotors in the distance, cutting through the silence.

Doug stretched forward, busting a yawn. Was he none the wiser? I didn't know. I imagined my hands around his throat. I imagined my fingers piercing all the way through his flesh and ripping out his voice box.

"What's the noise, mate?"

I didn't feel as though I could answer. Somehow, I did. "Choppers."

Chinooks. Our Chinooks. They're early . . .

"Didn't you say they'd be coming in after sunup?"

"Yeah."

"Then, they're early," Doug said.

"Yeah."

As the noise got closer, I realised the sound was no Chinook. It came in low over the terrain then punched past overhead doing top speed, kicking up dust as it shot over.

"Shit!" Doug said. "That can't be your blokes."

That changed my tune. I immediately grabbed the car keys and twisted them in the ignition. The V8 engine sprang to life.

"Did they see us?" Doug said. The look of horror in his eyes. Oh, he was such a player.

"I dunno. We're in the open. Now's the time to get to cover," I yelled.

The GPS data transmission must have been intercepted and we were nothing more than a ground target. No point getting to cover. With the gearshift in neutral, I put my foot down hard on the throttle. The tacho needle pushed past the red zone. The V8 engine screamed.

"What are you doing! Let's get going!" Doug shouted.

"It's too late. Time to run!" I yelled, at the same time grabbing the Beretta and GPS receiver.

The helo was coming closer for a second pass. Maybe the SUV's engine was hot enough. Any heat-seeking AGM would go straight to it.

"Doug!"

"What!"

"Get out and run! NOW!"

Getting out, I wished hard I had two good legs. I did the best I could getting away. I half ran, half hopped as fast as I could go. Doug paced out in front, occasionally looking over his shoulder.

"Find cover and get down," I yelled. The noise of the rotors was fast coming back. Closing in on Bosco's precious SUV.

I found a tree with huge roots sticking out of the desert ground and got down. Where in the heck was that grazier! I looked to my left and saw him getting behind some bloodwoods, just in time for an AGM to fire from the helo. It hit the side of Bosco's SUV and it erupted in an enormous explosion that lit up the night sky, trailing off in a huge fireball.

"Doug! Get on the ground and roll in the dirt. Roll. Roll. Roll!

"What for!" he yelled back.

"Just do it! Get that dirt over you as much as you can. Roll. Roll. Roll!"

I got down and rolled around, getting as much dirt, dust, and grime over me as I could. All over my clothes. All through my hair. All over my face. Up my nose. In my mouth. Doug was rolling around like a wild boar just shot. "Keep rolling around and don't stop! Roll. Roll. Roll!"

Die. Die. Die, I kept thinking. I should've left him in the SUV.

"Okay, I'm rolling. Dunno why. But you're the boss!"

"Your body heat! The helo can't see us if we're cold. Keep rolling around and don't stop. You gotta get cold, Doug. Make sure that dirt is all over you!"

The helo hovered over the wrecked SUV momentarily and slowly turned as though scanning the immediate area. A bright search light lit up and the scanning began all over again. It turned again while hovering. Dust kicked up, reaching up to it. The searchlight bounced around through the rising dust and reflected off native trees and bush.

"When I say go prone . . . go prone!" I yelled.

"Prone? What's that mean?"

"Just get down flat as you can! Do it now!"

I went prone, flat as my body would allow, and wiped more dust over my face for good measure. The search light hit, stopped for a split second, then went in another direction.

"Don't move, Doug! Not even a muscle!"

I held my breath. If I could've stopped my heart, I'd have done it. Then, without warning, the searchlight came back. I lifted the Beretta and emptied the magazine in rapid fire at the searchlight, which immediately shattered and went black. Projectiles ricocheted, pinging off the helo. More than a few bullets zipped past my body and hit the ground. I heard a yelp to my left. One of my shots had impacted Doug. I wanted to believe he was still alive if only for the opportunity to torture the bastard.

From where I lay cloaked in desert dust, I watched as the helo lifted up, turned, and shot off in the direction it came. I pushed up to the side of Doug's body and checked for signs of life, of which there were none. Prick.

* * *

I spent the rest of the night hunkered in a dried-up creek bed. My decision to fire on the helo still ripped through my mind. Had I not fired; Doug would still be alive. It was an awful price to pay. No intel. Now, what about Angel? I could only imagine what had died with Doug.

First light dawned with the steady thump of rotor blades in the distance. I relaxed, knowing a Chinook had a sound all of its own. Getting up and dusting down my desert-soiled jeans, I slowly headed back to the LZ carrying a shit load of guilt to deal with. More guilt to add to what I'd already stuffed down there in that dark pit where all my other bad shit lived.

The RAAF CH-47F Chinook landed on the road just next to the wreck of Bosco's SUV. Several armed figures dressed in black with faces covered by red bandanas and dark sunglasses climbed out of the rear, followed by one who could only be Bosco. He stood beside the wreck of his SUV and immediately spun his blue baseball cap backward, then put his hands on his hips in obvious disgust.

Tracing the shoulder of the dirt road, I walked with speed toward them. Bosco spun and faced me, raising his arms. "What have you done!" he called out. "Man, what have you done to my Chev!"

After approaching, it took a bit of explaining. I saw Bosco's jaw drop as I described what had happened. All the while, the men of Detachment 421 stood silent. No one would ever know their reaction up until the time they all checked weapons. Still no words were exchanged – it was as though they weren't human at all. Maybe they were all fucking cyborgs, who'd know? After checking the body of the grazier laying in the open desert dust, one of the black-clad guys said with words as blunt as a hammer to get in the Chinook. Which I did. Without any hesitation.

Climbing into the Chinook, I reached up and grabbed a headset. As I put it on, staring back at me were a set of sparkling ebony eyes I'd not seen since the hurt locker, south of Basra.

"Teresa?" I said it to myself at first. I locked eyes with her. She locked hers with mine. She smiled brightly. Her face. Her raven hair. She hadn't changed a bit.

"I would kiss you hello, Nathan. But you been out dirt wrestling again," she said in her most exquisite Israeli accent. Now, I realised, we had the company of MOSSAD along for the ride.

"Teresa . . ." I was about to ask what does MOSSAD have in this? But I was stumped for words. She kept smiling. Those ebony eyes kept sparkling. The same as always.

"Teresa . . . What are you *doing* here?" I finally asked.

"You need trauma doctor," she answered plainly. "But also, will put my talents to these Milestone."

Of course, I realised. Not only was she a fine surgeon, she was also adept and respected in the field of cyber counter-terrorism. Her English still needed a polish. That hadn't changed. She glanced to Bosco. Bosco winked back. I felt the blood rush to my face. My composure left. But somehow, out of my surprise, I managed to echo her smile.

As the engines spooled and the Chinook rose slowly, Teresa reached over and placed a hand on my knee. "How is it been going with you, this past years?"

"Teresa . . . I . . . I'm . . ."

"Stunned?" she said, still beaming.

"Yeah." I placed my hand on hers. "Why you? Why now?"

Bosco sat back and folded his arms as though pretending he wasn't there. He had something to do with it. Now, I was sure of it.

"Nathan," she said, grinning. "When you leave, I say to Bosco, if there is need he should call. I say myself, one day Bosco will call. And I wait until such time. Now, Bosco call. I get first plane. So now here to help with making the Milestone dead. You need trauma doctor. You need countermeasures. I shrug my shoulder. Who else but me, huh?"

"Teresa. I never meant . . ."

"Is okay, Nathan," she said. "I live. You have work. I have work. I understand."

The Chinook turned high in the air and headed to the coordinates of the seismological disturbance. I couldn't take my eyes away from Teresa's gaze. When I did, I saw Bosco sitting back and grinning. Had the others not worn their facial coverings, my guess is they'd be grinning the same. They all heard the words I said over coms. Even the pilot and co-pilot, I assumed.

CHAPTER FIFTEEN

First Blood

As I was getting out of the Chinook, Teresa's words sprang to mind.

Trauma doctor . . . countermeasures . . .

It made me wonder what may be out there waiting. We were already prepared for anything. But MOSSAD? There was a connection, but where? It whipped around in my head. Then it came. The centrifuges in Iran. The one that got away, as Maggie had said. Without our MOSSAD allies, the intelligence of the Iranian centrifuges might not have come to light. Maybe one day, there'd be another seek and destroy mission to look forward to.

The highly armed men of Detachment 421 took point and led the way through the bush. I kept an eye on the GPS coordinates, sidestepping Bosco who was in formation, occasionally covering our six. Teresa paced beside me. Within a few moments we arrived at a clearing.

We all halted and half crouched. There was nothing at the location apart from the usual desolate isolation. "Ground zero," I called out at the same time weapons were relaxed. One of the black-clad guys called out, "What the fuck?" But after scanning a full three-sixty, I saw a depression in the dirt not far from where we'd stopped.

"Over there," I called out, pointing. We made our way across.

Arriving at the depression in the dirt, I glimpsed the edge of what seemed like a metal container. The majority was deep under and hidden in the soft earth, as if the container had been dropped from an aircraft. Maybe from a Black Hawk. I bent down to touch it.

Bosco slapped my hand away. "Out of everything, you're gonna go and blow yourself up again?" he snapped. I'd slipped up for a moment. I was a little distracted and Bosco, doing what he did, shoved me back into the real world.

The 421 crew knelt down close to the metal container, appearing to scan it. "Anyone with electronic devices, switch them off. Now!" one of them said from under a red bandana. I hit the button to the GPS receiver and it went dead in my hand.

"What do you think it is?" I said out loud.

Bosco came up beside me. "From where I stand, it looks like your average military footlocker. It's badly busted up. You reckon it was dropped?"

"The seismological disturbance," I replied through my teeth.

Before I knew it, one of the 421 crew began to sweep the red desert sands away. I felt a hand on my shoulder. Teresa urged me to get back. As I got back, the circle of black-clad men around it retreated while one was left alone with the sole job of making the object known. After thirty minutes of careful manipulation, he stood up and confirmed Bosco's belief. "Foot locker," he said. "Need the ordnance disposal bot from the helo."

* * *

We made for a safe zone while the remote bot went about its task. By this time, the sun was biting down and it was getting seriously hot. Who knew how it felt for those guys dressed in black with their faces covered. They kept their faces covered no matter what. Their words were few. Nods were plenty and no names or call signs were ever mentioned. They communicated among themselves using hand signals unique to them.

I saw Bosco quite a few times reacting to their signals, and at times commentating on their processes as though he was part of the team. If their hand signalling was unique, how did *Bosco* know? Then it occurred to me. The bandana those guys wore. Red. The same as the one Bosco kept with him. I eyed him for a second while he oversaw what they were doing. He was deep in the action even though he was standing right next to me. My enquiring mind went to work.

"Bosco. Your bandana is the same as theirs," I said. "Care to tell me why that is?"

Bosco stopped what he was doing. He placed his hands on his hips and put his head down as though there was nowhere for him to go. Then he looked up with a smirk. The same smirk that said 'you gotta be kidding.' He didn't need to speak it. I already knew it.

"Hey relax, will ya?" Bosco finally said after sucking back a long breath. "So, it's a red bandana. You gonna hold that against me?"

I turned away, held a hand to my chin, and calculated in my head. The numbers told me if Bosco was in Detachment 421, he was in play at the same time as that idiotic Candy programme. The CIA's programme at Pine Gap. Now I needed answers. He'd better have the right things to say.

"Normally I'd let it go, Bosco. But you know too much about those guys. What *aren't* you telling me? Were *you* 421?"

He said nothing. He avoided my enquiry. I asked it again.

"Bosco, now's the time to convince me you weren't 421. Just saying."

"So what if I was? What difference does it make?"

"It makes every bit of difference. It means you were in on that Candy programme."

"Canter. What in the heck are you talking about?"

Immediately, my hands curled into fists. Bosco's Adams apple dipped. I remembered Candy for the massive CIA botch up that it was. Without Candy, maybe Franco would still be alive. Maybe Franco wouldn't have turned. Maybe Angel would still have her parents.

I ran over it in my mind. The drug based on C6H12N4. Meth-amphetamine that was supposed to be modified. The CIA claimed it was the drug of choice to subdue operatives who had access to sensitive material while being stationed at Pine Gap. It was the CIA's answer to protect their interests and assets. Whatever happened to trust and commitment? Was it ever considered?

It was Detachment 421 that administered the drug. Maybe even Bosco himself. In Franco's case, the drug was beyond anything toxic. It changed him. It turned him. He became volatile. Explosive. Had Franco not had it in his system, he wouldn't have bludgeoned his wife to death.

But then, there was something else. The disk had something to do with it. The disk, with all of the implicating intelligence that now rested in the hands of Firebird Station. Maggie expressed it was found in the possession of Angel, in her backpack. Who could have put it there and why? It could've only been someone close to Angel. It could've only been someone who wanted to leak the contents. Alisha. It made me wonder if she knew what was on it. Was it a forewarning? Was it an attempt to bring the agencies up to speed?

Had Alisha known about the Milestone mission and objectives? Had Alisha known about the Oudarretian motivations? Their need for helium-3? Their plan to eradicate humanity? Their plan to mine the moon? It was a war hammer between my eyes. Alisha. Angel's mother put that disk in her backpack. But where did *she* get it? I closed my eyes. My brain worked hard.

Think . . . It's what you're good at. Think. Think hard . . .

I turned away from Bosco's gaze and placed a palm to my forehead. I almost had it worked out. It was coming. I almost had everything put into place.

Welcome to the world of lies and secrets . . .

The words I heard so long ago. Who else could it have been but someone close to Franco? Who else but someone needing to blow everything wide open? I had my hunch. I needed proof. I needed concrete evidence. A hunch wasn't good enough.

"You don't wanna start this, Canter. Believe me. Just leave it." Bosco's words punched through my train of thought, wrecking everything I'd worked out.

"You *were* 421!" I shouted. "And you *were* in on the Candy programme!"

"Hey, big hoss. Hold it together. We can discuss it another time."

Fuming, I wanted to grab him around the throat and squeeze. "Why, Bosco. Why!"

Teresa's hand fell on my forearm. "Nathan, it is history, no?"

Just where in the heck was I? As I stood there and gazed into Teresa's eyes, I wondered with even more curiosity at her sudden appearance. The whole picture was there just a second ago. Something as simple as a phone call from Bosco, she'd told me. Was there more? Something told me I still wasn't completely in the loop, that I was more out of it than I should be. My mind tumbled and spun.

"Nathan. Where are you?" Teresa said, lightly placing a hand up to my face.

I wasn't happy. I was far from it. Out of everything that'd been said, everything that had been made known, it didn't seem to end. Answers. I needed them. Bosco and his story. Nothing but lies. Teresa with hers. Andrew with his. The disk I'd not yet seen. Eagle Shield . . .

"Nathan. Relax, no?" Teresa said. Again, with a hand up to my face.

Maggie's words came.

Sometimes you overthink . . .

My mind. My thoughts. My worries. Sometimes, I hated it. How could I turn this off?

* * *

"Clear!" someone yelled.

"You guys can open it now," someone else said.

I spun to Bosco, holding it together the best I could. My hands clenched at my sides. "This isn't over, Bosco. Not in a long way is this thing over. You'd better have something good for later. Just saying."

"Whatever, big hoss. But remember we had jobs to do. We might not have liked it. Orders are orders. Who are we to second guess that shit coming down from the top?"

No choice in the matter, I had to put everything away and keep it for another time. That time would come soon enough. For now, we had to get back to what needed to be done. With every moment that ticked by, Angel was spending more time in danger. I pulled my head out and got on with it.

When the footlocker was properly unearthed and the threat of any possible explosive jettisoned, I pushed past the crew of black-clad guys, claiming it was my job to open it. I crouched down and manhandled the mangled door. After a few hefty heaves, it finally opened.

The first sign something was off was Bosco suddenly pushing his head sideways with a hand up to his face. The next was when the 421 crew moved backward a pace, almost in an involuntary movement. It didn't register what was in there. In the first instant, I thought some mad bastard had slaughtered a pig and stuffed it in there. But as the stink erupted, I knew it was no pig at all. The mad bastard had dismembered a human body with the same kind of intricacy as packing a meat tray.

I mumbled my horror under my breath, stepping back with my hand to my nose and mouth. Bosco was beside me as though no cross words had ever been exchanged.

"Well, big hoss," Bosco said. "You were right. Looks like they *did* execute one of the civilians. And *before* coming to the table, just as you thought."

"Angel . . ." I said with urgency, looking down, trying desperately not to believe it.

"It's not Angel." Bosco kneeled and lifted something grisly and awful. "Check this out."

Bosco retrieved a note that was heavily stained in red mess. He stood back and eyed it before passing the note to me. I was hard-pressed to make out what was written in what must've been thick black marker. My eyes focused through the muck. One word only. 'Quinlan.'

My mind drew back. It wasn't one of the names of the locals from back at William Creek. I examined the note and held it to the sunlight in the hope of revealing any further clues.

"Now we have a contact," Bosco said. "Quinlan is the guy who's gonna do all the talking."

"Yeah. And this is the guy's calling card. Elaborate, don't you think?"

"He's obviously in no mood for bullshit, Canter. This guy is psycho. I reckon there'll be more dead guys turning up before we even get started."

* * *

After photos were taken of the grisly scene, Bosco and I, and one other from Detachment 421 did the best we could. Retrieving most of the body parts and placing them into the black body bag, we soon realised there was not a lot that could be recovered.

Apart from the head and limbs and a section of torso, the rest was a mush that I tried hard to ignore. A few personal items were left on the body. Left there with a purpose I assumed. They would aid in discovering the identity of this poor innocent individual. I was relieved it wasn't Angel. However, Angel was still missing and time was playing out of our hands. If it was urgent before, now it was even more so.

The Guardianship had just showed their muscle to us all, and what they were capable of doing. They weren't going to make things easy. The negotiations would start. What would it take for Angel's release? And when, exactly would we be contacted by the person who went by the name of Quinlan?

With a roll of 35mm film in my grip, the flight back to Alice Springs was silent of any chatter other than the words used by the pilot and co-pilot to control the Chinook. After touch-down at Alice Springs airport, a vehicle was waiting for those black-clad dark souls. They got out of the Chinook, got into the vehicle, and left without any bother.

Bosco and I ferried the two body bags to an awaiting Ford Transit van. One of the bodies was the civilian found in the foot-locker, the other, my code orange failure. I wasn't sure how this would play out with Maggie. But now he was dead, it could only spell disaster. And Angel . . . she was further away than I could ever care to imagine. It made me feel incredibly heavy, but more determined than ever. Quinlan. The day we'd come face to face, I'd take my pleasure slowly.

Moments after delivering the body bags and watching the Transit van drive away, all that was left was the trip back to Firebird Station. I knew in my heart things would instantly ramp up.

* * *

We arrived there disheartened from what we'd seen out in the arid outback. Maggie opened the door quietly and we all slipped through. Her displeasure deepened and turned into anger at the news of the deceased code orange. I'd waited until I was face to face with her before I gave her the news. I don't know why I chose to go that way. It would've been much easier to let her know over coms. At least by doing that, she'd have time to digest it.

Me being me, I chose to avoid telling her until I had to. Maggie turned away, saying nothing. I gave her a few moments to herself. She quietly sat down at her desk. It was as though she went away somewhere momentarily. When she finally came back, it was all heads back in the game.

The person who went by the name Quinlan had played a card in the inexcusable bloodletting of an innocent individual. The purpose, however, wasn't clear. Was it nothing more than the act itself? Was it a message? If it was a message, there was nothing more in it than to let us know he was indeed the psychopath Bosco claimed.

Maybe Quinlan was showing his muscle. Maybe he was showing how much power he wielded. Maybe he was playing for the disk. If he wanted the disk in exchange for Angel, it didn't matter which way I looked at the situation, it was never going to be as simple as that.

The ramping up of events I'd expected didn't happen. There was no sign of any attempt to communicate by this Quinlan. The day turned into two. Then into three. By the end of the fourth day, with no word of anything, my determination for Angel's safety intensified and supercharged. But somewhere in the back of my mind, I knew it was always Quinlan's intention to keep us hanging. To keep us guessing. To keep us on edge. That's how he was playing it. He showed his hand in the beginning. Now, not knowing was sheer and absolute terror.

During the nights, the lights were left on. Sleep came, but only for an hour or two. Maggie's meeting room became more like a command post. Someone was always there, forever manning all the communication devices we had. At the same time, Andrew sat at the computer and never left. He'd fall asleep still sitting in the same position as he was when last awake. As the time dragged on, we became nothing more than weary ghosts, walking the hallways, clinging to the expectation that something, *anything*, would begin.

CHAPTER SIXTEEN

Seed

Day six. A certain buzz was in the air. Things were stirring. From the coffee machine, I heard voices emanating from Maggie's ad hoc command centre. As I rubbed my weary eyes, Maggie sprang up from behind. She startled me enough to cause my coffee mug to hit the floor.

"We have something to go on, Nathan. My meeting room when you're ready." She looked down at the shattered coffee mug, then looked back up. "Mop and bucket in the laundry cupboard." Then she walked away.

When I arrived in the meeting room, Maggie gestured for me to take a seat. An awkward silence hung in the air, interrupted by Bosco's cough and Teresa saying something about the furniture. But Maggie went about her business without any delay at the whiteboard. "This is intelligence just in from Canberra," Maggie said as she started to write. In big bold letters, she wrote on the whiteboard. 'McMurdo Organic Seed Stores Antarctica Division.' Then placed her marker down.

I scanned the words not once, but twice. I narrowed my eyes, squinting a little. What stuck out was the acronym. MOSSAD. Was I seeing things? Surely not?

I stuck my hand up like some school kid in a lecture room. "Have you noticed the acronym?"

Maggie smiled back at me. "How did I know you were going to say that, Nathan. Yes, I'm aware. It has nothing to do with MOSSAD other than pure coincidence. But I was equally as alert as you when I was first given this information."

"What's this about then?" I asked.

"We'll get to it in a bit. But first, I want you all to know we're not leaving here today until we have no white space left on this whiteboard. I want ideas. Every idea, no matter how small. So, let's start people. Let's put our heads together and get something down."

I sprung up and asked the obvious. "What do we have on this Quinlan?"

"Nothing yet," Maggie said, almost despondently. "But make no mistake about it, Nathan. Whoever this fellow is, he will make contact soon enough. He has played this for far too long. You're right in suggesting Quinlan's tactic is to drag this out and keep us on the defensive. But now we have something that will bring him out of the shadows. No longer the deadlock. Time to smoke the bastard."

I knew what had to be done next. And I knew how it was going to get done.

"We can start by finding the Guardianship base of operations."

"That's not gonna be easy, big hoss," Bosco said. "The Guardianship don't have a base of operations. They're all integrated."

"You know as well as anyone here," Maggie added, eyeing me. "The Guardianship don't fly colours. They don't wear a uniform. Much the same as terrorists, the Guardianship could be here, there, or anywhere. You could walk right past one in the street and you'd never know. How can one find a base of operations when they appear to operate out of cells? One, we don't have any idea where those cells are, and two, we'll never know when the next Guardianship sleepers become activated. It's exactly as Bosco says. They are integrated into the very fabric of our lives. Invisible until activated. The worst kind of warfare."

I put my idea forward. "They have a Black Hawk."

"And that's not unusual," Maggie replied. "We already know they have access to top military spec equipment. And top military spec ordnance, I might add."

"What about the fuel?" I put in.

Maggie spun and wrote the word 'fuel' on the whiteboard next to what had already been written.

"Go on," she said. "What are your thoughts on fuel?"

"A Black Hawk has a range of 373 nautical miles," I said. "Which converts to around 700 kilometres."

I got up from my seat and walked over to the whiteboard. I picked up a marker and placed a mark. "Assuming this is where we were. Bosco's wrecked Chevy. Let's call it point A. It's just a matter of searching within a 700-kilometre radius of that point."

I penned out a circle on the whiteboard, calling it point B. Everyone locked eyes and listened. I continued. "We can assume a certain amount of fuel was consumed getting to point A. If the Black Hawk was at bingo fuel, then the radius of the search zone point B is smaller by half. Just 350 kilometres. We can also assume if the base we're looking for is outside of the zone point B, then we're looking for fuel dumps point C.

"If we find fuel dumps, then we can estimate a base of operations in the general direction between Points A and C. I believe the Black Hawk was either approaching, or at bingo fuel. Those guys were in too much of a hurry to get away. It would've been an easy search and kill. I was right there in their sights. But they didn't bother to put any effort into searching further. They were at bingo fuel. They needed to expedite their return. Trust me on this."

Maggie immediately spun and faced Andrew who was sitting at the computer. "Get us a list of abandoned military installations or anything else of interest within a 350-kilometre range of Bosco's wreck."

Andrew nodded and went to work.

"You see, Nathan," Maggie said. "It's all in the detail. You've earned your money today. Thank you for this."

As I sat back down, Maggie spoke loudly. "Anything else we can work on?"

"Any word back on the samples recovered from William Creek?" Bosco asked.

"Yes, actually. And I was getting to that. We have a match on the blood sample that points to this fellow." Maggie approached her desk and held up an eight by ten-inch photo, then passed it to Bosco. He scanned it and passed it Teresa who then passed it to me.

Maggie went on. "This man, a Columbian expat by the name of Alfredo Sanchez, was on the FBI blacklist after serving a prison sentence for cocaine trafficking in 1989. However, after he was released from prison, there was no record of him leaving the United States for Australia. Immigration have nothing on him at all. Unfortunately, there is no further intelligence on his movements. By this information, we can therefore assume this man was a Guardianship soldier."

"A dead end," I said.

"Not exactly, Nathan," Maggie said. "I have to say I wasn't prepared for what I found next. After digging further into Alfredo

Sanchez's activities prior to his conviction, I learned this man was also in the business of importing coffee into America. By all accounts, a legitimate venture, or so it seemed. He made the mistake of using the coffee as the vehicle for his illicit drug activities, which led to his arrest.

"Who could've guessed the cocaine was just a sideline for this fellow? For raising a bit of extra cash. It was the coffee itself that was of importance. Not the cocaine. As a matter of fact, had there been no cocaine at all, we might not have discovered the importance of the coffee shipment. I can only speculate the cocaine trafficking was off his own back and never part of the Guardianship operation. A clear cock-up on his part, I'd say. Wouldn't you agree?"

"That depends," Bosco said. "What's with the coffee?"

"Thank you, Bosco. I was getting to that. But first, let me sidetrack a little. It's all relative. Trust me." Maggie took a breath and looked down at something on her desk. "Canberra got in touch only hours ago with leaked intelligence from someone who chooses to go by the name 'Blue'. It was quite a surprise and completely unexpected. I have no idea how or why this Blue leaked to Canberra. I speculate my enquiries with the FBI sparked it, but who'd know? That being what it is, Blue's intelligence points directly back to this Alfredo Sanchez in ways that will astound."

Maggie then moved over to the whiteboard and double underlined the words 'McMurdo Organic Seed Stores Antarctica Division.'

She went on. "The leaked intelligence from Blue suggests somewhere in close proximity to McMurdo Station in Antarctica there exists a vault containing seeds of all known plant species, held in deep freeze. Having this intelligence can only lead to one speculation of why the vault is there."

"A doomsday vault?" Bosco said slowly.

Maggie nodded and winked. "Your deduction is correct, Bosco. That's exactly what it is. And there's more. Coffee plant seeds. Coffea Arabica to be precise. The intelligence Blue has given up suggests the Coffea Arabica seeds that are held in deep freeze in Antarctica have been genetically altered."

"How genetically altered?" Teresa asked.

Maggie paused then rubbed her eyes. It appeared she was as tired as I was. As tired as we all were. "This is complicated and there's much to get through. I think we should all take a break before we continue."

Nobody wanted the break. No one rose from their chairs. Maggie grabbed a wad of papers and tapped the edge of her desk lightly with her fingertips, casting her eyes over us.

"No break?"

"Give it to us straight," Bosco said.

"We don't have the time," I put in. "Every moment is crucial."

Teresa nodded vigorously.

Maggie put her papers down on her desk and paused. "Alright. I hope you've all got your heads in the right space before I start. This is not going to be easy to swallow. You must all take it for what it's worth. This intelligence is all confirmed by our top analysists at Ben Chifley." Maggie put her papers down and spread them out on her desk.

"Coffea Arabica genetically altered," she began. "These seeds, when germinated and planted, grow as ordinary plants. However, these plants have something extraordinary. These plants release helium-3. The coffee beans from the plant also contain the helium-3 element. And that's not all. The FBI managed to track down shipments of these Coffea Arabica seeds going into the United States from Columbia. This is the connection with Alfredo

Sanchez. From there, the FBI were able to intercept shipping manifestos showing the seeds and coffee beans being shipped out of America."

"McMurdo Station," I said.

"You're spot on, Nathan. But let me say this. Not only Coffea Arabica, but the intercepted manifest also records seeds of other plant species. *Thousands* of species. All originating from the Columbian source. All connecting back to Sanchez. But Sanchez was not alone in this. After further inquiries, we established a vast network of individuals exporting seeds out of Columbia. Perhaps these other seeds haven't been genetically modified in the same way as the coffee plant seeds. There's no intelligence to suggest otherwise. However, one can assume *why* they were listed in the same shipping manifest. My guess is they've used other seeds to mask the export activities of the Coffea Arabica. Either way, we've got a job to find out."

"What you're suggesting is too unbelievable," Bosco cut in. "And to be honest, coffee plant seeds? I mean, c'mon guys. This is a little odd and farfetched, don't you think? Why not turnips or tomatoes? Why not goddamn horse radish? I can't see it. It's all codswallop. This is a clever hoax to distract us from this Quinlan guy."

"I see and understand your scepticism, Bosco," Maggie said. "Let me put a little perspective on this. I'll ask you a simple question. How much coffee do *you* consume every day? How much coffee does the *average* person consume every day? I can tell you now, coffee is consumed in much higher quantities than turnips or radishes. Added to that, we can't ignore what has been virtually placed in our lap by this Blue."

Maggie trailed off. After pausing a beat she went on, ignoring Bosco's apprehension. "The intelligence shows the vault in Antarctica is a collaboration of the United States and other Western Hemisphere nations. Top secret due to the nature of the business. We can therefore assume it is, by all standards, an archive of seeds kept in storage for any future cataclysmic event. Whatever that may be. Manmade or natural. That day will come in humanity's future. That being the way it is, it seems the Guardianship have actively used the McMurdo facility for their own means. It gives us an idea of how cloaked the Guardianship actually is. The vault near McMurdo Station known as Vault Vitae-G is overseen by a detachment of CIA Special Activities Division operatives. By that, we can clearly assume the Guardianship has infiltrated the CIA and is somehow working with them shoulder to shoulder, unbeknownst to those in the genuine task force."

I wondered what was to be done next. Could Scotty-Blue be the 'Blue' who leaked the intelligence to Canberra? The more I thought about it, the more it began to fall into place.

Welcome to the world of lies and secrets. . .

"Questions?" Maggie asked.

"Who's Blue?" I already had my suspicions. I needed confirmation.

Maggie positioned herself for what I thought was going to be a lengthy discussion, only to be interrupted by Andrew at the computer. Andrew passed Maggie a printout. She took it from him and after reading the note smiled wryly.

"Maralinga," Maggie said with new enthusiasm. "Maralinga is where we start our search for Angel." She faced Andrew. "Get us in touch with CIA Director McKinnon. I think we might have enough to requisition that U2 aircraft of theirs."

CHAPTER SEVENTEEN

Coffea Arabica

By the time the day was over, the whiteboard was completely covered in coloured marker and no white space was left. We'd nutted out all the intelligence we had. Unfortunately, no word yet from this Quinlan. It appeared whoever Quinlan was; he was out there somewhere biding his time. I only hoped Angel was okay. We *all* hoped.

It was only a matter of time before he made contact. From there, the negotiations would start. I already knew the policy. Negotiations with terrorists never went well. In the past, most instances never made it to the table. What made this case any different? It was a most discomforting realisation.

Maggie had disappeared from the meeting room the moment Andrew connected the coms to Langley. They'd been gone for almost an hour. Even so, their absence seemed to span just moments. Maggie walked back into the meeting room with facsimiles in her grip. "We have our U2," Maggie said. "Nathan and Teresa, pack a bag. You're both travelling with me to Canberra. Andrew will coordinate from here." Maggie faced Bosco. "We'll need you abroad, Bosco."

"Let me guess. Antarctica?"

"First to Langley for a mission brief," Maggie answered. "You'll be inserted into the next CIA rotation to Antarctica. This is a recon mission, Bosco. Not sabotage. We do not want to disturb any legitimate business down there. Find the Coffea Arabica seeds. Report back with your findings. That's all. Unfortunately, you'll be there until the following CIA rotation. I suggest you pack some extra woollies."

"Yeah," Bosco said, then put his head in his hands. "How did I know that was coming?"

"Anything further?" Maggie asked.

"Will you be doing the negotiations?" I asked.

"Absolutely not. We are all far too emotionally invested. A negotiator has been appointed. That's the reason for the trip to Canberra. Added to that, Canberra has more up-to-date electronic equipment to handle the situation than we have here. The negotiator is . . ." Maggie held her hand out to Andrew, who was standing as though he'd just had his hand on a dodgy electrical cord. With a hand visibly shaking, he passed a facsimile to Maggie.

"The negotiator is an experienced . . ." Maggie looked down at the facsimile. Her face paled. "The negotiator is . . . Mathew Malloy. ASIO counterintelligence." The paper she had in her grip slipped from her fingers to the table.

Bosco looked up. "No shit. The same Malloy as . . ."

"The same Malloy who did the Sydney Opera House botch up?" I said.

"How can this be?" Teresa put in.

"How did we get *stuck* with this guy," I said disbelieving. "Malloy is no good for this."

It was Malloy in control of the seven hostages held at the foot of the Opera House stairs in 1995. It was Malloy who called the bluff of the jihadist standing with them, armed with a chest full of explosives and deadly packets of ball bearings while chanting the words Allahu Akbar. It was Malloy who moved the SRG into place, ordering them to take the fucker down. Out in the open, in the middle of the day, an SRG sniper took the shot. After the dust had settled, all hostages were lost, along with another twenty-two dead and injured. Malloy's intelligence of the man carrying fake explosives was incorrect. He called the bluff. He went in on a hunch. The lives of many were lost as a result.

Maggie passed the facsimile back to Andrew. "I want clarification on this," Maggie said. "Get on the blower and get me the Director-General. If he's unavailable, then the Minister for Defence. Failing that, the Prime Minister, for God's sake. I want clarification, Andrew. Make it happen."

Clearly stunned, Andrew went back to his computer and sat down. He mumbled something under his breath.

Maggie went to her desk chair and slid down into it. "Obviously now, if Malloy takes this on we have our hands full. Let us all hope cool heads will prevail."

* * *

Andrew put his headset down at the side of his computer keyboard. "Prime Minister Keating on the blower."

"We'll take it on speaker, Andrew," Maggie said, then waited for the pilot light on the speaker to show up red.

As I waited for the voice of the Prime Minister, I thought back. The conversation I'd had with him amounted to a few short, sharp statements. It was the last time I wore the khaki pollies with sergeant stripes and the sand-coloured beret bearing the winged dagger. I knew I was due to be stood down. I'd already checked the paperwork and the date was drawing near. Although I had my suspicions, I wasn't fully aware why I was summoned to the Prime Minister's Sydney residence, Kirribilli House. The whole thing was lightning fast. No notification of anything until that exact same morning.

Getting there in my shiny kit, I found myself in the company of other military personnel and civilians who were in the process of being interviewed by the media. Then my suspicions were confirmed and I wrestled with the urge to get up and run from the place.

During that day, I hovered in the background as individuals were given their awards for certain occasions of heroism and good deeds done. I watched on as the number of awardees dispersed. There I was, the last to leave. On my left was the Minister for Defence Gary Punch. Next to him, Chief of Army Lieutenant General John Sanderson. On my right, The Governor-General Sir William Deane.

PM Paul Keating hovered in front of me. Immediately, the media were given firm instructions to cut airtime and pack up their equipment. Keating's eyes scanned me up and down. "Sergeant Masters," he said, eyeing me with a set of birdlike eyes down his long nose. "We owe you our gratitude. You've done your country proud."

After awarding and pinning the Medal for Gallantry to my uniform, he said in words almost at a whisper. "Walk with me. Walk and talk."

I found myself on the front porch of Kirribilli House alone with Paul Keating. His officials and minders were out of earshot as he positioned himself for words I was not expecting. Keating regarded me before speaking in the same volume as before, whispering down low, "I have something that might interest you." In a single breath, he went on and confirmed everything Scotty-Blue had said about Pine Gap and Prime Minister Whitlam's undoing. The rest of the conversation was pretty much a blur but ended with him convinced I could contribute with time spent among the elite of Australian Intelligence. ASIS.

That was then. Now, as I sat waiting for Paul Keating's voice to arrive out of the speaker, I wondered how this would begin.

"Good afternoon, Colonel Mack," Paul Keating said. "I don't need to remind you it's an election year. I'm afraid bloody Howard's campaign has got legs longer than mine this time. My arse is in the wind. Make it quick."

"Good afternoon, sir," Maggie responded. "I understand about your election commitments. But I must insist you give us your attention in this matter."

"And what matter are we talking about, Colonel?"

"The matter regarding Eagle Shield. I take it you've been brought up to date?"

"I have. And I also have a missive on my desk from the Director-General. Also, the photographs taken by Detachment 421. I have to say, what a bloody mess."

Keating chuckled lightly. Maggie rolled her eyes. I couldn't believe our PM's statement. He made light of the situation, expressing it with irony. Something he was good at, I supposed. It was the same arrogance the media had tagged and bagged him with. Either way, in that moment, my vote to Howard and the Liberals was a done decision.

Maggie went on. "I'm opposed to the negotiator appointed by ASIO, sir. I need you to intervene and get us someone more adept than this Mathew Malloy."

"Malloy," Keating sounded staggered. "You're kidding."

"We need to change this, sir."

"The last I heard, Malloy wasn't on the payroll, Colonel. But I . . ."

The room fell instantly silent. Maggie eyed the speaker. The red pilot light was no longer glowing red. She tapped the device lightly, then a bit harder. "Did we just lose the Prime Minister?"

Andrew, from his chair at the computer, spun and eyed his stepmother. Shock sitting there in his eyes.

"Andrew. What the bloody-hell is going on?" Maggie said.

Andrew responded with a slight stutter to his voice. "Q-Quinlan on the blower."

Maggie took a breath. She marched out from behind her desk with both hands on her hips. "Put Quinlan through to speaker, will you please?"

Maggie flicked her blond-grey hair to one side, and eyed the speaker on the table again, as though willing Quinlan's voice to punch through. The pilot light glowed red. No one spoke for a moment or two. The silence was deafening. We waited.

A voice jutted from the speaker. A voice digitally cloaked, generated from some electronic device. "We have your girl. We want the disk . . ."

I shot a stare at Bosco and Teresa, both of whom appeared to be struck silent. Their facial expressions were long in disbelief.

Maggie raised her hand, locking eye contact with Andrew. "With whom am I speaking?" she said, then paused.

A moment passed. I checked the pilot light. Still red. Still connected.

"Quinlan."

Maggie walked, measuring her steps closer to the meeting table. "Proof of life, Quinlan," she said calmly. "You and I both know this can't go anywhere without proof of life."

Another tense moment passed. A crackle. A bit of static on the line. The sound of footsteps erupted from the speaker. Hard footsteps, then more footsteps. The footsteps of a child. Another crackle. The urgent voice of a ten-year-old girl. "Nathan? Maggie?"

I was about to scream out her name. It took every ounce of will to hold it back. Maggie shot me a stare that said everything I had in my head must be silent. I bit my bottom lip hard enough to draw blood. The coppery taste filled my mouth and I swallowed it down.

"Nathan . . .!" Then Angel screamed a most blood-curdling squeal. A rustle. Commotion from wherever she was. I imagined what she was going through. I pictured in my mind how she was trapped and held captive. Maybe she was tied. Maybe not. Who'd know? I stood from my chair. I placed both palms down on the meeting room table and bent my head forward. I saw my own reflection in the highly polished table. My face, twisted. Snarled in anguish. I closed my eyes and bit down harder. Teresa reached and placed a hand on my back. Unwillingly, I sat back down.

The low, manipulated voice came back. "You have your proof of life," he said. "Now. We want that disk."

Maggie held up her hand. Her instruction was clear. No one was to speak. If it were possible, not even to breathe. Everyone was to hold. The room was silent enough to hear things not ordinarily heard. A car from outside. The tick from the clock in the hall. A drip from the tap in the bathroom. A moment passed. Then another.

"We want the disk!" the voice said again, louder.

My breathing shortened. A mere short sharpness just able to sustain life. Maggie was holding back. Why was Maggie holding back?

Maggie. What are you doing?

"What of the others?" Maggie asked, cutting through the silence. "No one else will die today, Quinlan."

No words. More footsteps. Rushing footsteps. More commotion.

Within the time it took for a human heart to push blood, the voice of a male somewhere in the background. "No . . . NO, NO!"

BLAT!

Then another. BLAT!

A metallic sound clinked on a hard floor. I heard Angel cry out. My heart shuddered. Yet another hostage was killed.

Quinlan's footsteps rushed back to his phone. "Now . . . do I have your attention."

It wasn't a question. It was a statement!

"And what makes you think we haven't made a copy of the disk?" Maggie said.

He laughed. A most evil, sardonic laugh. I'd heard that laugh, digitally cloaked or not. But where did I hear that laugh? Where?

Quinlan cut back in. "You cannot copy the disk. You will destroy it! But you know that already. If you destroy it. E-v-er-y-one-will-die."

Then Quinlan laughed. Again. The evil fuck that he was. I knew it. I knew that laugh. Where?

Maggie's look of sheer shock drilled into my head. Her stare hardened. She immediately spun and signalled a cutthroat to Andrew. Andrew disconnected the line.

I wanted to get up and object. Where was she going? What was she doing?

"Relax, everyone," Maggie said, at the edge of a sigh. "We'll no longer be on the back foot of anything."

The policy I'd dreaded arrived as expected. No negotiations with terrorists. But it was Angel's life in Maggie's hands.

"Quinlan needs the disk and he's played his highest card," Maggie said to everyone there, even though she regarded me, looking down into my eyes. "Angel *will* be safe, there's no doubt. There's too much in it for Quinlan. He knows how to get in touch. Next time, we'll be ready."

CHAPTER EIGHTEEN

Game On

Two weeks passed with no word of anything. Two weeks, equivalent to fourteen days. Equivalent to 336 hours. Equivalent to 20,160 minutes. Equivalent to 1,209,600 seconds. I counted every one of them. And the counting went on.

We'd not made our way to Canberra. However, Bosco's mission to Antarctica, codenamed Crossbow, was underway. I'd not noticed him leave, only that one morning he didn't appear in his usual manner. Bosco had crept away during the night. I thought for a brief second his clandestine departure was to avoid any further discussion of his involvement with Detachment 421. Then I realised it was normal for Bosco to just up and disappear. Something he was good at.

Where in the heck was this Quinlan? We hung around, sleeping little. Eating just enough to keep upright. I wondered at times if it was the other way around, that Angel would no doubt be hanging on for me. I hung on for her. I clung to every ounce of hope. I stuck to courage as best I could. And the time dragged on.

There on the whiteboard, several photographs clung to its edges, taken from the edge of space via the CIA U2 over Maralinga. Zoomed in shots confirmed everything we'd expected.

We'd found the base of operations we were looking for. The photographs revealed not one, but three Black Hawk helos on the ground, positioned around what appeared to be a set of old dilapidated, concrete buildings and shipping containers that were scattered around as though they'd been dropped. The question was what to do about it? Moving in on the target had its own set of consequences.

Angel's extraction was critical and without any further communication from Quinlan, any mission on Maralinga became locked in a standoff. As well as Angel, there was at least one other hostage to consider. And after all, we had no intelligence to suggest Angel and the hostages were even at Maralinga. In the end, it came down to nothing more than mere assumption.

* * *

Another white board was delivered into the meeting room and butted up against the other. One blank. One full of coloured scribbles and blue-tacked photographs stuck around the edges. I sat at the meeting table feeling heavy and malnourished, Teresa at my side. Her eyes no longer sparkled but were red-rimmed due to lack of sleep.

Maggie and Andrew walked in, carrying folders and wads of paper, placing them on Maggie's desk as though they were much heavier than they truly were. I scanned the meeting room. Without Bosco, the room felt empty. I couldn't help but smile while considering the fact Bosco made his presence known wherever he was. He was a pain in the arse, I thought. Oddly, without him I realised I'd lost a mate, no matter how much of a pain in the arse he was.

On the table in front of me, a mug of coffee had already gone cold. Considering Bosco's task, I was reluctant to drink it even with the dash of Wild Turkey I'd added out of habit. Teresa sat silently beside me with her fingers locked tightly together. Andrew was at the fresh whiteboard, taking the protective plastic layer off with a set of long zips. Maggie was behind her desk, looking down and shuffling papers. Her avoidance in making eye contact was already building up questions in my mind. Something was about to go down. This day was different than the last days and weeks. Something appeared to be in the air. It was game on. Finally.

Maggie raised her head and locked eye contact. "Righto . . ."

When Maggie said 'righto,' it was the same as 'Stand-to' being shouted by a commanding officer to his troops. There it was. 'Righto.' Teresa, at my side, sat with her back straight. Her body language changed. She knew the same as me, I supposed. My spirits lifted and I ended up taking a swig of that spiked cold coffee.

Maggie began. "We're not sitting idle any longer. The waiting has gone on long enough."

Andrew was writing on the fresh whiteboard. A single word in big red letters in the top left-hand corner. 'Barras.'

Maggie left her desk and moved toward the big red letters, picking up a marker and double underlining the words. "While we wait for word back on Crossbow, Barras is our mission for the rescue of Angel and any other hostages the Guardianship might have. We know of one other hostage. We have to prepare for the possibility there might be more."

Andrew made his way from the whiteboard to the meeting table and placed mission briefs in front of Teresa and me. I took up a document stamped with the Australian coat of arms in the top left-hand corner, Barras printed in bold. Objectives underneath. 'Insertion into enemy base, Maralinga' below that.

Maggie continued. "Nathan and Teresa. Your mission is insertion into the enemy base at Maralinga under the cover of German tourists gone astray. You are to be captured and held captive by whoever is holding Angel and the hostages. We hope you will find yourself in the company of this Quinlan fellow, and then work out what is necessary to evacuate Angel and the hostages. Your primary objective is the release and the safe return of those held captive. Your secondary is the capture of Quinlan. Your tertiary is the destruction of any infrastructure, adopting scorched earth policy to any Guardianship-controlled edifices."

"I'm not overjoyed with secondary," I said.

"You'll do your best, I'm sure," Maggie responded. "Think of the intel we can pull from this fellow after we capture him."

I wondered how Barras would succeed, knowing it was inevitable I would come face to face with Quinlan. I'd need to fight the urge to put a bullet into his head. Maybe I'd default to the tertiary, leaving the bastard tied. I held my breath thinking it over and scanning the pages. Maggie cut through my thoughts.

"Before you say anything, Nathan and Teresa, we can draw an assumption about Quinlan. Firstly, this man appears to have access to classified material. How this is possible is still being worked over in Canberra. However, that being the case, it is probable you both may be a known entity to him. We'll get your undercover worked out to take this unfortunate set of circumstances out of the equation. You'll not be compromised by the time we're finished. We'll have all of your documentation ready and you'll be as German as any German citizen."

"I don't know German," I said.

"I realise this. We're not about to drop you in without the proper coaching. Both you and Teresa will be dispatched to Swan Island for intensive training and tutoring. You'll have time to explore your objectives and formulate your actions-on. But time is of the essence."

"How much time?" I asked.

"You'll deploy in two weeks from today."

* * *

Two weeks slipped past at Swan Island. My head was shaved. My fake beard looked real and as long as ZZ Top's Dusty Hill. A tattoo at the back of my head, done by a guy who'd turned up suddenly and unannounced. He etched India ink deep into my skin. Not so much as a recoil in his eyes from the sharp and penetrating pain he inflicted. This guy, white. Hair pure white. His eyes. Those piercing blue-pink eyes. I watched him in the mirror as he went about his task. I was drawn to his appearance and couldn't look away.

"Relax," he said in a low and slow tone, while staring back at my reflection. "I'm an albino. Get over it."

"I never knew one. Never seen one," I said awkwardly.

"You have now."

He walked slightly away and grabbed more ink from a hard case. Like a barber, he came back at me with the tattoo gun buzzing and bent my head forward. I sat still, putting my trust in a guy I'd not previously met. The choice of tattoo wasn't my call. He'd already worked it out. The things we do, I kept thinking. With my head tilted forward in the reflection, I noticed the guy didn't have any tattoos on his body. Since when do tattoo artists have no tattoos?

I asked.

"I already told you I'm albino. I don't get to do this stuff on me. The ink won't take and it'll end up getting blotchy. Perhaps doing this job is my way of compensating." That voice. Every time he spoke, it was enough to chill my bones.

After he'd finished and I got control of my headache, he held up a hand-held mirror to the back of my head. I saw for the first time what he'd put there. A tattoo of a white eagle. The best I'd ever seen. With the white eagle in flight, wings flared, the image wanted to jump out in 3D. The intricacy and attention to detail was masterful. Almost photo-realistic. There was something else there. A sword gripped in an eagle talon.

"I'm amazed," I said, focusing on the sword. "I've never seen any tattoo of a white eagle with a sword." The tattoo by itself was far from any cliché. I was thankful for that, knowing it was going to be there until the day I took my last breath.

"The sword of destiny," he said across a shoulder, while placing his kit back into the hard case. "Everyone has a path, Nathan Masters. Most have several. Wisdom will help you choose. The sword of destiny will give you focus."

Post mission, my hair would grow back and cover it. Maybe I'd now keep my head shaved.

The tattooist continued to pack up his equipment with as much precision as it was unpacked. I was about to ask, but I could draw my own conclusions about the message in that tattoo. By the time I was convinced about the message, the tattooist was already making for the door.

"Wait!"

He turned.

Eagle SHIELD · 169

"Thanks for the tatt. And thanks for the pain," I said. "I just let you get all intimate with the tattoo. The least you can do is offer your name."

"I'm Gabriel. But you already knew that, Nathan Masters."

Knew it? No. I had no idea. Gabriel who? Was it a puzzle I was supposed to solve?

"Gabriel who?"

He didn't respond. Like his low and slow voice, he'd already gone, almost melting away.

* * *

A passport bearing my new name, Karl Muller, was thrust into my hand on the day we left Swan Island. I was quietly confident with my new ability to speak German. I'd changed so much it was possible to be frightened by it. Along with my new persona, my cumbersome fake leg was replaced by a more modern equivalent. Titanium, with a knee joint that operated so smoothly the limp was now only slight. After they'd placed it on my stump, I couldn't help fist pumping the air. But Teresa – she was transformed into something quite extraordinary.

No longer the raven hair. No longer the Arabic accent. Teresa was a German blonde beauty in every sense of the term. Her name had become Adeline. Adeline Muller.

The mission clock was activated the moment our rental car arrived at the facility gate. A late model Jeep Cherokee kitted out for touring and with all the extras. It was no Land Rover, but it would do.

The Jeep smelled of a mix of leather and plastic and that new car smell. Two large suitcases were stowed on the rear seat. Inspecting the contents of the suitcases revealed clothes that said tourist, and a folder containing wedding cards and best wishes written in German by individuals we'd never know. A red velvet hard case containing matching gold wedding bands and a marriage certificate dated two weeks prior from somewhere in Las Vegas. My passport also reflected the recent visit to America out of Stuttgart and then on to Australia. Everything was put into place with much delicacy and finesse.

Just before I twisted the key in the ignition, I felt a warm kiss on my cheek. "Ich liebe dich," Adeline said with her beaming smile. She placed her hand on my fake leg. In that moment I wished I had my real limb. Even though there was no physical touch I could feel blood pushed to places that had recently only been used for the necessities of life. I returned her smile.

Before I had words, Adeline's mouth was locked over mine. I was in trouble for the first time in recent memory. Perhaps longer than that. I returned Adeline's passionate kiss with my hand on the back of her head, pulling her in with obsessive force. Like teenagers, our tongues wrestled together and I didn't care where we were. We were married after all. Newlyweds. In my wildest imagination, I never expected it. It was going to be a good mission, I thought. Different, but good. Our first night would see us pulled up somewhere in Adelaide and I was already in a hurry to get there.

CHAPTER NINETEEN

Distractions

We'd stopped a half a dozen times along the way to the city of Adelaide. At times to fill the tank. Other times to go at it like a couple of eager bushy-tailed creatures hell bent on the task of procreation; we went at it at every opportunity we could find.

With the weather cold and rainy, and the Jeep parked at the side of the highway, we made good use of the back seat. The windows fogged. Moisture dribbled on both sides of the glass. Our bodies intertwined in a honeymoon dance, ignorant to the world outside. And nothing. Utterly nothing could take me further away from the reality of why we were here.

It was as though my lungs breathed new air. It was as though my life found new meaning. Getting into the driver's seat, I found my cheeks cramped with muscles I'd not previously known.

Just before sunset, we reached the traditional German-speaking town of Hahndorf. Another opportunity to get out for a stretch. An opportunity to mix with the locals and test our skills as German tourists, speaking nothing but what we'd learned. To my surprise, we held up well enough to pass off as the couple who'd made their way from Stuttgart to Australia. Finding a German beer hall, we feasted on weisswurst with spicy cabbage and mash, while drinking ale from insanely huge steins big enough to break a forearm. Leaving that place with a belly full of beer and sausage was much harder than I anticipated. After reaching the Jeep parked out the front, I tossed Adeline the keys. I was in no shape to drive.

With Hahndorf in the rear-view mirror, we motored down the mountain on the duel carriage expressway with Adelaide city and its beautiful lights soon coming into view.

"Es ist hubsch," said Adeline, pointing to the lights on the horizon.

"Ja. Es ist sehr hubsch," I replied, smiling. I wondered how on earth such a pretty sight could make its way into my awareness when in a matter of days, things would change drastically. Who knew what was waiting at Maralinga. Who knew the conditions and circumstances. We were, for all instances, detached from any safety net. We were on our own with no chance of any contact back to Firebird Station. No tap-out button. No rewind knob. Nothing but our cover story, which we hoped was good enough to fool. Considering our objectives, was it enough? We had no weapons. We had no tools of trade. Our mission was clear. Get to Maralinga and be captured. From there, one could only guess.

* * *

We made Port Augusta by 1200 hours the next day and travelled west on the Eyre Highway out of Poochera, Wirrulla, and Ceduna before pulling up for the night at Penong. The next sunrise saw us taking a sharp right turn at Nullarbor and heading due north into the wilderness, the desert hot enough to reach fifty-plus degrees. Hot enough to cook a meal on a rock. Dead straight dirt roads stretched to the horizon and caught the unwary with their own death. No one sound of mind would attempt to travel the Trans Access Track without water and a vehicle that could hack it. It wasn't uncommon for unwary tourists to perish out here. So many had died or gone missing with no trace.

* * *

Dawn in the middle of nowhere was cold and amazingly dry. Packing up camp, Adeline said few words. Maralinga was a few short hours further north. In my mind, I rehearsed actions-on, then realised Adeline was away with her thoughts too. As Adeline stowed the tent back in its bag, I filled the tank with diesel from a yellow jerry can, making sure every drop of the slimy, stinky stuff was emptied.

"Karl . . . Up there . . . Look." Adeline said in German while pointing.

I put the empty jerry can back in its holder, then walked to Adeline's side and saw what she was seeing.

"What are they?" she said.

"Eagles," I told her after searching in my mind for the German translation. On the updraft, they were hovering in a line abreast appearing to have us caught in their sights. I realised I'd seen them before. They were the same seven eagles I'd seen back at William Creek.

"What are they doing?" Adeline asked, while swishing away flies. "Are they hunting?"

"No. They're showing the way. We'll follow. Let's get going."

There was no hesitation about it. After selecting four-wheel drive with the mere touch of a button, I steered the Jeep off the track and headed inland. The Jeep bounced hard over the rough surface that for all I knew had never previously been in contact with humans. The stony red surface, strewn with quartz and sand-stone rocks, rushed and scattered. I slowed down and sped up, pushing past trees that seemed to be screaming urgently for rain. And the heat . . . By ten in the morning, even the air conditioning struggled to keep the cabin within a range of twenty-eight and thirty degrees.

We drove down gullies and craggy creek beds. We pushed up sand dunes, sending frill necked lizards into a mad scramble. All the while those eagles were never far away. This was so surreal. I was chasing eagles across the desert. Was I mad? At times, we'd get close enough to see their eyes sparkling in the sunlight, then they'd move on again and I'd follow. They *were* taking us some-where. Showing us the way. The question was where? And to what?

In the distance, the eagles set themselves down on the ground. Getting closer, I could see the dirt around them darkened by what appeared to be . . . moisture? At first, I thought it was a billabong full of water. Logically, I already knew how rare that was and with the heat, how unlikely. Just before we reached the darkened patch in the middle of empty nothing, the eagles took flight and pushed away, disappearing into the remoteness.

"Stay here and I'll go . . ." I said to Adeline. "Better still, get behind the wheel. We don't know what we're dealing with."

Adeline nodded sharply and slid across to the driver seat as I hopped out. Walking to the depression in the dirt, I was horrified to find the darkness in the dirt was blood. Body parts and bone were haphazardly strewn about as though nothing else mattered. I was hard-pressed making out how many bodies. Two or three maybe. The few limbs sitting out in the open were stripped of flesh. Sections of torso had entrails hanging out in the sun.

As I got closer, the stink rose to my nose and punched me in the face. I covered my nose and mouth, but it didn't seem to help. I noticed something small and plastic in the shape of an L on the ground. I looked at the object awhile before it struck me. I knew what it was. I picked it up. Angel's puffer. She was here. My brain thumped. This was a place Quinlan was setting up for Angel's exchange. But what had gone wrong? The eagles, I wondered. Did they do this? It's no wonder Quinlan never got back in touch. No wonder so much time passed with no word of anything.

With Angel's puffer in my grip, I spun around. Before my legs led me away, I noticed something else. On the ground lay an electronic device partly covered by red dirt. I knelt down and studied it for a moment, then swept the dirt away. At first I thought 'booby trap.' But looking down at the object, I realised what it was. A tactical beacon. The exact same device I'd used down range in Iraq.

Getting back to the Jeep, I showed the items to Adeline. I explained about the puffer, telling her it could have only belonged to Angel. And that meant she was at one time in the vicinity.

"How do you know this belongs to Angel?" Adeline asked.

"Because it has no label on it. While we were driving down from Alice Springs, I saw her use it. I saw her peel the label off. Maybe it was a habit of hers. But this is Angel's asthma medication. So now she has none. If she has a bout of asthma without this, she's in serious danger."

Adeline took the item and studied it. Then I gave her the TACTBE.

"Communication device?"

"It's a tactical beacon," I said, struggling with the translation. "The tactical beacon is pre-tuned to the AWACS frequency."

"So, why is such a device here?"

"Hard to say. Maybe they've hacked it and are now using it for communication between them," I said. "The only way to find out is to…"

"Open a channel?" Adeline cut in, then held her breath. "Karl. This is very dangerous . . ."

"Yeah, I know. But the reason why we're here is to get compromised, remember? I can't think of a better way right now."

Adeline passed the TACTBE back to me with eyes wide and alert.

"You ready for this?" I said.

Adeline nodded slowly. "Yes, let's do this."

I took the device in my hand and switched it on. It lit up and there was a burst of static. My first instinct was to start talking, but I thought I'd tease it a little. I pressed the button on the side a few times to see if it grabbed anyone's attention. Nothing. I did it again, this time dropping a series of five carriers. Within a moment, a carrier came back. A series of two. I smiled. I'd just pinged the bastards. Whoever they were, they were listening.

I shot a sideways glance to Adeline who was looking extremely uncomfortable. I let it rest there for another moment, listening to the static. From out of nowhere, a series of five carriers came back. Four short. One long. Morse code, probably.

So I began.

Two short, one long, one short – the letter F.

Two short, one long – the letter U.

I let it rest and waited for a reply.

A moment later, a voice crackled and said, "Who is this?"

I knew I'd sparked their interest. Now let's drive this home.

I depressed the handset button. "Break . . . Break . . ." I said in German.

The voice came back. "Hey . . . who the hell is this?"

"Break-Break-Break . . ." I said again.

"Okay. Whoever you are . . ."

"Your mother sucks donkey dicks," I said in German.

Adeline rolled her eyes, but it didn't stop her from laughing. While she was laughing, I pressed the button for one long carrier, figuring it was a good bit of something to send.

"Stay right there, asshole!"

"Come get me. Mongrel." I yelled into the handset, then immediately switched it off.

I looked at Adeline. "So now's the time to get going, don't you think? Just for the exercise, let's give them something to chase."

Without a word, Adeline twisted the key in the ignition and planted her foot down hard on the accelerator. The little Jeep surged forward and swung north. No longer than forty minutes later, a Black Hawk came over the rise from behind, bearing down.

"What do we do now!" Adeline yelled.

"Now we stop and get out . . ."

CHAPTER TWENTY

Collapse

I stood by the side of the Jeep and raised my hands in the air. Adeline was standing the same as me. From the door of the Black Hawk, which had hit the ground in a hurry, and several dark figures rushed toward us, springing from the dust. One aimed the butt of a rifle at my face. I felt the thud. I felt my brain pin-ball around in my skull. Then lights out.

* * *

It took me a second or two to realise my eyes were open. I could see nothing. Everything was black. The smell of hessian hit my senses. My head was covered with a sack. I tried to move my hands, but that was no good. My wrists burned with whatever they had used to tie them. I focused my hearing on the steady dripping of water into a bucket. I was in the same kind of horror story I'd not been in since SAS training back in '85.

I listened hard for any other sounds while I pushed my tongue hard up against my teeth. About three front teeth loosened and threatened to come out. The pain was an immense tug of war between the steady throb and the drilling headache. Nothing I couldn't handle. Another round of dental bills at some point, I thought. Listening with the full strength of my hearing revealed nothing but the sound of the water and someone, somewhere, listening to music I could barely make out. Every now and then I could make out a note. A guitar. An electric guitar. Where did I hear that before?

I stretched my hearing out as far as it could go. I sat not moving a muscle and concentrated on the sound. The music. What was it? I focussed my hearing and what I heard could be nothing else but a song by Metallica. I smiled. Angel. She loved Metallica. That meant one thing. Angel was being looked after. I felt my spirits lift and I knew I was not far from her company. But Adeline? Where had they taken her?

"Adeline?" I said softly from under the hessian hood. No response. No sound other than that constant dripping.

With my hands tied behind my back, I couldn't clap a hand to get a feel of any echo. It would've said a lot about where I was. Instead, I raised a foot and stamped it down. The echo told me concrete walls and floor. A splash also said water at my feet. My mind went to work. Bunker room. Putting it together, I guessed I'd been taken to the abandoned bunker complex at Maralinga, the same place they'd used for shelter from the nuclear weapons testing in the late fifties and sixties. Now, I had to work out what to do next.

Reaching down slightly, my fingers touched the metal frame of the chair. I wondered how long I'd been seated. Judging by my discomfort, it would've easily been a couple of hours. Curling my fingers revealed what was keeping me tied. If it was rope, there'd be a chance. Any knot could be undone. But I felt with outstretched fingertips nylon zip ties. I could break them, but not like this. Whoever had tied me had thought this one out. I was daisy tied. My breath left me as I realised there wasn't any hope of breaking free. My once raised hopes bled away. It was now a waiting game.

I listened, focusing on the music, wherever it was coming from. I concentrated on filtering out the steady dripping of water. *Enter Sandman.* That's what it was. It finished and I caught the edge of the next song. I heard the sudden eruption of footsteps from down there. Rustling and some muted voices. Then a scream. A scream that stopped the blood in my veins. Adeline!

"NIEN!" I yelled out.

From under the hessian sack, I screamed Adeline's name.

I rocked back and forth in my chair, hoping for something to give. I tried to force my bounds to break. "NIEN!" I screamed again. "FICK . . . DICH! FICK . . . DICH!"

A set of fleshy thuds bounced to my ears. Adeline cried out again. But then there were someone else's protests. The protests of a girl. Angel!

"NOOO! Leave her alone!" Angel cried out. I wanted to scream out to Angel. It took every bit of will to hold it back, but I had to keep things in play. I was German. A German tourist. It must stay that way. The game had begun and I had to hold it together or everything was lost.

From back there, wherever it was, I heard someone scream out, "Who the fuck are you! Who sent you!"

Adeline's cries went silent after a horrible fleshy sound told me she'd been knocked out. I heard Angel sobbing loudly. I felt useless and powerless. How I needed to be untied. How I wanted to let fly. But all those things I was feeling, all those emotions and reactions going on inside me, weren't doing me or anybody any good. It was time to suck it up. It was time to hold it down. It was time to get into the hard work and get going with what needed to be done. I was next. I readied myself.

* * *

With the hessian sack over my head, I wasn't sure how many there were. Two or three, maybe. I felt arms about my shoulders lift me from my chair. My body was dragged across the room and I found myself on my knees. The hessian sack was swiftly taken off my head. My eyes focused. Two muscle-bound freaks stood in front of me. Without knowing one way or another, I felt the presence of someone else from behind.

The first blow came down without any words. It felt as though I'd been hit by a train. My mouth instantly filled with blood. I spat it away. Number two wound himself up and he came down. If he'd used a bag of bricks, maybe it'd feel the same. I felt the ooze of more blood in my mouth. My tongue was mostly numb; I tried to get it safely away from my broken teeth.

"Who are you!" the big guy shouted down as he was winding up another blow.

"Nien Englisch . . . Nien Englisch . . ." I screamed, keeping things together, at the same time expecting more. He let me have it. I flung backward, reeling from the shock of a god-awful punch to the chin.

I brought my head up, shaking it a little. But that did nothing. Nothing at all. I saw them look at each other. One shrugged his shoulder. The other looked down at me. His eyes glistened with fury.

"Talk," he said. Then he wound up another and let it fly down. My head snapped sideways and I spat out some teeth with clots of blood. My mouth lock-jawed open. Blackness came to my left eye. My head screamed. Screamed out with pain! I fought it hard. I gave them nothing. I denied them all.

"Talk." Another explosion on my jaw. The same as the last, and the one before that.

"Ich bin verloren . . . verloren . . ." God knows how I got it out. My jaw was either broken or dislocated. It hurt more than I was willing to admit. I switched it off. I swallowed the pain. I gave them nothing.

"Talk." Another blow and my jaw was free and swinging. At the corner of my vision, something glinted in the dim light. I knew what it was. Knuckle duster. I held my breath, shut my eyes and braced for it. It didn't come. No more train wreck.

"No," the guy from behind said. "You'll kill him. And we need the fucker alive."

Before I knew it, the hessian bag was thrust over my head and I was lifted up off my knees. The metal chair squealed across the floor and I was sat down. For a brief second, I thought the bad was done. Reality checked back in. The chair was kicked over. I fell backward, my head connecting with the wet concrete floor. On my back, I knew what was coming. Still, I felt as though I could hold my breath for long enough.

As the water poured through the hessian sack, I pushed through the involuntary need for air. I held on until my mind said I could take no more.

Maybe a boot to my ribs caused me to break. I gasped and the putrid water entered, running down my throat. I tried not to swallow. I tried not to breath. The urge to cough came and I thought I might drown. I sputtered. Right at the edge. I could see something black coming. The very next second, they sat me back up.

A voice in front of me. "*Who* are you? *Who* sent you?"

"Nien Englisch," I said through my broken and blood-engorged mouth. I never knew saying words could hurt so much. But I still gave them nothing.

"Karl Muller . . . Ich bin Karl Muller . . ."

Silence. The dripping water. I heard one of them sigh.

"Quinlan wants to check this fucker's identity."

Footsteps splashing through water and a sudden draft told me at least two of them had gone. One was still there. I heard him pick something up. Something metallic. A snipping sound. The sound of metal on metal. He was coming at me with his implement and he was going to use it! I felt my eyes bulge from my injuries. I felt the cold metal on my hand. Then the sudden punch of pain exploded up my arm. The bastard had taken a finger. Now, along with the dripping of water into a bucket, there was the dripping of blood from my hand.

* * *

The door swung open. More were coming. Footfalls splashed on the floor toward me. I steadied. I braced. I tried not to breath. I wanted blackness. Maybe he'd get me there. I heard his footfalls step up behind me. I felt him grab my hand and swivel it around. Maybe he was going to squeeze it. I felt burning pain. I smelt alcohol. Then I put things together in my head.

"Joseph, Mary an' Jesus," a voice said. "Mongrel bastards did a good job on ya, didn't they, eh?"

I knew that voice from somewhere. The pitch. The tone. Everything about it sparked a memory from somewhere. I went to say something but stopped myself short. Maybe my mouth was in no shape to say anything. Who'd know if German was part of the guy's education. But one word I knew was universal across most languages.

"Wasser . . ." I was right out at the ragged edge of my alertness. I was on the verge of collapse. Blackness. It was there and I could almost touch it. Taste it. I wanted it. How dare it cheat me.

"Water? Yeah righto, mate. I'll get ya some, eh?"

That voice. How could I mistake it? I knew the guy. But what was he doing here? I must shut my mouth and not say anything. In the next moment, the hessian sack over my head was slightly raised and a steel mug found the corner of my mouth. I took a small sip, then coughed up blood clots that turned the water a cloudy red.

"Shit! Dun worry about it, mate. I'll get ya a fresh lot, eh?"

The guy I knew from years past took the sack off my head, then turned his back without looking at me. How could I hide? I looked to the side as much as I could. There was no hiding and nowhere to go.

With a fresh mug of water in his grip, he turned and met my gaze. The steel mug dropped from his grip. It hit the floor, loud. "Oh shit! You've gotta be bloody jokin', mate."

I mouthed words. It hurt like a bugger. "That obvious, huh?"

"Canter? What the fuck? What are you *doing* here?" he whispered. "An' that beard. Anyone can see it ain't real. It's hangin' off ya face all wonky."

Scotty-Blue reached over and peeled off my beard. "See? It's bloody worse than the hair of the dog. Reckon you should 'ave a go at ya wardrobe guy, eh?"

I put my head down. I smiled a bit, even through the agony. Despite everything, it was good to see Scotty-Blue. "Why're you here, Blue? You're not G? Tell me you're not."

Scotty-Blue looked down at me and winked. "Wish you knew the whole bit of it, mate. Lies and secrets, remember? And what's with the getup, anyhow?" He stepped back a pace, hand to his chin. "Oh shit. It's you who's got the disk, 'aven't ya? And you're 'ere for Angel?"

I nodded, but said, "No disk."

"Crap . . . Ya know they're gonna kill ya if they find out who ya are?"

I nodded again. I attempted to speak, but instead coughed up more blood. I looked up and Scotty-Blue had some kind of sad expression going on. In that moment, I knew he wasn't Guardianship.

"Well, we better not let it 'appen, eh?" Scotty-Blue said. "But that might be a bit 'ard right now. They took ya finger off so they can get at the print. They're scannin' records right now. You'd better 'ope that ya cover has been sorted. Cos if the prints don't match, they're gonna come down on ya harder than ya know."

"How much time have I got, Blue?"

"Mate, those blokes 'ave got kit that'll make ya eyes boggle. It's not gonna take long."

I said nothing. How could such an easy mission end up going so badly?

"Dun worry about Angel, Canter. I got 'er back. She's in me care," Scotty-Blue said as though reading my thoughts.

"Good on ya, Blue. But do you think you can get something to Angel? Her asthma medication is in my pocket. Can you get it to her?"

"Of course, mate. But I 'ave to ask, who's the sheila who came in with ya?"

"She's one of us."

"Already knew that bit. I'm askin' ya *who* is she? I'm privy to players. I know most of 'em. But in my book, she's unknown."

"Outsourced intelligence. MOSSAD," I said after thinking it over. "She's not to be harmed."

"Too late, mate. They bashed 'er up a bit, y'know? But she's alive, that's the main thing. They took her finger off too. They're doin' the same thing to her as they're doin' to you. I'd 'elp her a bit if I could. I can only push it so far. I got me own bizzo to get through, y'know?"

"What're you talking about? What bizzo. Are you G or not?"

"Look, Canter. Remember back in boot camp where I said to ya should we ever meet up again, you don't know me and I don't know you?"

"Yeah. I remember."

"That shit still stands, mate. I'll patch ya up best as I can. But ya gotta trust me on this. I got Angel's back. Nothin's gonna 'appen to 'er, if I can 'elp it. But you and your sheila? I dunno about that. I'll do me best. You've got an ally in this. That's somethin' at least."

Scotty-Blue patched up my hand with few words, then went to work on my broken face. He swabbed a bit here and there, obviously trying his best. His hardened expression told me there wasn't a lot he could do. While he swabbed at my bruises, I wondered what he was thinking about. He had that look on his face. He was away somewhere.

"I'll get ya a cup of coffee," he said.

How odd, I thought. He offered me coffee as though I was a visitor. Then it struck me. Maybe it wasn't as simple as that. Maybe he was probing me to see how much I was in the loop. It made sense. It made more sense than to simply offer me coffee. I tested the thought.

"I'm in the loop with Crossbow," I said. His brows dropped in a V.

"Thought so," he whispered. "But I 'ad to make sure."

"Did you leak to Canberra?"

"Hey, quieten down, Canter. There's ears 'round 'ere," he whispered down low. "An' yeah, mate. That was me. The word is Crossbow has isolated and contained the parent genome. That's good news, and stuff we can use."

"What parent genome? What are you on about?" I whispered, at the same time wincing from the sting of my facial injuries.

Scotty-Blue studied me with a serious expression on his face. He glanced to the door, then back to me. "Tell me you know about the O's," he said.

"The Oudarretians?"

Scotty-Blue immediately pushed a finger up to his lips. "Okay. Enough said. If you know the word, that tells me you're already in the loop. It's like this, Canter. Without the parent genome, the O's can't grow any more plants. When the source runs out, that's all there is."

"The Columbian source?"

"Yeah, mate. Columbia was the initial setup. To make it work and to get enough 'elium-3 for their needs, the O's need more crop. That can't 'appen without the parent genome. It was kept in the Antarctica vault for safe keeping."

I thought about what he was saying. Something wasn't adding up. Surely finding the parent genome was just a matter of looking for it elsewhere. "Where did this parent genome come from, Blue?"

"Mate. Do I have to spell it out for ya? Oudarret, of course. It's called Hadgitol. Alien vegetable. Why did ya think it's so closely guarded? There's only one parent genome. Should anything 'appen to it, the O's are most definitely up the Birdsville Track without a camel."

"And if it's destroyed?"

"It ain't gonna stop 'em from getting the 'elium-3. But it will slow things a pace. It'll put 'em back a few years. A decade, maybe. Like I said. Stuff we can use to our advantage."

"Are you in contact with Crossbow?"

"Me? Nah, mate. Firebird Station is. I intercepted the intel from there."

"Jesus, Blue. How in the heck . . ."

"You dun wanna know, Canter. I 'ave me ways. By the way, I'll get word back to your blokes so they can get a picture on ya status. Then we can work out what to do next. Like I said, I can only push it so far. Just . . . follow me lead an' she'll be apples, eh?"

After he'd finished, Scotty-Blue replaced the sack over my head. Then he was gone as quickly as he came. I was left wondering what next. Where to from here? I figured I'd find out soon enough.

CHAPTER TWENTY-ONE

Presence

It wasn't any longer than a couple of moments after Scotty-Blue left that cold, dark place when I heard the door punch open. From beneath the sack over my head, I both heard and felt feet rushing toward me. I began to struggle as hands grasped me about the shoulders. At first I thought it was another shot of waterboarding. The sack partially lifted and a wad of material was pushed up to my face. I pushed back in my chair at the scent. Chloroform. Then there was nothing.

* * *

"Nathan Masters!" the voice yelled.

I heard it, but my eyelids still had the weight of a barbell.

"Nathan Masters!" Something suddenly connected with my right shin. I shrieked out with the sudden blast of agony. My eyes. I tried to open them. It was as though they'd been stitched closed.

"Wake the fuck up, Nathan Masters!" Then a rush of something cold, wet, and stinking over my head. I knew the ammonia smell. The urine smell. I pushed it from my mind. I shook my head wildly, side to side, and opened my heavy eyes.

In a chair opposite, Adeline was tied and gagged, horror sitting there in her eyes. In a chair next to Adeline, a civilian most probably from William Creek appeared equally as terrified. A G-man with black nylon tights over his head paced back and forth holding a knife in his grip. In my heart, I knew it was about to get bad, worse than before.

The guy with the black nylons moved up behind me, and with the knife he cut my hands free. Instantly I swung back with an elbow. It met air. I tried to get up from my seat. The horror, I'd been tied down.

Laughter from the G-man. "Holy shit. You're a live one, ain't ya?"

The voice. That fucking voice! Where had I heard it before?

He left the room, closing and locking the door with a few heavy, loud clunks.

On a table in the corner, I noticed a closed-circuit TV. The blank screen lit up. First graininess, then Angel in a seated position somewhere else, also tied down. The guy I'd seen a moment before appeared behind Angel with the knife. She shook her head, her eyes full of terror and tears.

"NOOO! NOOO!" I yelled out, rocking back and forth in my chair, trying desperately to escape.

The voice of the man with the black nylons from a speaker in a corner, "Nathan Masters. Where is that disk! What happens here today is about you, Nathan Masters!"

How did he know my name, for fucksake!

I reached down with shaking hands and began to untie myself from the chair. Quinlan, on the monitor, laughed. "It doesn't matter, Nathan Masters. Feel free to move around. Go ahead. Make like a free man."

"You bastard!" I screamed. "Touch the kid and I'll be the last one you see!"

"You're right, Nathan Masters. Someone *will* die. And guess what? You get to choose."

My mind buzzed with the punch of adrenalin. Removing the last piece of rope, I leaned forward and released Adeline, then the civilian. I immediately made for the door and tried to force it open. No good.

"There's a gun under the chair, Nathan Masters!"

I spun and looked, catching a glimpse of the metal lying there on the floor. I immediately moved and picked it up, then checked for rounds. One shot in the chamber. That's all there was. I sat down in the metal chair. Teresa and the civilian both stared, terrified, facing me. It suddenly struck me how this would play out.

"The clock on the wall, Nathan Masters. You have . . . I was gonna say twenty minutes. Let's call it ten. Choose wisely!" On the monitor, he placed the blade to the base of Angel's throat.

"Let's talk about this!" I screamed.

He laughed. A sardonic chuckle, most evil. That laugh again! "The disk, Nathan Masters," he said. "The disk. Until I have it, someone will die. *You* will choose."

I put my head down and thought hard. "I have it in my pocket," I lied, grasping at anything to turn the situation around. The only thing I could come up with. But the bastard ignored me.

Before I knew it, Angel's gag was swiftly taken off. She screamed out. "NATHAN!"

"Angel! I've got this!"

"NATHAN! HELP! ME!" she screamed.

"Tick-fucking-tock, Nathan Masters!"

I noticed a small amount of blood trailing down from where Quinlan had the blade to Angel. Where was Scotty-Blue? Didn't he say he had her back?

"Tick tock! Time is all you have, Nathan Masters. Someone will die. You must choose!"

I put my head down. Yeah, I thought it for a brief second. One round I could use on me. A selfish thought. I didn't know where it came from. Something human, I supposed. I eyed the clock. Time. It was getting away. My mind ran through the possibilities. How could I make something appear that I didn't have? It was impossible. Quinlan wanted blood, maybe just for his amusement and nothing more. I took the handgun and studied it. What was I to do!

Angel must live . . . Angel must live . . .!

Everything went spinning around.

My choice was none. Time. I felt like throwing the gun at the monitor. Somehow, I'd have to live with my conscience after making a choice. For the rest of my days. Collateral damage. My logical brain was trying to cut in. Trying to give me the answers. Out of everything, there was simply too much at stake.

My eyes met the civilian sitting there, visibly trembling.

But then.

I took a breath.

I closed my eyes.

I calmed myself down.

I eyed the civilian. "What's your name?"

"G-Garry Penrose," he said. "I've got the bottle shop in William Creek."

"Family?"

"Yeah. A wife and two kids. Seven and ten. My girl looks like the one on the telly right there. Here . . . Look . . ." He reached for his back pocket and went fumbling around for something. Maybe a wallet. His hands shook trying to grab it. He failed.

"It's okay, Garry Penrose."

But he went on, almost begging me not to kill him.

"I've got two horses, two dogs, five alpacas, seven chooks."

I held up my hand. "It's okay."

Adeline cut in. "You must do what must be done, no?" she said. Sadness twinkled in her eyes. She was no longer Adeline. She was Teresa. My Teresa. She was speaking with the same calm voice I knew and adored. I gazed into her eyes. I saw something in there that said forgiveness. I saw her expression change and she gave me a short nod.

It was then that I realised how much I loved her. In my mind, just for a second, I pictured what kind of life we'd have shared together had we not wound up here. She had my heart and now it was clear. She gave me forgiveness. She gave me permission. I must take it all away.

As I looked at Teresa with the weapon pointed directly at her forehead, she simply closed her eyes. A teardrop rolled down her cheek and fell away. My eyes fogged over. My tears welled up. My breathing shortened, and I felt helpless and vulnerable. I put the weapon down at my feet and sighed. Frustrated. Angry. Sad. Everything.

Teresa stared back at me in surprise. Or shock. I didn't know which. "Nathan," she said. "Do it. Please. You must do it."

My eyes went to the civilian who was shaking his head. He pushed back in his chair. No words left him. All the training I ever had told me civilian lives must come first. Teresa was a soldier. It must be her. I picked up the weapon and held the weight in my hand. I flung my eyes to the clock.

"Nathan Masters! Time's a wasting!"

Quinlan brought his knife in harder on Angel. More blood trickled. She screamed, "NATHAN!"

I felt the coolness of the gun metal. My mind shuddered. How I wished for more than one round. I winced. A sharp thump at my forehead pounded and threatened an aneurism. I picked up my weapon. I mouthed the words to Teresa, 'I love you.' She looked down. She knew.

Another glance to the monitor. Something had changed. Angel had dropped her head slightly. Her pupils skipped side to side. Her lips compressed. Something was happening. Something was going to happen.

"Angel! No! Hold on!" I yelled and dropped the weapon at my feet.

"Tick tock, Masters!" He brought his knife in on her harder still.

I felt a presence behind me. A presence, creeping up silently, collapsing around me. My ears pinged with a high-pitched squelch. Ambient sound melted away. So magnetic, the presence. Coming from behind and encapsulating my body, closing in around me. I felt a touch on my shoulders. I wanted to swing around and see. I couldn't. I couldn't manage it. The touch reached from my shoulders and drifted down to my arms. I picked up the weapon. I levelled it in front of me.

A voice. A slow, low tone I'd heard somewhere before was now in my head. "Give me your burden," the voice said, low and slow. "Give your burden to Gabriel . . ."

I found my hands were no longer my own. The barrel of the gun no longer shook. Steady and precise, my hand raised. My finger on the trigger. Pressure. Not mine. I wrestled. I fought. I looked at Teresa. Her eyes closed. Another tear.

"Teresa!"

The shot came.

BLAT!

Teresa's head snapped back. The weapon fell from my grip and hit the floor.

CHAPTER TWENTY-TWO

Fallen

With the video monitor in the corner showing nothing but graininess, I sat forward in my chair, my head in my hands, wondering what the FUCK I'd just done. Looking at Teresa, I found myself absolutely horrified. I fought through the overwhelming sadness that encapsulated my body and trapped me, holding me there just as hard as being physically daisy tied to my seat.

The shock of everything. The shame and the sorrow. The disgrace of my actions. The humiliation Quinlan led me to. There was no changing anything. But all those feelings I fought hard, knowing much more was in store and much more needed doing. I did something I knew I was good at. I swallowed everything and forced it down. Down, all the way down. I pushed it all to the place where everything else bad in my life lived. I bottled the energy of my anger and sorrow away. Saved it up for a purpose attached to the name of Quinlan.

I left my chair, my body heavy, and looked around the room for the camera that looked over me and the civilian. With the lens still trained down, whoever was behind the camera could see everything. I had to take it out and get them dark. I already knew the camera must've been a keyhole device. I began to look for any crack or crevice where it could be found.

Garry Penrose appeared to know what I was doing. He pointed. I slapped his hand down. "Don't point," I whispered. "Don't even look at it. It'll make it obvious." I moved closer to him and down low I whispered, "You know where it is?"

"Yeah," he whispered. "I saw a red light before. It's in the crack in the corner to your right."

"Good." I sat back down in my seat, reaching down for the handgun that I'd dropped a few moments ago. I leaned forward and whispered, "You sure?"

"Yeah."

Doing what was required needed speed and I had but one chance to make it happen. I reversed the handgun in my grip. The barrel in my palm. Rushing up from my seat, I raced to the corner, then using the gun as a hammer, I belted the concrete crack open to finally expose the keyhole camera. "Son-of-a-bitch," I uttered, ripping the camera from the wall, thrusting it on the floor, and smashing it to pieces with the handle of the handgun.

It would only take a moment or two, I thought. They'd rush in through the door and I'd be waiting. I got myself there with the handgun, still holding it to use as a hammer. I waited with an ear pushed up to the wall just short of the opening. I gestured with a hand for Garry to get up and get behind me. He left his chair. "Ready for this," I whispered.

"No," he said.

"Just get behind me and stay out of the way. Got it?"

"Yeah, righto."

My ear pushed to the wall. I readied myself for what was about to happen.

C'mon Quinlan. You freaking son-of-a-bitch . . .

It wasn't all that long before rushed footsteps padded down what sounded like a long hallway. The footsteps stopped at the door, just as expected. I held the gun up above my head, ready to bring it down on the first person who came through. The door opened slightly, but before I could pistol-whip someone's head, something was pushed through the aperture and the door snapped closed.

I spun, wondering what the thing was. It hit the floor with a metallic clunk. My eyes focused on the cylindrical black object just in time for my heart to jump in my mouth.

"FLASH BANG! COV . . .!"

My ears went deaf. My eyes went white. Blackness came.

* * *

In front of me, a badly beaten up Scotty-Blue was seated and tied. Garry Penrose was tied in the chair next to him. Fortunately for the civilian, not a scratch on him I could see. I was in the same busted metal chair as before. Daisy tied all over again. But no hessian bag. No gags. No water that said waterboarding. Scotty-Blue was grinning about something. I put my head down, not believing how bad this was turning out. I'd spent too much time on the defence. Now it was time to turn things around.

My eyes went to Scotty-Blue. "What happened to you?"

"The G's don't like smartarses," Scotty-Blue said. "I hammed it up so they'd freak out and put me back 'ere. Guess I did a good job at it, eh?"

"Why, Blue?"

"Why? I saw what was goin' down. 'ad to think of somethin'. One thing I learned, spendin' time around this place, you don't mess about with that Quinlan. The man's a fucken lunatic."

"That tells me you know the guy."

Scotty-Blue nodded. "Quinlan isn't the guy's real name. He got it from somewhere. Dunno where. He was a pimp who 'ad a few prostitution rings goin' on. Got 'imself into trouble, stepping on toes up around Kings Cross with some of them underworld blokes. He's got a temper that goes off at the snap of a stockwhip. Him and that knife of 'is. Crazy bastard, y'know?" Scotty-Blue trailed off. Then added. "Ya know what, Canter? This Quinlan came out of the western suburbs of Sydney. I remember that's your stompin' place."

"A long shot," I said. "How many millions in Sydney? And we don't even know his real name."

"You don't, but I do. Billy Butcher."

FUCK!

No. It couldn't be. It just wasn't possible.

My mind went back to the time Quinlan contacted Firebird Station. He laughed. He had that laugh. I recognised it even though his voice had been altered. Fat Fuck Billy. Could it be possible? It wasn't *impossible*. It wasn't even *implausible*. Just hearing the shape of the words from Scotty-Blue took me back to that place. Then my logical brain checked in. How many Billy Butchers lived in Sydney? How many lived in the western suburbs? How many in the western suburbs during the seventies?

It didn't matter how hard I threw it around in my head, there was no running away from it. Fat Fuck Billy. Billy Butcher. The guy with the knife. But why? Why all this, Billy?

Scotty-Blue regarded me as my mind ticked over. "You know 'im! I know you do! You got a dog face!"

That brought me back.

"What're you on about!"

"Dog face. Y'know? Grrr."

I went over everything. The laugh. The knife. Quinlan's body language as he walked around the place. The stooped shoulder. It was him. I put a hand up to my face and lightly touched the bruising. The injuries. The swelling. The pain. I squinted my eyes and forced my mind back. There had to be a reason for all this. Now, it was personal. I needed answers and I needed them fast.

"So, what's this place about?" I asked Scotty-Blue who was still eyeing me with his piercing blue eyes. His gaze immediately hardened. He was thinking about it. Just doing that told me he wasn't going to admit anything. I asked it again. I noticed Scotty-Blue's hesitation as he lifted his gaze then sheepishly looked back down.

"Sorry. I can't 'fess it up to ya, mate. It's for ya own good. Trust me."

"Blue . . ."

"Canter, If I told ya, you'd be dodging blow-back for the rest of ya life. Better to just get ya head into getting Angel out of here. Forget about this place. It's no good knowin' too much. The G's 'ave a death squad set up for blokes like that. You dun wanna go there. An' I'm not gonna be the bastard who caused ya to disappear, neither."

How did I know he was going to say that? Figured. He kept banging on about lies and secrets. Another one to add to the list. I'd find out soon enough. He was right about one thing. My mission was about Angel and getting her to safety.

"Okay," I said. "Got any ideas about getting out of here? Now's a good time."

Scotty-Blue lit up. Almost like a kid who'd been told there're biscuits in a tin on top of the fridge. "Yeah, of course. I got just the ticket; I reckon. I know where they're hidin' Angel. An' that's just a start."

"They'd have moved her by now."

"Probly. But they can only take her so far. They'd have a fair bit of walkin' to do," Scotty-Blue grinned. "While the G's were busy with you lot, I snuck out and unplugged the start-up circuit breakers in the helos. I hid the circuit breakers where they'll never be found. I put them under Angel's bunk. If they try to jump away, they'll get no joy with gettin' those engines to spool. That's them pretty much stuffed, don't ya reckon?"

Shit. Scotty-Blue would be made to answer. And what would happen if they found the circuit breakers under Angel's bunk? Each way I looked at it, the same end result. More would die and most likely the red-headed guy with the piercing blue eyes sitting in front of me. It didn't take long to realise Scotty-Blue had dug his own grave. And it didn't take long to realise the need to get going.

"We have seconds to get mobile, Blue. We need to get away from here or we're done."

"Yeah. Don't I know it. Get up and swing your chair over here so ya can get something out of me pocket."

"What about cameras?"

"Mate. Nothing a bit of juicy fruit chewy gum can't fix. Check out me handy work, eh? Left corner to ya rear."

I swung around, saw what he did, then smiled. I got up and swung into a position to reach his pocket. I dug in and felt something metallic and pulled it out.

"Holy shit." I was stunned. But I managed a light chuckle. I swung back around and faced Scotty-Blue. "A cigarette lighter?"

"Not just any old cigarette lighter," Scotty-Blue winked. "A zippo, mate. Just the thing to melt cable ties, don't ya reckon? Dumbarses never bothered to check," he said, then laughed.

Within a moment, I was free. The moment after that, Scotty-Blue and Garry Penrose were rubbing their wrists.

"The door," I said. "How do we get out? It's locked."

"Ave ya tried it? Why not try it and see?"

"You've gotta be shitting me . . ." I said, quietly stepping up to the door and applying pressure to the handle. Sure enough, it wasn't locked.

Scotty-Blue's grin widened. "I rigged it. When you turn a key in the lock, the bloody tumbler just spins. It feels like it's been locked. But whadoyano? It ain't."

"I'd kiss you if you didn't have balls, Blue."

"Mate. It takes balls to do what I did, eh? No need for the slobber. C'mon. Let's git."

"You know the place. You get point."

"Roger that, Canter. Get outta me way."

I felt much lighter than a moment ago. Before the door was opened, we swapped to communicating with hand signals only. Scotty-Blue signalled 'control room to the left. Armoury to the right.' We'd need to clear a line of sight before leaving our confinement. I double tapped Scotty-Blue's arm and made sure the civilian was in close proximity to my rear. To the civilian I signalled a zipper across my mouth, which he understood with a nod.

Scotty-Blue knelt down at the doorway and used the shiny zippo lighter as a mirror to check the line of sight. He gave a sharp nod and we were on the move, slinking down the hallway to arrive at another steel door. Scotty-Blue pushed his ear up to it and listened for any sign of movement. Another nod and we were through.

Another set of hand signals told me 'trap door in the floor, bunker below.' I double tapped my response and moved silently to the location. Scotty-Blue gripped the handle and lifted the heavy trap door. "Go. Go. Go," he whispered, and we went down the ladder to an opening stretching out. Doors left and right. One door on the left was open. We swung left and leapt inside.

"Hang on a sec," Scotty-Blue whispered. He moved over to a large array of switches at the wall. One by one, he switched them off. "We got seconds now. I just switched off the cameras and security. They'll be blastin' down 'ere when they notice." He reached in and grabbed a set of keys from the drawer of an old steel desk, thrusting them into his pocket. "Now to the armoury. Quick. Don't just stand there, mate."

Scotty-Blue scurried away. I ran after him with the civilian in front of me. A hand on his back urged him forward. "This way! This way! C'mon!" Scotty-Blue yelled over his shoulder. A moment later we were at a door with Scotty-Blue pushing a key into the lock.

A large steel door opposite had big orange letters.

'Bunker M. S. Lvl 10 beyond this point. Intruders shot on sight.'

A strange-looking locking device was at the side of the door with a fingerprint scanner. Had there been more time, I might've gotten Scotty-Blue to 'fess up the info. He was already in the armoury, switching on the light. Stepping in, I couldn't believe what I was seeing. Racks of military weapons of all descriptions lined the walls. A double-sided rack went straight down the middle.

I grabbed the first weapon from the rack to my right. A scoped SA-80. Just the thing. At last I had the power to punch. The power to hit back. We'd need to get going and pretty much right now, but where? Scotty-Blue passed me a full magazine. Grabbing it, I locked and loaded. Garry Penrose held something in his hand. He awkwardly fumbled with it. It occurred to me he knew next to zilch about firearms. I took it from him and grabbed something else more user-friendly. "It's a Magnum revolver. Just aim and pull the trigger. Both hands, okay? Or you'll wear it on your face." He nodded in response, looking nervous.

"What are you waiting for, Blue?" I said. "Show us the way."

"Mate. Already told ya. They're comin' and it'll be from down there," he pointed. "But we got the guns and ammo. We hold 'em from 'ere."

The word fuck whipped around in my head. Ammo at our backs, yes. And about a tonne of TNT. Being boxed in was bad enough but add in a well-placed grenade and it was all over.

"Blue, this is no good. We're boxed in."

"No time for it. By the time we reach the manhole they'll be on top of us."

"Jesus!"

"There's only fourteen of the bastards," Scotty-Blue said. "They'll be funnelled from the far end and we can take them down one by one."

Yeah, I thought. Fourteen, but how many had grenades or anything else that went bang? It was the things that went bang I was worried about. Then I had an idea. I spun and eyed the racks of weapons, but it wasn't more guns I was looking for. I needed something else. If there were racks of guns and ammo in there, there must be something more. I went looking for stuff in a box, but I couldn't see any.

"Blue. Stuff in a box. Got some of that here somewhere?"

"Stuff in a box? Yeah mate. Right at the back. Under the RPG launchers."

"RPG launchers? Why didn't you say that before?"

"Ya already 'ad ya SA. Figured that's all ya wanted."

I left Scotty-Blue and ran toward the back, looking for RPG launchers. Just as he said, boxes of stuff were underneath. I dragged a box out and opened it. M18 Claymores. Curved directional charges. Just what I needed. I grabbed a couple out of the box and ran down to the end of the hall. At the end, I turned right to the foot of the ladder. I set up the Claymores. There would be a nasty surprise and maybe enough of an explosion to get more than a few dispatched at once.

After running back and taking up position, we were left in a waiting game. It appeared they weren't in a hurry as Scotty-Blue first thought. The fact was we were still at stand-to as time ticked away. Some thirty minutes passed and nothing. It left Scotty-Blue in a state of bewilderment.

"What do you suppose?" I said. "No one's coming."

"Beats the heck out of me. Thought this shit would've gone down by now."

I glanced at Garry Penrose who appeared to be relieved, then to Scotty-Blue who looked more befuddled than ever. The next moment, I heard a voice coming from down the end. Angel's voice! "Nathan. I'm coming down."

My mind erupted in panic. The Claymores at the foot of the ladder!

"NOOO! NO, ANGEL!"

"Nathan. They told me it's okay. I'm coming down to be with you."

I launched into a hopping sprint.

Scotty-Blue's voice from behind. "Canter! It's a trap! For fuck's sake!"

I managed a few metres, then Scotty-Blue crash-tackled me from behind.

"Fa gawd's sake, Canter. It's a bloody trap!"

"It's not a trap! That's Angel's voice. She's gonna . . . she's gonna . . ."

I got up and ran again. Scotty-Blue crash-tackled me again. "It's a bloody voice pitch modulator, Canter. It's not Angel!"

"How do you know this!"

"Because, mate, it's the same voice pitch modulator Quinlan used when he contacted ya the first time. Remember? I was there. I seen it with me own eyes!"

CHAPTER TWENTY-THREE

Stand To

Standing at the armoury door, weapons trained. My heart was in my mouth. *Boxed in, boxed in . . .*

"Nathan," Angel's voice said from somewhere down there. "Why won't you let me come down? I want to be with you again, Nathan."

Hearing her voice was doing my head in. I fought it. I fought it hard. Every now and again, I glanced at Scotty-Blue. His weapon and red dot sight also trained down range. He was more in the game than I was. In the back of my mind, there was still doubt about Angel's voice. What if Scotty-Blue was wrong? Psychological warfare at its best.

Silent moments passed. I noticed Scotty-Blue double check his weapon before he went prone just at the edge of the armoury doorway. One eye firmly on his scope. Something had to give. The stalemate would finish. It would end in a bloodbath.

"Nathan, are you hearing me?" Angel's voice again. A slight pause. Then, "Prepare to bleed, Nathan."

Scotty-Blue looked up at me and winked. "Told ya, didn't I?"

The doubt gone from my mind, I scoped and red dotted my weapon on the wall at the far end. Footsteps came down the ladder. I heard them. I winced and held my breath. An almighty explosion erupted, sending a shockwave down the hall. My cheeks flapped like flags. My head rocked back. My body almost flew backward off my feet.

Soon after the dust had settled and my ears stopped pinging white noise, the sound of something metal hit the floor and danced down the hall toward us, clicking and clacking as it went. I watched it getting closer. I thought for a split-second it was a grenade. But then it rolled. Grenades don't roll, they bounce. They skip. Especially on hard surfaces. Then horror.

"Gas. Gas. Gas," I yelled.

"Gas. Gas. Gas," Scotty-Blue yelled the same.

We flew inside the armoury and shut the door. Now we were more boxed in than ever. "Lock it!"

Scotty-Blue thrust the key into the lock. "Dunno if it's the only key. Maybe it is. Maybe it ain't."

"It'll buy us time. That's something."

"You know they're gonna breach," Scotty-Blue said, shooting me a death stare.

"If they do, this place will go up like an atom bomb."

"They'll still do it. They're all mad fuckers."

With no weapons covering the hallway, it was easy enough for the guys in gas masks to give us one hell of a showdown. This was going to be up close and personal. Going toe to toe in an armoury spelled out nothing but bad. A stray shot. A bit of shrapnel. I forced myself not to think about it.

I eyed Scotty-Blue. "More stuff in a box. NVGs. Gas masks. Grenades if you've got any."

He spun and ran to the back. From the back he yelled, "Empty on M33s. No gas masks neither. But C4 we got. A bloody ton of the stuff, mate."

"Detonators?"

"Yeah. Not only that, wind-ups. Just the ticket, eh?"

Putting my SA back on the rack, knowing it was useless up close, I grabbed a nine-millimetre handgun and loaded a full mag. "It's gonna be one-by-one as you say, Blue." But then I noticed the sprinkler system on the ceiling.

I met Scotty-Blue down the back to get an eyeball on how much plastic explosive there was. Three crates. Roughly sixty kilos. In another box, five wind-ups. The box under that, detonation cord. I eyed the detonation cord for a second or two. I had a purpose for it in mind. I retrieved the spool of explosive rope and put it around my shoulder, knowing at the same time if I got hit, the detonation cord would explode and I'd be truly sliced and diced.

Two hours max on the timed detonators, I thought. A good round number. Could I pull it off? Grabbing large chunks of the green/grey stinky, sweaty plastic explosive, Scotty-Blue helped set up the charges at each corner. The rest was heaped in the centre and everything was wired for a co-ordinated explosion. We worked the plan. Scotty-Blue went on without words, knowing exactly what to do. Twisting the timers over to the maximum two-hour time limit and pressing a button, and at the same time synchronising my wristwatch, I knew the next stage was to get out of the place.

"NVG, Blue. Grab one and put it on. Time to take the fight back to the bastards."

I gave one of the NVGs to the civilian and gave him brief instructions. He put it on with a set of visibly shaking hands. I helped him with his grip around the Magnum revolver. "Stay close and you're okay. See a bad guy, put a bullet into his brain. Two hands, remember? Now's not the time for getting a broken nose."

It was as though Scotty-Blue knew what I was thinking the moment I set an empty crate on the floor directly under the sprinkler system. He reached into his pocket and passed me the zippo. Activating the sprinklers meant any trace of gas outside would get washed away. I flicked the lighter open, got my naked flame, and held it up.

A couple of seconds was all it took before the place was awash. Using the butt of my handgun, I destroyed the light switch and everything went dark. Under the green glow of NVG, we moved out of the armoury. Detonation cord coiled over one shoulder, SA-80 slung over the other, I closed the door, locked it, then slid the key back under. There was no turning back. Two hours until the place was turned into a five-hundred-foot crater. And we hadn't secured the primary objective.

I slunk up close to one wall, Scotty-Blue and the civilian right behind me. The barrel of my supressed Glock pointed downrange, I popped out lights as I went.

I expected heads to be protruding around corners. I expected contact. We reached the foot of the ladder, with the body parts of at least four tangos strewn about, and the only way left to go was up. We had no grenades to clear up top should anyone be waiting, and in the back of my mind those timers were counting down. I stood at the base of the ladder and peered up. I briefly hesitated and took a breath. Hanging around was doing us no good.

My first thought was to get the place dark, but there were no light bulbs up top within easy picking. I lifted my NVG the same as Scotty-Blue and I looked at him for a split second. In the next split second, the civilian mounted the ladder and was gone. I didn't know what the hell he was thinking. If he'd yelled out the word 'banzai' it wouldn't have surprised me. Then I realised it was the old adage. The quiet ones. They're all unpredictable and this one was no different. Penrose said nothing the whole time he was with us. It was as though he wasn't there. Now this. Before any profanity left my mouth, and no sooner did the civilian reach the top, gunfire sounded and his body fell back down with a heavy, meaty thud.

I had no time to think about what to do next. I had no time to get my head around what just happened. The sound of a click, then another. Almost in slow motion, two M33 grenades were dropped down to rest at my feet. I picked them up at the same time Scotty-Blue went scattering away down the hall.

I grabbed the grenades. One in each hand.

Three . . . four . . . five . . . six . . .

I threw the grenades back up the manhole and ducked for cover. The explosion rocked the bunker, bringing my ears white noise. The resulting smoke that came down was mixed with a pinkish cloud of what could only be the blood of the dead.

I scaled the ladder and poked my head through the manhole, scanning the place. It was as though the walls had been freshly painted.

"Blue," I yelled. "Clear up top!"

He ran back toward me. It was almost a scene out of Mack and Myer for Hire getting to the ladder. He got himself sorted and climbed, meeting me at ground floor. There were six bodies that I could make out, laying splayed open like old cans of sardines. Out of the fourteen, that meant there were four left. And those timers back there wouldn't stop for anybody.

Rushing feet headed toward us. I sat back on my haunches and waited. One came through the door. BLAT! He was down. Another came after. BLAT-BLAT! He was down. Now there were two.

We moved out of the recent bloodshed to arrive in the hall going off to the control room. Scotty-Blue took point. I nodded as he went past, knowing he knew the way. I checked my watch. Twenty minutes had gotten away. I could've sworn it was only five. Already, panic began to rise. There was still much to get done. Maybe the C4 wasn't such a great idea. Second thoughts. I hated them. But still much to get done.

Quinlan. I'm gonna break your spine . . .

CHAPTER TWENTY-FOUR

Quinlan

Flashbangs. Again. No doubt in my mind. I'd been tied yet again to another chair. What in the fuck happened? Scotty-Blue was beside me out cold, tied the same as me. I scanned around. The amount of electrical equipment around told me 'control room.' I noticed the banks of switches and the glowing red and green lights. Green-grey metal panelling shot off from one side of the cold and cracked concrete room to the other. I shook my head, trying to get the pinging white noise out of my ears.

Realising where I was almost made me shudder. A 'cold war' control room. A room that said, 'this is the button I push to end the world.' My eyes focused on those buttons. Red with drop-down plastic coverings. Key holes on either side. Two of them. I assumed one for the shot man, the other for the station chief. The paint-peeled and grimy walls still smelling of stale cigars and cheap scotch was the final clue. The Maralinga testing range control room. And that, over there, was the main desk where that button was pushed.

In the centre of the control room sat an aged steel desk with a computer terminal and a large CRT monitor. Grainy images flashed to someone wearing black nylons over his head. As he stood by the keyboard with his back turned, doing whatever it was that he was doing, I focused on the knife in a scabbard he wore on his belt. I squinted a little. I focussed on the scabbard. The leather. The shape. The big letter 'B' that was embossed into the sheath. And I knew . . . I knew where my fate was about to take me. There could be no mistake. Billy the Fat Fuck Butcher.

Finally, the moment had arrived. I narrowed my eyes, with anger and revenge cutting a short course through my mind, chased by the images of Teresa's final moments as though some kind of silent movie. Images of the knife Quinlan held to Angel's throat. Images of the death this bastard left wherever he went. I felt the bashings and the beatings as fresh as when it happened. My eyes narrowed further. I felt my nostrils flare. My breathing shallowed. Quinlan was standing there with his back turned, still standing alive. I was going to change all that.

I focused on the opposite wall and formulated a plan. The SAs leaned up neatly and stood in a row. The ammo we'd taken from the armoury rested in a heap on the floor. On the floor a few centimetres from the SAs was the detonation cord I'd once looped over my shoulder.

I quickly glanced sideways to Scotty-Blue who'd not yet come back from unconsciousness. Blood trailed down his neck from his ears . . .

Let's play . . .

One: Get untied. Two: Keep Quinlan talking. Three: Kill the fucker. Four: Get to Angel. Five: Get the fuck out.

Simple.

In my back pocket, the zippo lighter was still there. I smiled to myself. If these guys had a brain, I'd have been dead days ago. Dumbarses. Just as Scotty-Blue said.

One: Get untied.

I put my head down and closed my eyes. I reached into my back pocket and grabbed the zippo. But how could I use it without making a noise? My mind answered. Swap One with Two.

"You can take those lady's pantyhose off your head," I said, low and slow, much the same as Gabriel. "I know who you are, Billy."

Billy Butcher immediately spun from the monitor and faced me. With a hand, he reached up and took his black nylon stockings off his head. He eyed me as though surprised, but I knew there was no shock there. "Well, well," he said. "If it isn't Nathan Masters? AKA Canter. Who knew we'd ever meet up again."

"Why you, Billy? Why are *you* here? Of all the people in the world . . ."

"It wasn't my idea," Billy cut in. "Let's call it fate. Huh?"

While he spoke, I chose my moment and used a naked flame at my wrist. I felt the burn and pushed it away. I felt the squeeze of the zip ties release. Number One was done. Now to finish with Two.

"I've got time. You've got time. Give us your story, Billy." In reality, time I didn't have. Those timers down below kept on ticking, and still there was no Angel. I wasn't aware of how much time had gotten away. I needed to check my watch. Even though my hands were free, I had to play this one as though they weren't. Time. I had a feeling there was much less than I thought.

Billy tilted back and laughed hard. The same conceited, egotistical, narcissistic laugh from years ago. "You're such an arrogant prick, Masters," he said. "You think this is personal between you and me? This is so far from anything personal, it's pathetic. You're not even on the radar. But there you are. Nathan Masters. The big-headed, arrogant Nathan Masters!"

"I thought you said this wasn't personal. You're sounding like a jealous schoolgirl."

"Jealous! Of what! It was always about the disk. I was doing my job. The fact you're playing means nothing. I didn't know you were in this until, lo-and-behold, you showed up. Like I said. Fate. Go figure. But you're here and now I get to have a little fun. You never fooled me. Not even for a second. Not even with that poor excuse of a cover story you and your crew came up with."

"Then why did you need my fingerprint? And why take my damn finger off to get it!"

"Fingerprint? Whatever gave you that idea? Taking your finger off was a bit of amusement. To see you squirm. To see you feel pain. I wanted to see that pain in your eyes. I could've done more than a finger. So much more."

"It was never gonna go your way, Billy."

"There you are again. You're the same arrogant prick you always were. Go ahead and flatter yourself, Masters. You arrogant piece of shit."

"Then dazzle me, Billy. Tell me how this plays out."

"You want my story? Okay. Like you say. Time is what we have. But it'll make no difference. I've got your girl and you've got my disk. Then, what's a little chat between friends, huh?"

Billy walked a little closer. I was now within striking range, but my curiosity kept me seated. I toyed with the idea of stepping up and taking him down. It would've been finished right there and then.

Another quick glance sideways. Scotty-Blue was still out. Dribble from the corner of his mouth.

C'mon, Blue . . .

"I was making a bloody good living. I was rolling in cash up to my fucking chin. But those arseholes from up the Cross blocked any chance for washing my hard-earned money. I was making so much money but couldn't use it. It kept piling up. What was I supposed to do? What the fuck was I supposed to do, Masters!"

He came at me, his hands closed into fists. His face centimetres away from my nose. It was a moment coated in gold. But I held.

Timers . . . Tick tock . . .

He went on. I listened.

"From out of nowhere this guy gets up in my face. He tells me there's a way I can get to use all my cash. All he wanted was a tiny fee of three per cent. But it didn't stop there. This guy tells me shit about the end of the world. He tells me to give up pushing the hookers. There's a way to get in with a crowd who's set up to escape what's coming, he says."

"Let me guess. A black guy. And let me guess again. This crowd he tells you about is The Guardianship."

Billy eyed me sternly. "The Guardianship of Milestone!"

"I know all about it, Billy. That's why we can't let you have the disk."

"Fuck you, Masters!"

"I bet this black guy didn't tell you where he was from, hey Billy?"

"What the fuck are you talking about?"

"Looks like you've only got half the story. You wanna know what's *not* been said?"

"I have all I need to know. I have a ticket away from this place when that day comes."

"You think? Let me tell you what'll happen, Billy. Before you get to use that ticket you've got, you'll be nothing more than a slave to the Guardianship. Twenty years spent doing shit with no guarantee at all. Think about it. Reckon you can handle dirty work for twenty years, Billy? What if during the twenty years you're doing your dirty shit, murdering, stealing, and whatever else they get you to do, you get unlucky and get done by those same guys who've given you your so-called ticket?

"Don't believe me? Check it out. Project Amber, Billy. Go ahead and check on your gismos over there. Project Amber and your exit strategy doesn't exist. It will never exist. Why? Because we're going to destroy it. You'll never get that ticket. All that you're doing is a waste of your time. Go back to your prostitutes. Forget about the disk. Hand over the girl and I might just save your arse."

"You're wrong!"

"We've got the parent genome, Billy. Forget about everything. Do as I ask and you'll live. I can get you out of here. But you need to get Angel right now."

"You're wrong about Amber. And you're wrong about the Hadgitol."

"As I said. Go ahead. Check if you want. I'm sure your computer can patch you into Vault Vitae-G in Antarctica."

That rattled him. He immediately spun and went to his computer. While he was busy at the keyboard, I gave Scotty-Blue a shake.

C'mon, Blue . . . wake the fuck up . . .

Using the zippo, I melted Scotty-Blue's zip ties. At the same time, I took the opportunity to check the time. To my horror, only twenty minutes were left before things got ugly. I did what I had to do. With the heel of my boot, I slammed Scotty-Blue's toe. That worked. Scotty-Blue erupted in a horrible yelp. But that had the side effect of Billy spinning around.

Billy took the knife from his scabbard and launched himself toward me. With the knife held out in front of him, he came at me with speed. I dodged, getting up with such energy I left my prosthetic limb behind. Hopping sideways, balancing as best I could, I stood there. My eyes locked onto Billy's gaze of death. He held out his blade and lunged at me, the knife swiping sideways and just missing my face. Another thrust from Billy. I blocked it. I grabbed his wrist and using the energy of his forward momentum, I pulled him in toward me. I put a cracking head-butt to the bridge of his nose. Billy was gone. Lights out. He went backward, losing the grip on his knife, and he hit the floor.

I reached down for my prosthetic limb at the exact same time I saw Scotty-Blue kick Billy in the head. Billy instantly came back from unconsciousness and cried out loudly. The time had come. I grabbed my prosthetic limb from the floor.

Titanium . . .

Using the limb as a baseball bat, I swung out and struck Billy. He blacked out again and became spreadeagled, faced down. While he was on the floor, I brought my fake limb hard down between Billy's shoulder blades.

CRACK.

I'd broken his spine.

"Holy cripes, Canter. Did ya hear that?"

"Yeah. But I need to finish the bastard."

I picked up Billy's knife and eyed it for a second. Standing over him, I thrust the blade deep into his back, twisting it for good measure. Now I knew I'd cut his spinal cord.

I stood back up. Scotty-Blue eyed me with amazement. "I reckon ya done 'im."

"He's not dead yet. Just paralysed. Now we wake him up."

"Oh. Righto then. It'll be me pleasure," Scotty-Blue said. Before I knew it, Scotty-Blue stepped over Billy.

"Blue! What are you doing!"

"I'm wakin' 'im up. Plus, I'm bustin' for a leak."

I rolled my eyes. Yeah. It'd work. Then Billy *did* wake up.

Billy started with profanities, but he didn't move. He was totally paralysed, from the neck down. But bad news. That meant he couldn't feel pain. And I wanted him to feel every pinprick. After I'd slid back into my leg, Scotty-Blue helped me lift Billy Butcher's limp body into the chair.

"Grab that detonation cord over there, Blue." I said, pointing.

Within a moment, Billy's paralysed body was coiled up in detonation cord in the same chair I'd been tied in a few moments before. I wound a decent amount of detonation cord around Billy's neck; all the while, he was wide-awake and obviously fully aware of how he'd end up. He ranted and raved like a lunatic, not able to do anything. "Fuck you, Masters! Fuck you, Masters!"

"No thanks, Billy."

I ignored him at first. But what the heck. I wound one up and let him have it. Billy went lights out again. No more ranting.

Scotty-Blue finished with the detonation cord on Billy. "Ya reckon he'll lose 'is 'ead over this?"

"I reckon he just might, Blue. You know where Angel is?"

"Yeah . . . But . . ."

"What?"

"Sentry at 'er door. But no biggie with the SAs, though," Scotty-Blue said, while slinging an SA80 over his shoulder and then checking for rounds.

"Go get it done," I said. "I'll get this guy set up with a timer."

I checked my watch. Shit. Twelve minutes. It was going to be close. Under pressure, I was somehow relaxed enough to keep a level head. Just for good measure, I gave Billy the same kick in the shin he gave me, even though I knew he'd never feel it. I could've done so much more to Billy. Looking down at him, I thought about Teresa and desired retribution. But I held back from anything further. It was never going to be enough. Not even close. But Billy's days would be over soon. And much too quickly.

I placed a timer to the detonation cord, as I heard the eruption of gunfire coming from somewhere else. Somehow, I knew Scotty-Blue had things covered. After setting the timer to detonate in three minutes, Billy Butcher, the kid from next door, would most certainly lose his head and a bit more. That itself was payback enough. Payback for everything he'd caused. And for me, I had mere moments to get the hell out.

It wasn't long after the gunfire had stopped that I heard little feet running at top speed up the corridor behind me. In the next moment, I heard Angel's voice and found myself overjoyed. "Nathan!" I spun and picked Angel up in my arms. Nobody could take the smile from my face, no matter how much it hurt. But the smile lasted only seconds. It was now more urgent than ever to get away.

Without any delay, we ran. Down the corridors we ran. Outside, where real sunlight burst down on my skin for the first time in I didn't know how long. But no cars were in sight for the breakneck getaway we so desperately needed.

"To the helos!" Scotty-Blue shouted. "I 'ave a pocket full of circuit breakers an' we can get into the air."

"You fly?"

"Who did ya think got to fly drones into Iraq? We did that shit from up in Pine Gap!"

The moment Scotty-Blue said it, a deep thudding detonation from behind told me Billy Butcher was gone. I caught a glimpse of my watch. Four minutes and the place would go up in a massive explosion. Arriving at the helo, I placed Angel inside. How I would've loved to start consoling her. No time for pleasantries. Time to get away and fast.

"Blue! Two minutes. Get us in the air!"

"I'm bloody trying, mate. These things take a bit to get going. It ain't no car!"

"Blue. Hurry!"

The first sign was a series of loud clicks overhead. Then engines spooling up. Starting in a low hum, the Black Hawk began to whirr into life, building up in pitch.

"BLUE!"

Up top, the rotor began to move. Jesus! It was slow. I wanted to get out and give it a spin.

"BLUE!"

The helo shuddered. The rotors spun up faster. Dust erupted from the ground. But still no lift. I wanted to get out and lift the thing in the air.

"One minute! BLUE!"

"Hang on tight, you lot back there. It's gonna get a bit bumpy."

I checked my watch. "Thirty seconds! Get us up! Get us UP!"

"Nathan!" Angel squeezed up to my shoulder and buried her face.

"Hold on!" I screamed.

"Hold on, you two!" Scotty-Blue screamed.

The engine was now at full spool. The rotors thumping and vibrating the airframe. All I could do was hold Angel in tight while counting the last few seconds. The helo lifted. Scotty-Blue angled the airframe away from the blast zone. We rose up higher.

Four . . .

"Brace for impact!"

Three . . .

"Holy shit, Canter!"

Two . . .

"Grab on to something!"

One . . .

CHAPTER TWENTY-FIVE

Fallen Angel

No explosion. I got it wrong somehow. But as soon as I thought it, the earth below heaved up in a dome, then collapsed back down into a crater. I was expecting the same explosion as a World War I trench warfare catastrophe. The same as beneath hill sixty, the infamous explosion known as the largest non-nuclear detonation in earth's history.

From out of the helo's window, I watched as the dome sank back down into a giant dish. It was everything I expected and more. It was as though someone had taken a high-speed film and hit playback in slow motion. After the eruption settled, a visible shockwave spat itself across the desert plane. A low rumbling vibration erupted, audible even from the helo. Then fiery fingers reached up from the explosion, licking the sky with deadly debris. The earth screamed her fury.

Suddenly and without warning, the helo skipped sideways. On my left, the cloudless blue sky. On my right, the brown-red dusty desert. Warning tones erupted in the cockpit. The steady electronic drone of chimes and alerts accompanied by an electronic human voice.

Woop-Woop. Rotor. Vortex. Woop-Woop. Rotor. Vortex. Woop-Woop. Rotor. Vortex.

"Blue! Get . . ."

"I've got it, Canter! Hold on."

"BLUE!"

"Gimme a sec! Jesus!"

The helo tilted further right. The alarms and warning tones from the cockpit screamed out in pain. Scotty-Blue fought with the controls. Somewhere deep inside, I knew he had it. But did he? It felt as though I was upside down. Thumped and bumped. Rocked and jostled. But Angel. Out of all the urgency. Out of all the panic to get away, I never strapped her in.

As soon as I thought it, I looked sideways. Angel was at the open door. Her feet were sticking out and thrashing like flags in a cyclone. She was clinging on for dear life. Her red-rimmed eyes big as hubcaps, full of fear, gazed back at me. Her mouth was compressed into a slit, her black hair flinging and whipping wildly. She closed her eyes and put her head down. I reached out. I was too late. She was gone!

"NOOO!"

She was gone!

". . . FUUUCKKK!"

She was gone! Gone! Just gone!

"Canter. Hold on!" Scotty-Blue screamed.

"Blue! Angel!"

"I'm getting it!"

"Blue . . .! Man down!"

"What!"

"Angel . . .! She's out the door!"

Scotty-Blue yelled out. I heard him thump his window hard a few times. He had a job on his hands. Momentarily after, by some miracle, one by one, alarms and warnings tones settled into silence. The airframe levelled out. Rattles and jostles stabilised. Rotors were rhythmical, thumping away without stress. Turbofan engines spooled down into what I supposed were safe parameters. I got myself to the edge of the doorway and looked out, hoping for any sign of Angel. My heart wanted it to be so. But there was no sign. Angel had been flung out. Flung out an easy one thousand feet above the ground.

I wanted to get down there. To the ground, as fast as possible. The second I thought it, another warning tone. My mind snapped to attention. I knew the tone. Missile lock. No denying it. Scotty-Blue confirmed it with a series of loud profanities. Then, flares punched out from the sides of the helo. I looked left, just in time to see the sidewinder explode not fifty feet away. The helo was thrust violently sideways and I was instantly taken to my arse.

"Canter! Bogey!" Scotty-Blue yelled back. "Recommend you grab onto something! And close the bloody door!"

I tasted my own heart in my mouth, getting to the edge and leaning into the wind. I stuck my head out. "Bogey, five o'clock!" I screamed.

"I know it, Canter! Close the bloody door!"

My mind was racing. Somehow, I managed to put everything aside. I closed the door and grabbed a restraint. Missile lock again. The warning tone screamed out. The flares and chaff punched out. Another explosion. Shrapnel penetrated the helo and came whizzing past my shoulder. That was close. Too close. I held my breath. The helo began to lose control. Flat spin. More electronic warning sounds from the cockpit. Black smoke filled the insides as the flat spin increased. Spinning and spinning. Going down and down.

Scotty-Blue yelled out, "We're goin' down, Canter! Goin' down!"

He needn't have said it. I already knew it. I jumped into a seat, fighting Gs all the way. I dragged the restraints over my shoulders, then shoved the buckles home. I put my head down and held on tight. Scotty-Blue fought on in the cockpit. Black smoke. Warning tones. Spinning and spinning. The engines' high-pitched shriek increased. They were about to explode.

I pushed my head sideways and caught sight of another missile screaming past. A miss. But they were going to finish us good. The spiral. The spinning. Down and down. I closed my eyes and braced for impact.

The helo tilted sideways. The rotors hit the dirt hard. Crunching and grinding. Pieces splitting off. Clattering and thumping. Dust erupting into the cabin. I put a hand up to my face. Then a sudden thud almost broke my back. I found myself upside down. Then right side up. Then tumbled again, finally coming to a rest. Dust and smoke, with the scent of jet fuel thick in the air. Everything was going to get worse.

* * *

How long was I out? I had no idea.

"Blue! You okay!"

"I'm good. This ain't over, Canter. Get out and find cover!"

Getting myself unclasped in a hurry, I reached up and gave the door an almighty tug. The thing wouldn't slide open.

"Fuck sake! Blue! The door!"

Then I heard it. Chopper closing in. I struggled, wrestling with the door, trying to pry it open. Scotty-Blue was gone. He was out of his seat to somewhere. "Blue!"

I heard him up top, bashing at the door with something heavy. "Give it a shove, mate!"

I grabbed the handle and put my weight behind it.

Two seconds later I climbed up and out in time to see the chopper bearing down. Rounds fired, strafing the ground, kicking up dust. I jumped sideways. Scotty-Blue jumped in the exact same second. The metallic clinkering of rounds hitting the helo. The chopper punched overhead with speed.

"Fucking RUN, CANTER!"

I did my best. Run hop. All I could manage. Scotty-Blue sprinted in front, then got down behind a tree. I saw him waving his hand. Beckoning me over. Run hop. The helo exploded at my rear. I felt a massive burst of pressure and I was off the ground. I was in the air and flying. The tree. I caught a branch with both hands and gripped on tight. My leg flung off.

Scotty-Blue laughed his head off. What was so funny?

"Shoulda seen it, Canter. That leg coming off was the stuff of funny 'ome videos. I'd be a rich man if I 'ad a movie camera."

"Idiot. This isn't the time! Help me out of this bloody tree!"

Things got serious. The chopper was again coming in. I heard a sharp thumping change pitch and tone in the distance. An indication of a change of direction.

"Jump!" Scotty-Blue shouted. "You're only up by eight feet."

Minus the leg, I jumped. We found cover behind the tree and got down. The chopper came in low from the east. I knew by the sound of the engines and rotors; it wouldn't be strafing this time. It was configured for a landing. This one was going to be hand to hand. Up close and personal. Eye to eye. I readied myself. Without any weapons. I wished I hadn't left them behind. If they had firearms with them, we'd be done. We had nothing to answer a fire fight. We both went prone behind the tree, as flat as we could get.

Silent, we lay there as the chopper landed. The dust settled and engines spooled down. The all-black chopper sat noiseless in the dirt, no occupants exiting from the doors as the rotors slowed and became still. My first thought was to get up and break from the area. Minus the leg, it was a tough ask. I'd not get away fast enough. Moments passed. Silence ensued with nothing but the sound of desert flies at my face and Scotty-Blue breathing heavily at my left.

"What do you suppose?" I whispered.

"They've got us, Canter. No point cryin' over it. They've got us. Time to meet the boss, eh?"

"You're giving up?"

"Nah, mate. I'm savin' me life. So, we get to make another escape. That's gotta be better than a 50cal through the head, don't ya reckon?"

The moment he said it, my thoughts went to Angel. I sighed heavily. Her body was out there somewhere. She couldn't have survived such a fall. She was lost. The mission was lost. I had failed so dismally. Now it came down to this. My own death or another attempt to escape. Escape where? That was the hard choice. Maybe Scotty-Blue was right. Maybe it was for the best to just give in. Temporarily, at least. But who'd know what they'd do to us on the next round. They'd be harsher. Perhaps unforgiving. Perhaps they'd take us to a slow demise.

The right door of the chopper swung out and then opened. For the first time, my eyes met the black guy I'd heard so much about. Then there were two, then three. Tall. Just as I'd heard. Just as I'd seen all those years ago. And armed with what I thought were scoped weapons. Sniper rifles. M107s. 50cals, just as Scotty-Blue assumed. It dawned on me they were going to take us down as though we were nothing but a couple of feral boars.

My suspicion was confirmed when one went prone next to the helo and expanded the feet on the barrel of his weapon. The other two moved further away and after going prone in the red dirt, did the same. The first shot fired sounded like a cannon. The projectile struck the tree and went straight through it, sending bark and woodchips flying.

That was the moment I agreed with everything Scotty-Blue said. No sooner I had the thought, Scotty-Blue went up on his knees, putting his hands behind his head. That was it. Job over. Everything shot to shit. I went down on a knee and placed my hands behind my head, the same as Scotty-Blue.

While I had my hands up behind my head as though a white flag was put out, I caught sight of several figures high up on the winds, circling. I narrowed my eyes and witnessed the figures getting closer. One by one, the wings on the figures tucked in and became missiles. A shriek and a cry told me what they were and confirmed my suspicions.

CHAPTER TWENTY-SIX

Hell for Leather

The bloodbath that followed was sudden and swift. I'd not previously heard flesh ripping. It had a sound all to its own. It was a sight never to be forgotten.

The seven eagles, of which one was all white, came in on the wind from the south. A series of piercing shrieks swept through the sky. They came in low, wings tucked with talons poised for a strike. Swooping down, they attached themselves to the three men, then went to work with precision. I watched on as the eyes and ears of those on the ground were punctured one by one with giant beaks. Tongues were ripped out. Flesh was stripped away. Blood sprayed and gushed high in fountains amidst their chilling cries of agony.

When all was silent, the ripping and tearing continued with large chunks of red flesh being tossed about and scattered into the distance. They were dead, but it went on. It went on until the white bone was prominent against the red blood-stained ground. It went on until entrails shook and hung like long lines of sausages from the eagle's beaks.

By the end, three skeletons remained. Red dirt and chunks of stuff hard to describe littered the place. The eagles left the scene just as quickly as they came. They took flight and circled, shrieking out before dispersing into the southern sky. Gone, as though no one else was ever there. As though nothing else mattered.

It took a few moments of reflection to come to terms with what I'd witnessed. I knew Scotty-Blue was the same. He was empty of words. If ever Scotty-Blue had nothing to say, it was a complete phenomenon. It seemed Scotty-Blue's inner larrikin was never at rest. This time there was nothing. I had nothing. He had nothing.

I broke the silence by getting up and hopping away. At my back, I heard Scotty-Blue say the first words in roughly twenty minutes. "Did that just 'appen? I didn't just dream it, did I?"

"No, you didn't dream it, Blue. It happened. And we're still breathing."

I heard a thud. I turned around to see Scotty-Blue smacking himself around the head.

"Blue, what're you doing?"

"I'm tryin' to wake up."

"I already said you weren't dreaming. Can you get over here and give us a hand?"

"With what?"

"I'm trying to look for my frigging leg."

Scotty-Blue got up and ran over. Then, he tripped on his own foot and face planted into the dirt. I couldn't help it. I laughed. The moment of laughter was oddly refreshing. I laughed so hard my eyes watered. Then I felt my emotional tide collapse around me. I went the other direction. Everything I had kept bottled in escaped. Just momentarily. I sucked back a sigh, got a hold of it, and put it away. Now wasn't the time. With a heart as heavy as a blacksmith's anvil, I continued the search for my fake leg. Finally, I found what I was looking for. A bit of expensive titanium glinted and stuck out of the soft earth. I picked it up and slid back into it, the same as I'd done thousands of times.

"What now?" Scotty-Blue asked.

"Now? We go back and find Angel's body. We need it before."

"Before what?" he said.

It occurred to me that I'd seen something quite extraordinary with the eagles. Not once, but a few times. My mind went back to the presence I'd felt at Maralinga. The albino, Gabriel. As I put it together, I realised it for the first time. The white eagle. I put my hand on the back of my head and thought about the tattoo Gabriel had put there. A white eagle with a sword. The sword of destiny.

I tried not to believe it. I don't know why that was. Maybe what I was thinking was just too weird. Or too hard to understand. But having those thoughts took me to another conclusion. Somehow, in my heart, I knew Angel was alive. I didn't know how. I couldn't imagine how this was at all possible. But the feeling was most overpowering.

"Angel is alive," I said to Scotty-Blue, who was busy dusting himself down.

"Nah, mate. We were too 'igh up. She couldn't 'ave survived such a fall."

"Don't ask me how I know. I just know."

Scotty-Blue cast his blue eyes on me. "You're serious, ain't ya?"

"Like I said, Blue. She's alive and we have to find her. Fast."

"I guess we take that chopper then?"

"Yeah," I said. "We'll grab the weapons from the dead guys too. Something tells me we're gonna need them."

Stepping over the grisly remains and climbing into the chopper, I wondered about the search area. As Scotty-Blue lifted the chopper off the ground, I thought about how it was not the recovery mission I first assumed. My feelings grew stronger as I became even more certain it was to be a rescue mission. Once again, I didn't have a clue why I felt it so strongly. As Scotty-Blue leaned on the flight control stick, I willed him onward. We had a vast area to search for Angel.

Scotty-Blue piloted away and pointed the airframe into the general direction we came.

"Head bearing 180 degrees, Blue," I said over coms.

"Roger that." Scotty-Blue gave thumbs up.

The seven eagles came in from the south. If they originated from Angel's location, we were heading the right way.

From an open door, I peered out, looking toward the ground for any sign of her. After forty minutes of travelling in a southerly direction with nothing on the ground other than clumps of malnourished trees, dry and dusty planes, and the odd bit of wild life, I began to wonder. The thought of dingoes lit my mind like a strobe light. But I managed to push those thoughts away.

Then.

"Three o'clock low, Canter," Scotty-Blue said over coms.

Scotty-Blue tilted right and I saw for the first time what he'd seen. Down there, a lone individual was seated in the shade of a rather large sandstone boulder. My heart thumped as I looked down. As my eyes focused further, the individual looked up. I saw her face peering up as we got down closer and there could be no doubt.

"Angel!"

"Maybe it is, maybe it ain't," Scotty-Blue said. "My common sense tells me it ain't. Don't get ya 'opes up is all I'm sayin'."

"Yeah, you're right Blue. Get us down there." But in my mind, I was already down there with her. I kept my eyes on her as the chopper came closer. Just before the dust raised from the thrusting rotors, she waved her hands into the air, and I knew . . . I knew Angel was safe. How? I had a suspicion, but the thoughts in my head didn't make sense. I grappled with the logic. She was alive, and that's all there was to it.

After landing and spooling down, I got out and saw Angel standing next to a huge sandstone boulder with her arms raised.

"Angel!" I called out.

Angel came running over, completely unharmed. Then she stopped ten feet away. Scotty-Blue came to my side. I glanced at him sideways. Shock was in his eyes. Angel ran to him. "Uncle Scotty!" she squealed. Scotty-Blue knelt and caught her in his arms. My heart melted right there. She looked up at me in wonder. "Nathan? Is it you? You have no hair. Why did you shave it?" In her next breath, without any pause. "Your face. You're hurt. How did you get hurt?

I shot a stare at Scotty-Blue. He eyed me back as though muddled.

Amnesia?

"Angel. What can you remember?" I asked.

She didn't answer. Her little eyes scanned me. She looked down at my ugly swollen hand. She reached over and put my hand in hers and straight away I felt a cool sensation sweep up my arm. Morphine. I was no stranger to it. As Angel took my hand, she looked at me with sadness in her eyes. The punch of something cool swept over my body. When it reached my head, the kick in the brain cut off any trace of pain.

. . . I could tell you, but discover it for yourself . . .

Maggie's words. I remembered them. The pain was gone. Morphine. Wonderful, magnificent, sublime morphine. But no head throb. No dizzy attack. Nothing to bowl me over.

"You were going to take me for photos at that place you said. But why am I here?"

After a bit of confusion, I realised Angel was answering my question. I bet she didn't even realise she'd taken my pain away. It was all so innocent. So unknowing. "Was that the last thing you can remember?" I asked her.

"I remember my headache. But Nathan, you told me we were going to Melbourne and you said we could go and take some pictures."

"And that's all you can remember?"

"Yeah. That's all. Why? Is there something else?"

I bent forward and put a knee in the sand in front of her. "Well, let's go there and take some pictures, huh? But first, what about a trip to go and see Maggie."

Angel nodded vigorously. "But what am I doing here?"

What could I tell her? There was the long story or the short one. I figured the long story would come one day. Maybe she'd remember it in time all by herself. I opted for the short one. "You were stolen by some bad men. We came to find you."

"Bad men? I don't remember. What bad men?"

I got up and looked at Scotty-Blue who was scratching his head. Disbelief, maybe. But I was good with it. To someone else it would've been weird. Maybe far-fetched. Angel was safe and that's all I cared about. "It's okay," I said, feeling a smile rip through the bruises on my face. "Let's get going before it gets too hot."

Chapter Twenty-Seven

North by South

Scotty-Blue set the chopper down on the airstrip at William Creek. I looked across the road. My Land Rover was still there waiting like an old friend. The hotel still stood lonely. The paint-peeled shack with the red cross still had crime scene tape wrapped around it. For a moment, I thought Scotty-Blue was going to join us for the trip north back to Alice Springs. He didn't climb out of his seat. He stayed there, watching me with a set of eyes that said goodbye. "Ya still got ya keys?"

"No keys. I have no idea what happened to them. But nothing I can't handle. I take it you're not coming?"

"I can't, mate. You know it's not possible."

"Why?"

"Lies and secrets, my friend. Lies and secrets."

I smiled and felt relief for the first time in how long? How did I know he was going to say something like that?

"Nothin's changed, Canter. I don't know you. And you don't know me. Always remember it."

I nodded, smiling a bit more. "I don't know you, should we ever meet up again. Like you always said."

"It 'as to be that way. Make no mistake. It's all important, Nathan Masters."

"You just called me by name. I can't remember a time you'd ever . . ."

"You gettin' all gushy on me? Bloody hell, Canter. Better get ya hard arse back on. It don't suit ya," Scotty-Blue said. "You need a weapon? There's the M107s."

"I'll pass. I think I'll be fine from here."

"Nah, mate. You won't. Take this one then." Scotty-Blue handed a Glock through the window. I took it. "It was on the floor. Take it and you'll be fine. Gonna sleep tonight. I reckon you might too."

Scotty-Blue gave a quick wink, then pressed a few buttons and twisted a lever. The engines' RPM increased and the rotors began to spin. "Lies and secrets, Canter. Remember it. Oh, an' your job's not finished. Remember the Hadgitol? Gotta get it sorted, mate. Stop those pricks who's got it!"

I stepped back, holding Angel's hand. She waved her Uncle Scotty-Blue goodbye as he slowly lifted away, turned the chopper, and moved away on a north-westerly heading. I stood there wondering if we'd catch up again. Should that happen, it'd be as though complete strangers, I realised. He had his reasons. Who was I to second-guess it. But I knew there was more to Scotty-Blue. It brought up a whole new set of questions.

* * *

Stepping up to the Land Rover, I eyed it for a second and smiled. I placed a hand on the canvas roof, amazed there was no cleaning to do. Having no keys, it was just a matter of attaching a couple of wires and we were on our way. Gotta love the little non-turbo diesels. Everything so simple. Just the way I liked it. This time, we'd head north back to where the trip started.

"What about my bag, Nathan? I need my camera."

I looked down at Angel's beaming face and couldn't help but wonder what she'd been through. It was a relief to know she had no memory. How traumatic for such a young soul. "No problem. Wait here and I'll go get it."

Thank god the door wasn't locked. Inside and saw the mess with everything tipped over. It didn't take long to find our bags. I took them and left that room forever. Stepping outside, I saw the hotel windows were boarded up. A big 'for sale' sign sat on a post out the front. The entire place was a ghost town. I eyed the phone box on the street and wondered if I should check in with Shilo. Placing the bags in the back of the Land Rover, I decided against it. Maybe it was better to turn up and face whatever needed facing.

I got myself under the dash and looked for those two wires. Having found them, I touched them together and the little diesel motor turned over and idled without any argument.

I wasn't ready to head north. One more job to get done. The promise I made to Angel a couple of months ago. I steered south and headed out to Lake Eyre. It also meant I could get an eyeball on the calamity Bosco had left behind. I had to be sure. I needed to know the scene had been cleaned and nothing was left over. Arriving there, nothing to tell the story. No Robinsons helicopter. No dead pilot. No turned-over Bronco and dead G-man on the ground. Everything was gone, as though it hadn't happened. Not even tracks in the dirt. I wondered who cleaned the site. Was it the cops or the clean-up squad Bosco had arranged? I'd never know.

At the edge of the vast white open space, Angel hopped out of the Land Rover, camera in her grip. She giggled at the beautiful sight she held in her viewfinder while she went to work shooting the landscape. In the distance, high in the bright, cloudless sky, eagles were up on the wing. Only two that I could see. I knew in my gut they were ordinary wedge tails and not those of the seven. How could I explain it to Angel? How could I tell her the long story? How could I tell her once she was ready to hear it? I sighed with the thought. That day would come. I'd have to work on it from this moment. When that day came, I'd have something ready for her mind to digest.

We stopped there for a little more than an hour, taking in the scene, enjoying the space and silence. Breathing the air. It gave me much-needed respite. It gave Angel a great amount of joy watching the eagles up there on the wing, circling. When it was over and her film was spent, she pushed up to my side. "I had an eagle friend once," she said.

"I know. You told me about Charlotte."

"I did? When?"

"In the motel room when you were sick."

"I was sick? I don't remember."

"I know. Maybe a good thing, huh? C'mon. Let's go. It's gonna be late by the time we get back to Maggie's house."

* * *

The landscape whizzing past the window was now all too familiar. Heading north on the Oodnadatta Track, my mind went to Doug the grazier. I remembered the early stages of the darkest times of my life. Had Angel known the complete story, I don't know if she'd be sitting next to me right now. Maybe she would.

Her camera, even though she was out of film, seemed to keep her busy and I was thankful for that.

I took the trip slow. I was in no hurry. Angel was as silent in her seat as she had been while driving down. I wondered what she was thinking. I wondered how she was feeling. I was about to open up and tell her at least some of the story. Maybe it would help the amnesia. I glanced sideways and sure enough, she was busy with the landscape out of her window; her eyes pointed to something in the sky. "Nathan. Do you think those birds up there are following us?"

"What birds?" I asked.

"Those ones up there. See?" She pointed and tapped the window lightly. "I've been watching them. It's like they know where we're going."

I bobbed my head down to see better. "I can't see them. You want me to stop?"

"Yeah," she said. "But I don't have any film left."

I stopped, pulling up on the side of the track. As I got out, Angel was already out of her seat and walked a few paces away. "They're beautiful, Nathan. Come see."

They circled high up. The seven I'd seen and already thought of as friends. "Eagles," I said. "And yeah, kiddo. They are beautiful."

Angel turned and stared back at me. Her eyes had a little pain in them. "You called me kiddo," she said, and I noticed a tear sitting lonely at the edge of an eyelid.

"Sorry, Angel. Is it something I shouldn't have said?"

"Mum used to call me kiddo. My dad did something horrible to her. Please don't say that anymore. It reminds me of what my dad did."

"I'm so sorry . . . I wish I could've changed it."

"What do you mean?"

Collecting my thoughts, I wondered how to answer. One of my weaknesses, I supposed. I was never any good at matters of the heart. When it came to feelings, I had no idea. Maybe Angel was about to change all that. Maybe being with her was part of my path. To show me the way out of emotional emptiness.

I'd spent the best part of my life training in the art of killing. Through the process, I'd learned to empty my soul. Nothing lived in there. I could take a life without any bother. I could look down on the dead guy at my feet and not feel anything. It was a job and nothing more. At that moment, I realised why I never got close to anyone. I felt sad that I lived my days emotionally dry and had not welcomed relationships into my life. But Teresa changed that in me. We'd see where this new path lead. But I made no promises. I am what I am. I chose the life willingly. Next life, I'd do it much differently.

I gazed down at Angel, who was standing and waiting patiently for an answer. I felt my eyes quickly fogging over. I constructed a sentence in my mind and I thought it may be the one to offer. "I knew your mother and father long ago," I said. "Angel. They were two people very much in love with each other back then. Sometimes, I wish I could go back in time and change things. Put things right. If I knew your father was going to do those horrible things when I first knew him, I'd have done everything I could to keep those two apart. But you know what? If I'd come between them, there'd be no Angel. And we'd not be standing here right now. And you'd not be looking at those beautiful eagles up there. Those eagles now showing us the way. They're your guiding light. They're here for *you*. And something deep inside me tells me they'll never leave you. They'll be with you for life, forever guiding, forever protecting."

"They're my eagles?"

"More than you know, Angel. More than you know."

"And if I wish for them like I wished for Charlotte, they'll come?"

I smiled a little before answering. "If they don't come, they're always in your heart. Look for them there. Trust them to show you the way and they will. You may not understand what I'm saying just yet. You will in time."

Angel looked up as though what I'd said didn't make sense. Her little face was trying hard to understand something profound. Then, her eyes dropped slightly. "I'm tired, Nathan. I think I can go to sleep now."

She wrapped her arms around me as little kids do. Before I said anything further, she was in her seat, waiting for me to get behind the wheel. We left and continued our trip north. As we drove, the eagles left and disappeared into the horizon. Angel closed her eyes and sleep came.

CHAPTER TWENTY-EIGHT

Return to Base

Angel had slept the entire way to Alice Springs. We arrived close to midnight. I stopped the Land Rover out front of Firebird Station, killed the engine, and just sat for a moment or two. A perfect time to reflect a little. The lights shone brightly through the tattered curtains. People were up and about and I wondered all over again what was next. I remembered Scotty-Blue's words before he up and left in the chopper at William Creek.

It ain't over, Canter. Remember the Hadgitol?

Already, I was preparing for whatever that may be. At the very least, Angel was safe and in the care of not only me, but others who had a vested interest in her security. Mission accomplished, I thought. I relaxed, knowing the final play was at hand. But what would that entail? And how would it be accomplished?

At the heavy front door, I knocked in the code known only to those in the game. Angel was fast asleep in my arms. I held my breath. The door opened. Bosco's face came out of the darkness and he made himself known. He smiled and went to say words. I put a hand up to my mouth and signalled a shoosh. "She's asleep, Bosco." I whispered. I carried Angel's sleeping body to the bunkroom at the end of the hall.

For some reason, I envisioned Teresa sleeping in there. My heart plummeted. The hard nature of her demise hit me. Teresa was never coming back. She was never going to hold her warm body against me again. She was never going to hand me coffee with a kiss. Those times were gone. Ripped from my heart. And it was *me* who pulled the trigger. It was *me* who took her life. If there was anyone to blame, all I needed was a mirror.

Teresa's death came with such a high price. I would take that regret with me like a black dog, whenever I heard her name. But through it all, I would always ask myself if I could've done more so that she didn't have to die. And I would ask it every single day until I took my last breath.

Placing Angel down in the bunk, I covered her to her chin, switched off the light, and closed the door. In the hall, Bosco watched with an expression of surprise.

"Thought you were still down range," I said in a whisper.

"I was, and I'm back, big hoss. You turned up just in time. Fireworks about to start."

"Oh? And what fireworks are we talking about?"

"I'll let Maggie do the honours. Grab a hot brew, do the formalities, and come downstairs. I think you'll be amazed."

"Formalities? What formalities?"

He didn't answer. Bosco spun and left, disappearing down to the control room. I took a sharp left-turn and headed straight for the coffee machine. It had been one hell of a time and my little luxury was only a moment away. That's when I heard someone to my rear. I turned to face Maggie. The moment I dreaded and had somewhat avoided arrived.

I was expecting much sharper words. Maggie regarded me in the way only she knew how. "How did you end up?"

There it was. Simple. Direct. Straight to the point. No 'Hello, Nathan.' No 'How's Angel?' No 'Where's Teresa?' Nothing.

How did you end up . . . ?

What could I say?

"Mission accomplished, Maggie."

Maggie stepped back a pace and folded her arms. I was no expert at body language, but how could anyone mistake such an action for anything positive?

"I see you've accomplished the primary objective," she said. "What say you of the secondary and tertiary?"

"As I said. Mission accomplished. All is destroyed. But Quinlan – there was no way he was gonna be brought in."

"That's a shame. But good work. We'll debrief in the morning. For now, however, more important things are on. Normally, I'd say go get some rest. But believe me, Nathan, you won't want to miss this. There's some paperwork in the meeting room for you to sign."

"Paperwork?"

"Regulations, really. *Official Secrets Act* Form Ten-B. Your intelligence security level has been raised to level eight. I need a signature before you're eligible to come downstairs. Level eight eyes only for what you're about to witness. Are we clear?"

"Sure. What's going on?"

Maggie laughed, stepping back another pace. I was tired and it was a bad choice of words. I realised she couldn't have answered without my signature. "Sorry. I'll get the paperwork out of the way."

"Good. Come on down when you're ready. Oh, and by the way," Maggie said over her shoulder while stepping away. "A letter for you from Teresa. She left it in the bunkroom before you both left for Swan Island."

* * *

Coffee in my hand, I sat slowly down at the table and eyed the envelope Teresa had left behind. On the envelope, the words, 'My Dearest Nathan.' I sighed and tears sprang to my eyes. I knew what was in there. Somehow, I even knew what she'd written.

It'd start with a greeting. Her words in broken English. I smiled a little knowing just that. I loved the way she spoke. None other could speak as she did. Her accent was one of the things about her I found so attractive. I hung on every word she ever told me. I often laughed to myself. The struggles she had. The corrections I made. It was all so lovable and enjoyable listening to her talk.

After a greeting, she'd let me know that I'd only ever read such a letter in the case of her death. She'd go on by saying how sorry she was for how she passed. She'd even tell me how much she loved me. She'd remind me of all the good times we shared. She'd tell me not to mourn her in death, but to treasure the moments we had together. The love we shared. The laugher. The tears. The disagreements and the shouting that came with it. She'd remind me of all those things.

Then she'd end her letter in forgiveness. She'd remind me that she was always and forever looking down from wherever she was. She'd say to not give up on love, but to open my heart should it arrive again. She'd tell me it wasn't our time, but our time would come again.

After I finished the letter and put it away, I realised all those things were written in there. Almost word for word, just as I felt.

CHAPTER TWENTY-NINE

A Different Perspective

The place was lit up with bluish lights, down there. New electronic equipment had been installed since the last time I visited. New banks of computers along the far-right wall. Two huge flat panel screens screwed into place. New tech, I thought. Plasma screens. Probably more expensive than a Mercedes-Benz SL500. I was beginning to see firsthand how much money was splashed this way.

Maggie turned and regarded me with her hands firmly on her hips. Bosco was standing beside her with his blue baseball cap spun backwards, chewing on what was probably gum. Andrew was at one of the several computers, bent over a keyboard, tapping madly.

Maggie beckoned me over. "Come," she said. "Take a seat, Nathan. We're waiting for the satellite connections at this time."

"We'll have the Daydreamer uplink in a few moments. Minotaur shortly after," Andrew said. He got up from his chair and came toward me, taking the trouble to reach out and shake my hand.

I repeated my original question to Maggie, sitting down in the chair at the long Tasmanian Oak table.

How in the heck did they get it down here . . .?

"Mind telling me what all this is about?" I asked.

"Yes. Of course. I apologise, Nathan. My mind is firmly else-where, so it seems. Welcome to Operation Cobalt Blue. Mission brief on the desk over there if you'd like, but I'll give you the rundown. We are conducting a coordinated drone strike. Our tar-gets are Vault Vitae-G; McMurdo Station; Antarctica; and Halifax Winthrop Engineering in North Eastern Iran, approxi-mately six hundred kilometres south of Mashhad. We are going to obliterate The Guardianship capability. It all comes down to this."

"Maggie. Vault Vitae-G is blast-proof. We've already estab-lished it can't be compromised with AGMs. That was the reason for Crossbow, wasn't it?"

"Crossbow was reconnaissance, as you know, Nathan. This is about the destruction of assets."

"Then why can't we lead a sabotage mission old school?"

I said it. Maybe I should've left it. Maggie flicked her hair to one side as she did when she started to get annoyed. She took a breath, then said, "It's much too late for that, Nathan. Black ops are out of the question. Cobalt Blue has CIA and Presidential ap-proval. We're going ahead as planned."

If the mission had Presidential approval, it could only mean one thing. The thought spat cold ice through my mind. Many in-nocent people were going to lose their lives. How many were stationed at McMurdo, I wondered. A hundred? Maybe a thou-sand?

"You're going to nuke the place?" I asked, still not believing it for a second.

Bosco strode over and got up in my face. He was on a hair-trigger, I thought. I wondered what it was about. Maybe he'd heard enough arguments over the mission's pros and cons. "Canter, there's just no option," he said. "What I saw down there was *not* just a couple of coffee plants and a handful of seeds. The bastards are stockpiling fuel cells. Antimatter fuel cells."

"You're shitting me," I said. "Antimatter is theoretical."

"Not anymore, big hoss. It's as real as that damn fake leg of yours."

"So you think nukes are gonna finish it? Nukes are airburst weapons. They won't make a dent in a blast-proof bunker."

"Ahem," Andrew butted in. "You might be a bit wrong there. This one we're using is a little different to the airburst variety. This one is a ground-penetrating bunker buster nuke. 3.5 megatons. Two warheads. One for penetration, the other for the destructive yield. Just in case you wanted to know."

Holy shit. They were going to do it! And not only that, it was planned well in advance. While I was down range. I wondered about that timing. Was it done this way with a purpose? I, for one, wouldn't have given it my endorsement. Not this. Not the death of innocent civilians. I said it aloud. "And what of the people down there? There's at least a thousand innocent civilian scientists who have nothing in this. You're gonna go ahead and murder them? Cold and calculating? Are we not as bad as the bloody Guardianship?"

"Collateral damage," Maggie said matter-of-factly, sighing heavily. Her complexion reddened as though she was losing her patience. "The stakes are much too high to consider a mass evacuation of McMurdo, Nathan. The Guardianship will be alerted and we're back to where we started."

"Are you people shitting me!" I shouted.

"Canter!" Maggie snapped. "I'm reminding you of where we are! Yes, people are going to lose their lives. Yes, those people are innocents. We CANNOT conduct this operation without making the Guardianship cognisant. All bases have been covered. This has Presidential approval. Are you going to sit there and second-guess the leader of the free world? Do you *not* think the President of the United States has taken the trouble to calculate the outcome? We are talking about the human race, Nathan. The stakes are just too. Bloody. High."

Maggie trailed off long enough to take a deep breath. Then added, "I wish it didn't come down to this. But with the Hadgitol and now the antimatter fuel cells? We must stop it. There *is* no other way. Andrew! Get some fresh coffee down here for god's sake!"

Andrew left his seat and shot up the stairs. After he'd gone there was a silence in the control room thick enough for a chainsaw to hack through.

"Everyone take a breather," Maggie said. "Clearly, with a certain amount of opposition to Cobalt Blue, this is not going to be an easy mission."

"And what about Halifax Winthrop?" I asked without pause. "Are we to nuke that place too?"

"They're the centrifuges," Maggie said. "A present from Teresa, if you will. The same weapon will be used. The casualties, however, will be at a minimum."

"How many?"

"There are employees there. Intel suggests they're all Guardianship working for the same cause. Halifax Winthrop Engineering will procure enough enriched plutonium for the manufacture of a super-bomb in a few short years. The Peacemaker."

Peacemaker. Where did I hear that term before? It was a memory, but from where? I got up from my seat and walked back and forth with a hand to my chin. Then it came to me. Angel's dream. The one she had with the black guy. Peacemaker. All one word as Maggie had said. There it was.

"What of this Peacemaker," I asked.

"Little is known," Maggie said. "The intelligence we have on the Peacemaker doesn't lead us anywhere other than to an intention for it to be used. Even on that score, there is grey. We know Peacemaker is proposed as a super-bomb. A super-bomb with enough destructive yield to dwarf anything this planet has ever witnessed."

"What kind of destructive yield are we talking about?"

"One-gigaton. MOSSAD infiltrated Halifax Winthrop for a short time before becoming compromised. The plutonium required for such a device will no doubt come from there. Other than that, zip. And that is the reason why this facility needs to be shut down. We can't let such vast quantities of weapons-grade plutonium fall into the hands of the Guardianship. I can't imagine there'll be a safe place on earth should that happen."

"Okay, so nuke the place. But leave Antarctica and McMurdo intact," I said. "There is another way we can accomplish the task without taking lives."

"And what do you propose, Nathan. Go on. I'm happy to hear it." She wasn't happy. I could tell. She stood bolt upright with arms firmly folded, her eyes like blades of fine Tamahagane steel cutting through me. Now was my opportunity to come up with something. Anything. I thought hard. I walked back and forth. Head down with a hand to my chin. I had my opportunity. And it was fading away. *C'mon, Nathan . . . Think, for Christ's sake . . .*

"What about non-nuclear bunker busters?"

"Already considered that," Bosco said. "They don't have enough reach and yield to do the job. I'd know. I was there. We'd have to use more than a dozen. That would mean a number of drones, which we don't have."

"A full-frontal invasion with special forces," I said. "We'd have that place shit-canned in a minute."

"Nathan. You know that's not possible," Maggie put in. "We'd have to wait another six months for the weather. We don't have that time on our side."

"There has to be something. Anything but a nuke!"

Bosco walked to my side and put a hand on my shoulder. I pushed it away.

"C'mon, Nathan. I know you don't like it. We all don't like what's gonna happen. There's simply no choice."

I looked at Bosco and frowned. Anger built up inside me. It took an almighty will not to reach out and squeeze his throat. Him and his days in Detachment 421. No, I hadn't forgotten it. But this wasn't the time.

"Think about it," I said to everyone there. "Thermonuclear and antimatter. What does that sound like to you? Can you *not* imagine the cost? Not only to innocent bystanders, which is bad enough. What about the marine ecosystem and wildlife you'll be destroying for a hundred thousand years into the future? Species forced into extinction. Doesn't it sound like stupidity knocking at your door?"

"I've had enough!" Maggie shouted. "Enough! Do you hear me!"

Maggie slammed something down on the table. I wasn't sure what it was.

"Leave, Nathan! Leave and don't return until you have something productive to offer. This mission goes ahead. As planned!"

CHAPTER THIRTY

Cobalt Blue

My mind twisted with everything I'd heard. Seated at the dining room table, I added a decent amount of Wild Turkey to my coffee. Maybe it would help. Maybe it wouldn't. Everything spun in my head. Was this really happening?

I got up from my chair and decided to check in on Angel. I opened the door softly and peered in. Thank god she was still asleep. The amount of shouting and yelling could've woken anybody. For some reason I couldn't work out, I reached down and placed a hand on her forehead. She was hot to the touch. Too hot. Maybe she was coming down with something. Another seizure. I pushed the thought from my mind and went looking for some aspirin. Maybe it would bring her temperature down.

Stepping into the bathroom and opening the box with the red cross that was positioned near the door, I reached in and grabbed the aspirin. An empty glass was by the sink. I grabbed it and filled it halfway with water.

My hand instinctively went to the Glock handgun I had tucked at my back. Before leaving, I caught a glimpse of my own reflection in the mirror. The reflection staring back wasn't me. I didn't know who that guy was. But now, with a handgun, maybe I could stop this madness.

I moved fast toward the hallway, then to the stairs. By the time I got below, the uplink to the Daydreamer and Minotaur satellites were underway. Andrew was seated at the computer. Maggie stood with her full attention on the monitors. Bosco was standing beside Maggie, still with his baseball cap turned backward.

Maggie turned and eyed me. Then she beckoned for me to take a seat. Bosco didn't react. His eyes were firmly fixed to what was going on.

On the left monitor was a daytime vision high above the earth, looking over a vast desert in Iran. On the right, a night-time image under infrared. Both drones getting into position, I thought. How much time did I have left?

"Agent Blue," Maggie said. "ETA to ingress?"

"Ingress to target ten mikes, ma'am," the voice said over the speaker. That voice. I knew the voice. No. It couldn't be.

"Agent Grey?" Maggie said.

"ETA thirty mikes. Diversion due to weather."

"Agent Blue. Possible to go around to meet up with an ingress on thirty mikes?"

"Negative, ma'am. Bingo fuel."

That was it. It was going ahead. Nothing I could do to change anything. Or was there? I slowly rose from my seat and walked over toward Maggie. She turned and smiled briefly, then she went back to the monitor.

"Abort the mission," I said at Maggie's rear. Maggie immediately spun and eyed me. "Belay that last statement Agents Blue and Grey!" Maggie shouted.

"Ma'am? Still a go on the target?"

"Affirmative. Carry on," Maggie said, watching me intensely.

I pulled the gun out and pointed it directly at Maggie's head. "Abort the mission! For Christ's sake! Abort!"

"Belay it!" Maggie yelled.

Bosco turned and stood as though in shock. "Fuck sake, Canter! You idiot! What're you doing!"

Andrew got up from his chair, tipping it over, then pointed a handgun directly at me. "Drop it!" he shouted with intense resolve.

Maggie raised a hand, then let it relax. She took a breath. "This is how you want to play this, Nathan? Are you sure? It comes down to this?"

"Maggie. You can't let this happen. Please. If you murder these people . . ."

"Murder, is it? The exact same murder as you yourself are party to? How many lives, Nathan? Can you count them? Give me the gun and we'll discuss it."

"No. You'll abort this mission. You'll . . ."

"Nathan?" A voice from the top of the stairs. Angel.

"Angel, go back. Please!"

Then a voice in my head. Deep from within. Not my voice. Not my inner voice.

"Nathan, this not how I wish it to be. Let it go, my darling. Let it go."

Teresa . . . ?

"Let it go," Teresa's voice repeated in my head. "It must be these way. Let it go, Nathan. A price will be paid, no? You and I have other work. In much years from now. Let it go . . ."

Teresa . . . !

I relaxed my weapon. My arm dropped to my side as though it was much heavier than it truly was. The gun fell from my grip and clacked, hitting the floor. My leg quivered from under my body and I fell. I spun to see Angel teetering at the top of the stairs. She was going to tip. "Angel!" I yelled. I scurried madly to her side just in time to stop her fall. She was still burning up. I held her in my arms at the foot of the stairs. Nothing I could do but watch on in terror. I had no power to stop anything!

"Ma'am. Agent Blue. Ingress to target. Proceed as planned?"

"Affirmative, Agent Blue. Proceed," Maggie said, showing the professional she was. I realised what I had just done. Maybe there was no way back. But Maggie carried on regardless. "Agent Grey, proceed to target."

"Copy that, Colonel. Proceed to target."

Maggie spun and faced me. Her expression told me there'd be a price to pay for my insubordination. I knew it. I felt it. And thousands of souls were about to meet their end.

The monitor on the right showed a row of lights under infrared. The drone was almost within range. "One mike, ma'am."

"Agent Blue. I authorise you to engage your target at your ready."

"Roger that, ma'am. Thirty seconds before rifle."

I climbed up from the floor with Angel in my arms and found an empty chair. She was fast asleep again. Her temperature was quickly coming down. I was relieved, but at the same time on edge with what was about to occur. My eyes fixed to the monitor on the right, I held my breath.

"Rifle, rifle, rifle. Weapon away. Countdown begins. Sixty seconds to impact."

Maggie then took a seat and buried her head in her hands for just a second before looking back up to the monitor. Regret maybe. I saw it. She was human. It occurred to me that Maggie was doing her job. She was a Colonel. She was answering the orders from those above her. She had no choice. I knew, watching her, that she opposed this too. Her own feelings. Her own reservations. The same as me. But she'd never admit it. She'd check that at the door. The true professional she was.

"Thirty seconds . . ."

Bosco moved closer to the monitor. It was as though he was willing it on. Maybe he was getting some enjoyment, I supposed. It wouldn't have surprised me.

"Ten seconds to impact . . ."

My eyes grew large. Holy hell. Please God!

"Five . . . four . . . three . . . two . . . Impact."

The screen under infrared immediately lit up bright blue-white. Blue-white! For a long time, blue-white. I wondered about the immense explosion down there. I wondered about the lives lost. All souls instantly vaporised. I hung my head for a second. It was done. Looking up again, still blue-white.

"Something wrong with the monitor?" Bosco asked.

Then the voice of the drone pilot from the speaker. "Woo hoo! Woo hoo! Fucken boom, mate. Lies and secrets can go an' kiss my lily arse!"

Bosco and Andrew laughed. It wasn't funny. Not at all.

"Agent Blue!" Maggie shouted. "You're still on audio! Check your words, thank you very much!"

"Ah, sorry ma'am. Thought I 'ad that bit sorted. Forgot I 'ad to press the bloody button, eh?"

"Thank you, Agent Blue. You may recall your drone. That is all. Out."

Maggie signalled a cutthroat to Andrew, who disconnected from the Daydreamer satellite. The monitor went blank without sound.

"Agent Grey?"

"Ingress to target, two mikes, ma'am."

"I authorise you . . ." Maggie broke off. Her voice became hoarse. Her words quivered slightly. Then she took a breath and regained her composure. "I authorise you to engage your target at your ready, thank you."

"Roger that, Colonel."

The camera from the Minotaur satellite showed the Halifax Winthrop structure from high in space.

"Thirty seconds to rifle, ma'am."

"What's that?" Maggie said, moving closer to the monitor, as though seeing something for the first time.

"What?" Bosco said.

"That!" Maggie repeated.

Maggie put her finger on the screen. I noticed what she was viewing. I hadn't seen anything like it before, but there it was. After Maggie lifted her finger away from the monitor, I had a better view. Something out of the ordinary, sitting lonely on the desert flat. Something that began to glow.

"Rifle, rifle, rifle. Weapon away. Sixty seconds to impact."

The glowing object intensified, then lifted off the ground slightly. Instantly, it shot away as if it was never there.

"Ten sec . . . what the . . . Hang on . . ."

"What is it, Agent Grey?" Maggie said, holding her breath.

"Ma'am? It appears we've lost the weapon. The weapon has been compromised. It's been destroyed."

CHAPTER THIRTY-ONE

What Now

Maggie sat behind her desk, avoiding eye contact. Her avoidance cut deep. I knew I'd stuffed up severely. I knew answering my mutiny was here and now. In the shit again. I'd been here before, but never so deep. I sat nervously bobbing a knee up and down.

Maggie kept her eyes down, shuffling papers. Shuffling photographs and everything else. Angel was away with Andrew for an appointment with the GP. Bosco was out on an errand, Maggie had said. I sat there, still and silent. The emptiness and avoidance was murder.

"Do you have anything to add before we start?" Maggie finally said, not bothering to look up from her desk.

"No," I said. "Just put it out there, straight up with no bullshit."

Maggie smiled, but not out of happiness. Exactly the opposite, I thought. She placed her papers down, locked her fingers, and eyed me. "You know this will have to go down to Canberra, Nathan. I can't avoid it. What you did is completely inexcusable. Not only do your actions warrant a court-martial, but you were on the verge of ruining everything. And nobody gets to put a gun to my head. I have given this a lot of thought and you give me no option."

Her undertone was one of sadness. Disappointment. She held up a document with her own handwriting scribbled down the full length. "This is my Form-T describing your insubordination. It discloses everything that has happened. I suggest you read it to yourself before we go any further."

Maggie slid the document across her desk. I picked it up and read what was written. A blow by blow account of everything that transpired two nights before. After reading it, I gave a nod and slid it back over Maggie's desk. She picked it up from her desk and held it up before ripping it to shreds.

"Maggie. I'm guilty as charged."

"There's method in my decision," Maggie said, at the same time raising her hand. "You might think you've got off lightly. You'd be wrong in that assumption. I'll get to this a little later. But I know you, Nathan. This was *not* you. I want to know *how* you managed to get yourself down to such a place. I'm thinking there was a lot that went on to cloud your judgment. Talk to me. Tell me everything."

I settled back into my chair and thought things over. There was much to explain. By the time I'd finished, I'd given Maggie an account of everything in detail. I watched her expression change from hard to something more empathetic. She leaned forward in her chair, locking her hands and listening intently to the finer specifics.

I saw compassion twinkle in her eyes for a second, but then her professionalism cut back in, hardening her facial lines. I'd told her everything but left out one aspect. The time Angel fell from the helo. No matter which way I looked at it, I wasn't able to describe the event leading to Angel's amnesia. I made something up to put in its place. Maybe it was more palatable and easier to swallow.

"So, you're telling me Angel has no recollection whatsoever?" Maggie said.

"None."

"Have you tested it?"

"Yes, I have. A number of times I put questions to her to see if any memory would come back to her. She really has no memory of the ordeal."

"Hmm . . ." Maggie put a hand to the side of her face and sat back. I could tell from her cutting-ice gaze the whole scenario had her confused "Stay here," she said. "I need a moment." She got up and left.

I sat there with my knee still bobbing, the unfortunate set of consequences twirling and whirling in my head. I was ready. The real prospect of being stood down and sent to prison for attempted treason was starting to sink in. It was now a reality and not just a fleeting thought. The hard call would be announced the moment Maggie came back. She'd be back with a couple of federal cops in tow. My hands would again be cuffed behind my back and I'd be on my way.

When Maggie finally entered and sat down in her high-back office chair, there were no federal cops behind her. She simply sat and took a heavy breath, then began with her hands locked together on her desk. "It's clear you'll need counselling, Nathan. Before you object, let me say this is non-negotiable. I will set it up for you."

"Sure," I nodded. "But what now?" Here it comes, I thought. Let's get to the big crunch.

268 · Carl Lakeland

"What now?" she said, as though surprised. "Have you forgotten? You still have your Eagle Shield mission. You *have* to get Angel into play. It's more important now than previously."

"We killed the Hadgitol. That makes Eagle Shield void, doesn't it?"

"We've taken the Hadgitol out of the equation, yes. But Halifax Winthrop is still standing. We don't get another go at it, unfortunately. We've lost the element of surprise to sneak up and destroy that threat. Without the parent genome, the Guardianship capability has been slowed, but not absolutely nullified. Perhaps they won't come out of dry-dock in a hurry. But make no mistake about it. They'll be back."

"Eagle Shield original objectives still stand, I take it."

"To the letter," Maggie said plainly. "But I'm still cross with you. I'm human, after all. I feel disappointment just the same as anybody. It will take some time, I'm afraid. Just appease me by going to the counselling sessions. We'll work it out, I'm quite sure."

"I dunno how that will work out, Maggie. Everything I'll need to talk about is classified."

"Exactly why we have our own. And he's in Melbourne. He's name is Xenon. Xe for short."

"Xe? That doesn't sound like an ordinary name."

"He's not an ordinary man. You'll see what I mean after you meet up."

"Okay. Done."

"Now. Other business," Maggie said. I could see some relief in her expression. She went on. "I need to bring you up to date on a few items. Do you feel like taking a look at some happy snaps? I'll understand if you don't."

I thought it over. Was I in the mood to look at images of destruction? I already knew McMurdo was no longer, and probably a good portion of Antarctica didn't exist. My mind again went to all the carnage. All those lives lost. I had no choice but to get over it and carry on. "Sure," I said. "I'll take a look."

Maggie passed a couple of photographs across her desk without any delay. The images weren't of Antarctica as I'd suspected. Instead, the photographs were of the infrastructure of Halifax Winthrop. Maggie reached across her desk and placed a finger on an object in one of the photos, the object that was believed to have destroyed the incoming weapon. "Any thoughts on what that might be?"

After scanning the photographs, I passed them back across Maggie's desk. "I have no idea. I've never seen any object like it before. But why do I get the feeling it has something to do with the antimatter fuel cells we found?"

"My deductions as well. We'll need to investigate it. We don't need anything like that in our way on the day Milestone finally comes."

"I still can't get my head around a theoretical antimatter becoming reality."

"I hear you. Anyway. I'll pitch this one to Canberra for a priority follow-up with Andrew," Maggie said, then placed the photograph back in her drawer. "Now, here is something that will surprise you." Reaching into her desk drawer, Maggie took something out. Small. Metal. She passed it over. I held the tiny object in my hand. I'd seen it before.

"The projectile from the William Creek crime scene?"

Maggie nodded vigorously and smiled. Not a happy smile. Maggie gave me the impression she was slightly perplexed, and the smile reflected her frustration, I supposed. "Interpol came up with a match a couple of weeks ago. The bullet was dispatched from Canberra just yesterday and it arrived this morning."

I took the bullet sample and eyed it. Immediately the image of the seven eagles came to mind. Gabriel, who'd dropped it into my hand. "Do we have a trace? Do we know who?"

"We have a trace. Doug Walken."

"The grazier guy?"

"He was a player."

My god. Maggie was right. I leaned forward in my chair. "But surely if he was Guardianship, the bullet could *not* be traced back to him."

"The man used his own weapon. Why? Because he was a sleeper. And he himself must've known just how temporary he was."

"Temporary?"

"Oh, absolutely. While you were away on Barras, we initiated a full autopsy on this fellow. What we found was something absolutely extraordinary."

Maggie reached into her drawer and retrieved something small in a plastic evidence bag. She passed it over. The strange object was obviously damaged, but I knew straight away what it was. "A bloody homing beacon? That explains the helo knowing where to find us. I assumed the Gs tracked the GPS upload after I transmitted the data back to you. But now this? It explains a lot."

"The beacon was surgically implanted just below his left armpit," Maggie went on. "However, that's not the extraordinary part. The man had another implant. A high explosive device. The man was literally wired from the inside. A kidney had been removed and the device was implanted into the cavity. When we found the device, the entire mortuary was locked down. In the end, the bomb disposal squad was called in and the only safe way out of the situation was to relocate the body and detonate the device in a controlled environment."

"Hmm . . . Hence the beacon being so damaged. How did you recover it?"

"Metal detector, and a lot of man hours."

I sat back and placed a hand on my forehead in disbelief. During the journey up from William Creek, I was literally sitting right next to a bomb. It made me wonder how things would've turned out had I bailed the guy up in the beginning. It also made me wonder how he was supposed to detonate it. He had no trigger device on him. None that I knew of. Certainly nothing obvious on his person.

Maggie cut into my thoughts as I was going over everything. "The device and the beacon were set up to be used as a coordinated attack, Nathan. Make no mistake about it. This fellow's mission was *never* about Angel or Eagle Shield. *His* mission was us. I speculate as soon as he came into the range of his objective, whomever was behind tracking the beacon would've remotely detonated the charge. Had you brought him here, things would've turned out much differently. I'd hate to think.

"Now you can let go of the guilt. He was a soldier. A Guardianship soldier. This goes much deeper than we first assumed. It means even seemingly ordinary people are intertwined into Guardianship ranks. We are at war, Nathan. We are at war, and with this new threat, we have no alternative but to consider the fact there're more of these so-called wired sleepers. Now we have our work cut out for us, wouldn't you agree?"

"I can't believe it. The man had me fooled. He had herds . . . and dogs."

"We did some research into his background. He lived alone in a shack on a property located not far north from Roxby Downs, which was burnt to the ground after we got there to investigate. It makes you wonder, doesn't it? He must've had a cover that was worked out far in advance. So far, in fact, the local populous at William Creek were none the wiser and indeed knew him well. Can you imagine the catastrophe had his mission played out? Perhaps we'd not be sitting here now and discussing it."

I shuddered in my seat, realising how close I came. How close we *all* came. The fact that I'd gotten him killed was nothing more than dumb luck. But was it more than that? How had Angel managed to send her warning? No matter how hard I thought it over, with Angel's amnesia I'd never connect those dots. Now, the whole scenario was nothing more than hindsight. Or was it?

"No, Maggie. I don't believe it for a second. It's too farfetched. How in the hell could a sleeper be in close proximity to where we were at the time? The entire length and breadth of this country. This guy was in the middle of nowhere waiting for us to arrive? It just doesn't sound plausible."

Maggie looked at me as I sat back folding my arms. Considering everything, my head was in a spin. "That's what I am getting at, Nathan. One: There're more of these fellows out there than you care to think about. Two . . ."

Then it hit me. "A mole?" Holy shit. Now it was coming together, and I hated seeing it in this new light.

"A mole," Maggie agreed. "Mathew Mallow. ASIO counterintelligence."

"The guy who was set up to be the negotiator with Quinlan!"

Maggie nodded vigorously and explained, "Mallow was recruited by the Guardianship after he got his nose all out of joint with that Sydney Opera House botch up. He was actively tracking you and Angel. When you arrived within range, this sleeper was activated. But it doesn't stop there. After the Federal Police arrested Mathew Mallow, we looked into his activities. At his place of residence, we found the intelligence of literally thousands of sleepers. All of them geared up and aimed toward our assets and infrastructures. There are ongoing operations right now to nullify the threat. It is with great sadness we expect things to worsen before this danger has been quashed for good. You can expect side missions coming your way. You have your Eagle Shield mission and there will be no rest for you, Nathan."

I heard what Maggie was saying and I accepted it for what it was worth. But something stuck out and I wasn't sure if it had already been addressed. "Firebird Station is compromised," I said. "We can no longer continue to conduct operations from here."

"I know. Sad, isn't it? I've sent Bosco away to investigate the prospect for a new location. Everything will have to be uprooted and moved, unfortunately."

Bosco. The mention of his name brought to mind older issues that needed to be sorted. I thought back to his involvement with Detachment 421. Maybe now was the right time to bring it up. I came right out with it. "Maggie. I'm afraid I don't have full trust with Bosco in Eagle Shield."

Maggie looked up and appeared stunned by my abruptness. "What on earth are you saying? Bosco is absolutely crucial to Eagle Shield. He is your wingman, for God's sake. Are you telling me my decision to have him in play is wrong?"

"It's not that at all. I'm sure your decision is sound. There's history with Bosco I can't get my head around. I'm certain he was at some time involved with Detachment 421."

There it was. I'd finally spilled my suspicions about Bosco. Maybe I should've left it. Already, regret for saying the words was sinking in. I hated my mind sometimes. Maggie sat back and folded her arms, eyes cold ice. "I'm not confirming it!" she snapped. "But what of it?"

"The CIA's Candy programme."

"That's classified," Maggie said plainly. "It's not open for discussion."

I saw her eyes leave me and go off in another direction. She stared at the window behind me before finally adding, "Let me put it this way, Nathan. I will not tell you that Bosco was an operative with Detachment 421. I will not tell you Bosco was inserted with the sole purpose of bringing the Candy programme down. I will go on by not telling you if it wasn't for Bosco, more lives may have been lost due to this CIA stupidity. I *never* told you those things. I never *discussed* them with you or anybody else. How you discovered this information is beyond my comprehension. And it stays that way. Clear?"

I nodded, not saying anything further. But I couldn't just leave it there. I was about to push this thing right out on the ragged edge.

"Agent Blue," I asked. "Who is this guy?"

"Classified." Maggie's word was dry as water crackers. She looked down and avoided eye contact.

"And where was Agent Blue's drone piloted from?"

"That's classified, Nathan. Bloody hell!" Maggie huffed. "Please do not push down this road again. Get to Melbourne. Go to your counselling sessions with Xe. Keep a clear head for your side missions as they come about. I'll be in touch in due course. That is all."

CHAPTER THIRTY-TWO

Melbourne 1996

Angel couldn't wait to get through the front door. No sooner did I have the key in the lock, she busted through into a very well-appointed apartment. The first thing I noticed was the television set on an expensive-looking table. Flat screen plasma. It took me by surprise.

Everything was new and the place smelled of new carpeting and furniture. There was even a large array of books on a bookcase. On the left, a balcony overlooking Port Melbourne. Angel wasted no time getting out there. I met her on the balcony. I imagined what it must look like at night as the city lit up with its colourful landscape. I wondered how all this was made possible. So much money. Where did it come from?

"Wow, Nathan. Wow!" Angel giggled. "Is this really ours?"

"Yeah. It is," I said, not believing it. Only the richest of the rich had a place like this. Maybe it wasn't so bad, this mission. Maybe I'd get to enjoy it. Things like this don't ever come for free. There's a price to be paid somewhere. Perhaps one day I'd find out what.

For now, a bit of respite away from all the bloodshed and killing was what I needed. Away from the stress of everything. I left

Angel by herself and went back inside. I felt almost childlike exploring our new home.

"You hungry?" I shouted from the kitchen. I opened the fridge and nothing, I mean nothing, was left out. An entire grocery store in a metal box. Then to the pantry. My mouth watered. The shelves were stacked high. Every need catered for.

"Am I hungry? Like . . . yeah!" Angel answered from wherever she was now exploring. The bedroom I think. I went to see.

Angel's bedroom was a ten-year-old's dream come true. A comfortable bed. A bookcase with rows upon rows of books. A desk in the corner. On the desk, a laptop computer. How in the heck was a laptop computer made available? Those things had just hit the market and were so expensive nobody could afford them. My mind whirled with amazement.

Which room next? My room.

I opened the door, walked inside, and placed the leather briefcase containing Eagle Shield objectives and that disk on the side table. A luxury bed. A desk and another laptop computer. All the trimmings I could imagine. It was such a delight. Things were looking up. Finally.

"Nathan . . ." Angel called from her room.

"Coming . . ." I said, like a real dad.

Walking into Angel's room, I found her sitting on her bed with books from the shelf sprawled out in front of her. "Look what I found," she said, holding up a couple of books. "These are about taking pictures!"

"Photography books," I said. "Nice."

"Look, Nathan. This one says how I can make some money from taking lots of pictures."

Hmm . . . Now this is not how it's supposed to go . . .

My first urge was to go looking for anything spy-related. Get there, I thought. Nothing like a beginning. But maybe I wouldn't push things too hard. Little by little, I'd get there in the end.

Angel sprang from her bed and blurred past me. I heard her call out with an echo. "Nathan. Oh my god! Two sinks! One for me and one for you!"

I got myself in there. The first thing I noticed was a luxury bath. Deep. With jets. I didn't know how long it was. I hadn't had the luxury of a spa in recent memory. Maybe longer. A shower cubicle to one side. Two shower heads in there. Then my eyes went to the door and I hoped it had a lock.

A lock . . . Good . . .

Stepping out, a sweet scent in the air. An arrangement of flowers on a small table. A note under a vase. I picked up the envelope and found something written by hand. 'Welcome home, big hoss.'

Bosco . . . ?

I opened the note.

Welcome to your pad. You've got everything to make yourself at home. You deserve it, Buddy. Check out the Nintendo. Every goddamn shoot-em-up game to keep your skills fresh. Keep that girl on course and we won't have a problem. I'm in the shadows as I always was. Just call. Phone in your desk drawer. See ya!

Bosco's errand, I thought. He was gone for how long? The bastard. I smiled, knowing he'd sorted everything. Now my head was clear, Maggie's explanation of Bosco's time in Detachment 421 made sense and I was able to rediscover the trust I once had with Bosco. Now, it was like I knew him as an old friend. And all this? Only friends and comrades got to do this for each other. Time to get on with it.

In the desk in my room I found a Motorola mobile phone the size of a small house brick. How in the heck could I ever carry that thing around? Another note under. A series of numbers and a short missive to suggest a safe. Stepping over to my wardrobe, I slid the big glass mirror door sideways. Suits. My size. Armani. Black. Seven of them. A safe at the floor with a dial and handle.

I dialled up the combination that was on the note and opened the steel door. A suppressed nine-millimetre Beretta with boxes of ammo. A big wad of cash. Hundred-dollar notes. Picking up the wad of cash, I guesstimated a couple of hundred grand. I felt the weight in my hand and juggled it a little, just because I could. Placing the cash back in, I closed the steel door and spun the combination lock. Next to the safe on the floor, shoes. Seven pairs. Gucci or similar. Shiny and black. Sneakers. Two pairs. Reebok.

A set of drawers to one side. I slid one open. Tracksuits. Grey. Australian coat of arms. Nike. Just what had I gotten into? I couldn't remember the last time I went for a jog.

Bosco, you idiot . . .

"Nathan! Come see! Come see!"

I dashed into the living room to see what Angel sounded so excited about. She pointed. "Look," she said, giggling.

On a shelf, figurines of eagles. About a dozen of them. Different poses and postures. Another note under. I passed the note to Angel and she read it out loud.

Dear Angel, something for you to enjoy. Love, Maggie. XX

"I'm so happy, Nathan. This is a really nice place, isn't it?"

"It is," I agreed. "Now, let's see about getting us some KFC."

CHAPTER THIRTY-THREE

Of All Things

Angel turns sixteen years old today. Where did that time go? As I finished setting the table, I reflected briefly on old memories. All the memories once hard like crystal had softened with time. My mission was going not exactly as scheduled, but it had its moments and I was optimistic. There were times when I thought I could never accomplish it. Angel, as I'd been told by several people, had a mind all of her own. Her school grades were exceptional. The top of the crop, her teachers said. No issues there. I couldn't have asked for any better. But how could I get her into the field of play when she was so passionate about her camera?

There were moments I'd even considered hiding her camera to make it a little hard for her. But every time she used it; her photographs were spectacular. Angel was indeed a master in the craft. How could I take that away? I didn't have the heart. She enjoyed it so much. Nobody in their right mind could ever do such a thing, knowing her talent and the pleasure she got out of it.

I'd even set up the laundry as an ad hoc darkroom. I'd covered the windows with black plastic so no light could get in. On a bench I made out of scraps of pine sat an old photographic enlarger. In a drawer, boxes of unexposed multigrade sheets of paper. Trays to the left contained developer, fixer, and stop bath. Those chemicals smelt like vinegar and probably were. But I never had the guts to taste it just to see. Who'd know if vinegar and water were the only things necessary to make prints.

On so many occasions, I attempted to guide and direct Angel into a position to build a desire toward spy craft. There seemed little interest there. So, no choice but to go with it. To see where it led. Maybe she'd change and become curious. I kept the hope going forward. Everything would fall into place, I kept thinking.

The table looked like a sixteen-year-old's party table by the time I'd finished with it. Everything I could come up with to make the occasion just right. Sweets and savouries. A balance of healthy and not so healthy. A birthday cake I'd made myself. Something I was proud of. Not perfect, but there was a lot of love in there, even though it sat crooked and wasn't flat on the top. Sixteen candles, ready to light. I stood back and sighed. My girl was growing up.

A present from me sat at the edge of the table. I couldn't wait to give it to her. It took an awful lot of will not to give it to her early. But now it was there, it was only a little while longer to wait.

"Angel," I said loudly from the table. No response. I bet I knew why. Opening her bedroom door, I found her with her headphones on. I bet I knew what she was listening to. I walked over and lifted an earpiece away. Just as expected, Metallica screamed from her headphones. Angel looked at me up as though annoyed. "Hey. Now I have to start the same song over," she said.

Figures, I thought. I lifted the earpiece away again. "Time to get yourself ready, Angel. They'll be knocking on the door in half an hour."

"I'll be there in a sec, Nate."

Nate . . .?

At least it was better than, mate.

I smiled briefly with the memory of that first day while traveling from Alice Springs.

Back to the kitchen. Stuff still needed to be done. Was there time?

I heard the shower starting and relaxed a little.

The doorbell rang. Here they come, I thought. Too late for the final touches.

Opening the door was the one person I knew wouldn't be late. "Hello, Jenny."

"Hey, Nathan. Am I too early?"

"You're never early for Angel, so it seems. How goes it today?"

"I'm great," Jenny said. "I have a present for Angel. Where shall I put it?

I pointed to the table where I'd left mine. "I guess that spot will do nicely." I couldn't help it. I told Jenny what I got Angel. "It's a camera," I said. "Not just any camera. It's a digital. No more messy chemicals, huh? And two tickets for the Metallica concert."

I didn't tell Jenny there were also two backstage passes to meet James Hetfield and the boys. I also didn't tell her they'd be invited to the after-concert party where Mr Hetfield would have his signed guitar ready to give to Angel. That was a moment I'd have to do my best to imagine. I tried desperately to put aside my imaginings of the party.

Amazing, the ASIS machine, Maggie once told me. If it wasn't for Bosco's help with Angel's birthday, I'd never have managed to accomplish as much.

Jenny beamed. "That's so cool, Nathan. She'll love that. Are you taking her?"

"Me? I don't think so. Not my thing. The other ticket is for you. But don't tell her before she opens her present or you're history. Get it?"

"You're such a kidder," Jenny laughed. If only she knew, I reflected. I also imagined Jenny becoming jealous after Angel got her guitar. Maybe I went too far.

At the same time Jenny set her gift on the table, the doorbell rang again. More sixteen-year-olds filed through the door, some giving me high-fives as they stepped past me. It didn't take long before there was no space at all. The place was a mad scramble of sixteen-year-old school friends. The atmosphere was electrified with the shouting and laughing, and I was already feeling the headache coming on. However, I was happy. Happier than I could imagine. The life of being a dad brought about such a big shift in my lifestyle, and I was thankful.

* * *

It was time for the ritual. At the table, everyone crowded around for the candles to be lit. I lit them up one by one. The doorbell rang again. Angel, getting ready to blow them out with a beaming smile, looked up from her sixteen candles as though wondering who it could be.

Answering the front door I knew who the final visitor was. I also knew Angel didn't know and how much of a surprise she'd have.

I opened the door. Maggie was smiling widely. I'd not seen her for so long. "Hello, Nathan."

"You made it," I said, smiling.

"A bastard of a trip. I'll never do it again."

"I appreciate the trouble, Maggie. She'll be a very happy birthday girl."

Angel ran to Maggie as she walked in. It was something so heart-warming to see. Although, with all the laughter and high-pitched gasbagging going on it was hard to hear anything. After all the formalities, the candles were blown out and Angel's gifts unwrapped. The camera was a great gift, but the tickets to see Metallica brought her to tears. The backstage passes, however, brought her to the kind of happiness that ripped my heart from my chest. I always thought it would've been the other way around. How wrong was I?

Then I found some peace out on the balcony. Finally, a bit of a breather. Just me and a hot brew with a dash of Wild Turkey. Life's little treasure. As I stood on the balcony that day and looked out at the city skyline, I thought of all those times way back when. The friends I made. The friends I'd lost along the way. The pain of losing Teresa. There wouldn't be a time without pain for her loss. Rather, a coping strategy to cover the suffering. I reflected on Matchbook, Crossbow, Barras, and the ultra-stuff-up I made in Cobalt Blue, which would never stop haunting me. It was but a reminder of how close I came to the edge and looked over. I glimpsed – for just a second – the darkness over there.

"You okay, Nathan?" Maggie said, joining me on the balcony.

"Yeah. Just having a moment."

"Sounds heavy."

"Yeah. Old memories. I often think back to old times when I'm out here."

"You think too much, Nathan. When are you ever going to learn to just go with the moment?" Maggie paused, then added, "How goes it with the counselling?"

"I'm holding my own, apparently. But I never thought I'd be still doing the counselling sessions after all these years."

"Call it maintenance. That way, if you have to spend a good amount of your life with the sessions, it's validated."

"You said Xe was no ordinary man. You didn't tell me he was one of them."

"Oh," Maggie said ironically. "One of who?"

I smiled with the same dryness as Maggie. "Don't think I don't get it. Xe is Oudarretian. Tell me I'm wrong."

Maggie opened a metal cigarette case and took out a cigarette, tapping it on the back of her hand before lighting up.

"You smoke?"

"So many things you don't know. Yes. But casually. I keep promising myself to give them up. But I only ever partake when things feel right and are going smoothly. Are they going smoothly?"

"You're changing the subject."

"Maybe." Maggie shrugged. "Let me put it like this. Xe is our biggest ally. He's deep undercover. His security clearance is higher than yours and mine combined."

"And yet he's my counsellor."

"A man of many talents, Nathan. But back to Angel. Tell me you've got her safely on schedule."

"Not exactly. Angel is a great photographer. But now she's showing interest in journalism. That's where she sees herself. I have to admit, she's so damn good at her art."

"And yet, that talent she possesses will inevitably take her to the realm of the tabloid press? I can't see her lasting in it. Too much of a dog-eat-dog world for our Angel." Maggie sighed audibly. "Perhaps that's partly my error. I encouraged her photography. When Angel was so young, Alisha was forever turning up with Angel's film cartridges. I too saw Angel's capability. Such an amazing young soul. But don't stress too much. Plenty of time."

"Two years isn't plenty of time. By the time she's eighteen, everything we've worked toward will be for nothing. I've tried so hard. Everything I could think of. I'm sorry, Maggie."

"I don't believe it for a second. Just keep going. We'll get there in the end, I'm sure."

"There's something else," I said. "I don't know how to tackle this one."

"That sounds awfully serious."

"Well, it depends on which way you look at it. I know how I feel about it. But I don't know if you'd be the same."

"Go on."

"Jenny. Angel and Jenny . . . they're more than best friends. I caught them together. What I saw didn't say just best friends to me. And they're too young. They're just little kids. They should never be . . ."

Maggie laughed wholeheartedly.

"Something funny I said?"

"You're more of a dad than you realise, Nathan. Angel is sixteen. She's a young adult. Has no one ever told you about female hormones? Girls grow up much faster than boys. However, I agree with you to some extent. But you'll have a challenge on your hands if this is something that's meant to happen."

"Angel being gay is of no nuisance to me."

"And so it shouldn't be. That's not what I'm getting at."

"Then what do you suggest I do?"

"Talk to her. Let her know that you're approachable but don't overdo it. You can push her away just as easily as having her come to you for your support. Young adult minds are very sensitive. Use care and caution."

How many opportunities over the years had come and gone? I never had 'the chat' with her. That part of me had failed dismally. I always assumed school would take care of it. I avoided it. I let it go.

"I assumed . . ."

"Don't assume anything," Maggie cut in. "You're in control."

I thought things over while Maggie enjoyed the view over the city. I don't know why, but after that moment, *nothing else mattered.*

Carl Lakeland lives with his wife in the sleepy town of Snake Valley, 36 kilometres south west of Ballarat in Australia. Lakeland grew up during the early seventies in the western suburbs of Sydney. Having enlisted into the military at the age of seventeen, he draws on his experience to create powerful and engaging speculative fiction.

"Sometimes, I can't let things be," says Lakeland. "I write stories with passion that others might see as being obsessive. I live and breathe it. I dream it when I sleep. But I never write down my dreams. If I can't remember those things I've dreamt, they're not important enough."

Lakeland's stories revolve around the element of 'what if?' He pushes the boundaries of his stories to the edge of the *Official Secrets Act*, which will leave the reader wondering about the aspect of creative license, or the possibility of fact in his writing. Either way, the reader will be left to make up their own mind. His books are fast paced, edge of your seat thrillers that are distinctively written in a way that will have the reader guessing which way the story is about to head.

"As a writer, unpredictability is the key essence. If I write something that can be foreseen in coming chapters, it's not good enough. I will scrap it. My goal is to keep the reader wondering, even sometimes to the detriment of my good guys!"

WEBSITE: carllakeland.com
EMAIL carl@carllakeland.com

Also by Carl Lakeland.

ABOUT THE AUTHOR

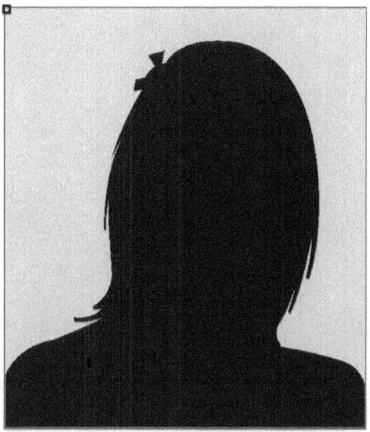

This is where the author biography text goes.

www.ingramcontent.com/pod-product-compliance
Lightning Source LLC
Chambersburg PA
CBHW030629110726
47901CB00002B/374